# TSISDETSI'S SHADOW

Eric Wilder

**Gondwana Press**

*For Marilyn*

*"No one escapes pain, fear, and suffering. Yet from pain can come wisdom, from fear can come courage, from suffering can come strength – if we have the virtue of resilience."*

ERIC GREITENS

# PROLOGUE

**M**r. Amos Brown staggered out of the roadside bar, the last twang of a Merle Haggard song swallowed by the heavy Oklahoma night. The place was a squat building, its neon sign flickering like a dying pulse, the word "Bar" barely legible on a rusted sheet of tin.

His shoes crunched on gravel, the sound sharp in the humid stillness. Chat Creek glimmered faintly under a sickle moon, its waters sluggish and stained with the memory of poison. The road stretched out before him, a cracked vein of asphalt leading nowhere he cared to name.

His car—an ancient Buick sedan, its burgundy paint chipped to reveal rust like open sores—slumped in the lot like a tired beast. The bench seats sagged under years of his weight, the upholstery cracked and sour with spilled bourbon and stale cigar smoke.

The tires were bald as his hopes, worn thin from endless miles between Tulsa and oblivion. Amos fumbled his keys, the metal cold against his calloused fingers, and the door groaned like a dying man as he slid inside. The air within was thick with the ghosts of old cigars, clinging to the dashboard's faded veneer.

He meant to drive to The Briar Patch Inn, a quaint turn-of-the-century guesthouse with gingerbread trim and lace curtains that felt like a mockery of his life's decay. But the bourbon in his blood had other plans, blurring his thoughts into a maze of half-remembered regrets.

The engine coughed to life, a rattling wheeze that matched the rasp in his COPD-ravaged lungs. He lit a cigar, the ember glowing like a lone star in the dark, and pulled onto Route 69, the

1

highway humming beneath him like a lullaby for the damned.

Somewhere along the road, a rusted sign leaned precariously on its post, the words Picher—6 miles barely legible through a tangle of bindweed and time. The letters snagged on a frayed thread of memory—whispers from his youth, tales of a town chewed up and spat out by its own greed.

Mr. Brown didn't know why he turned the wheel toward Picher. Maybe it was the bourbon. Maybe it was the weight of a life spent running from nothing to nowhere.

Picher emerged under a ghostly pale moon, a town reduced to a skeleton of its former self. Wind whistled through shattered windows and sagging rooftops, stirring dust that glittered with lead and despair.

Storefronts stood like tombstones: Murphy's Drugs, its sign dangling by a single bolt; Lou's Auto & Salvage, its lot choked with rusted hulks; a faded banner for Dairy Treats flapping like a trapped bird. The air tasted of metal and abandonment, and the silence was so deep it seemed to hum.

The chat piles dominated the horizon—monstrous heaps of mining waste, jagged and unnatural, rising like the graves of forgotten gods. They shimmered faintly under the moonlight, their surfaces laced with toxic dust that sparkled like fool's gold. No birds sang. No crickets chirped. The only sound was the Buick's engine, idling like a weary heartbeat.

Mr. Brown parked beneath the ruins of a Shell station, its canopy twisted like a broken spine. His head lolled against the headrest, the bourbon pulling him toward a dreamless sleep. The cigar burned low, ash crumbling onto his stained shirt.

His life felt like this town—hollowed out, used up, left to rot. No wife, no kids, just the bottle and the road. His chest tightened, a familiar ache from lungs that had long since betrayed him. He closed his eyes, letting the darkness take him.

A screech tore through the night, sharp as a blade on bone.

Mr. Brown jolted awake, heart pounding, the cigar tumbling to the floorboard. The sound wasn't animal, wasn't human—it was something older, something wrong. It came again, rising

2

from the gut of Picher, layered with rage and sorrow, like the land itself was screaming.

He peered through the windshield, his breath fogging the cracked glass. The town lay still, bathed in silver moonlight, but the air had shifted—thicker, heavier, as if time itself had slowed to watch.

The chat piles loomed larger now, their shadows stretching like fingers across the broken pavement. And then he remembered—a story, half-heard years ago in a dusty roadside museum, told by a Quapaw elder with eyes like polished obsidian.

Tsisdetsi, the Shadow That Watches.

The tale spoke of a spirit born from the land's wounds—rivers choked with poison, earth gutted by mines, lives buried under greed. Tsisdetsi wasn't flesh or bone but a weave of memory and consequence, a shadow that carried the weight of every betrayal inflicted on this place. It didn't hunt. It didn't kill. It forced you to see—to remember—what had been done.

Mr. Brown's skin crawled, his cigar's ember forgotten. The screech came again, closer now, a wail that seemed to pull at the edges of his soul. And then he saw it.

Between two collapsed buildings, a shape emerged—not moving, not gliding, but unfurling, as if the darkness itself were peeling open. It was blacker than the night, a silhouette that refused form, its edges writhing like smoke trapped in a storm. Where a face should have been, two pinpoints of ember-red burned, not eyes but wounds, glowing with the heat of ancient fury. Long limbs unfolded from its core, talons scraping brick with a sound like nails on a coffin lid.

Mr. Brown blinked, his vision swimming with bourbon and fear.

The shadow grew, rising from the base of a chat pile like a specter from a grave. Its form shifted with every glance—one moment humanoid, the next a twisted mockery of something older, something that had walked this land before men dared to scar it. Its red eyes pulsed, and in their glow, Mr. Brown saw flashes—rivers running black, miners coughing blood, children playing in dust that would kill them.

It wasn't just watching him. It was knowing him—every drink he'd taken to drown his failures, every mile he'd driven to outrun his shame. Tsisdetsi saw the man he'd become: a husk, as broken as Picher itself.

Mr. Brown shut the door of the Buick, hands shaking as he turned the key. The engine sputtered, then roared; the headlights sliced through the darkness but failed to catch sight of the creature.

He floored the gas, tires spitting gravel as he fled down Route 69. In the rearview, the shadow didn't chase. It simply stood, growing taller, its form stretching across the road like a stain on the moonlight.

Picher faded behind him, but the weight of Tsisdetsi clung to Mr. Brown like the dust on his boots. The Buick rattled on, its engine coughing as if it, too, felt the shadow's gaze. He drove toward Tulsa, toward the bottle waiting in his empty apartment, knowing he'd never outrun the memory of that night—or the truth it had forced him to see.

# CHAPTER1

I'd almost forgotten how Tulsa shimmered under the summer sun. The city stretched upward in glass and steel, with golden light bouncing off the mirrored skyscrapers that loomed over the streets like silent sentinels.

Pedestrians moved with purpose—business professionals in pressed suits, young creatives clutching iced coffees, and tourists snapping photos of the iconic Art Deco façades that graced the historic buildings. Even the pavement seemed to hum with energy, radiating heat beneath the soles of my boots.

The pulse of lunch hour was everywhere. The scent of smoked meats and Cajun spices curled out from sidewalk vendors, blending with the crisp bite of fresh-cut citrus from a fruit stand.

At street corners, musicians played for tips, the twang of a steel-string guitar cutting through the rhythmic murmur of conversation. A food truck selling Vietnamese banh mi rattled as the line grew longer, patrons fanning themselves with menus.

I stepped onto Boston Avenue, adjusting the brim of my hat as I scanned the patios lining the street. Though I hadn't been downtown in a while, Tulsa hadn't changed much—except maybe it had, in ways I hadn't noticed yet.

Above me, the Mid-Continent Tower stood proudly, its Gothic Revival edges casting intricate shadows against the sky, while the nearby Philtower Building was draped in its crimson-and-green-tiled crown, reminding me that history still had its place among the modern sheen.

At a bustling bistro tucked between corporate offices and boutique shops, Jake Huntington waited. I spotted him easily

—lean, sun-bronzed, dressed in casual wealth: tailored slacks, a crisp linen shirt, the kind of confidence that came with fortunes built and reputations cemented. Even seated, he carried himself like a man who knew he belonged anywhere he chose to be.

A stunning woman I didn't recognize sat beside him, one of her graceful hands resting on the stem of a martini, her eyes half-lidded in amusement as she listened to Colley Hornbeck, Jake's chopper pilot, who gestured animatedly between bites of his burger.

Jake caught sight of me and grinned, waving me over. I took a breath and stepped forward—into familiar company, into a meeting that held more weight than just friendship.

I'd met Jake and Colley a few years back when I was doing undercover work at a resort in the mountains of eastern Oklahoma. They were there looking for Bigfoot, and I was persuaded to lead their expedition.

Though Jake came from a wealthy Oklahoma oil family, exploring for oil wasn't his dream. Cryptids were: sasquatch, chupacabra, and other mythical creatures that go bump in the night. His TV reality show, Cryptid Hunter, was now the number one reality show in America. Everyone recognized Jake, as did those passing on the sidewalk. Jake loved it.

Colley's brown hair, which he always wore over his ears, was now sprinkled with gray. He had the bone structure and good looks of an aging movie star. Colley was a character, yet he could guide a chopper into places most pilots wouldn't even consider attempting. Seeing me approach, he stood and shook my hand.

"You're a sight for sore eyes," he said in his mellow country twang. "Mama, this is Buck McDivit, half Indian and the best tracker in Oklahoma."

Mama smiled, her café au lait complexion radiant in the Tulsa sunlight. Her black hair was braided, colorful amulets and veves reflecting the Oklahoma sun.

"Jake has told me all about you," she said. "He didn't tell me how good-looking you are. Love your Stetson, colorful western shirt, and alligator boots."

"Buck's the real deal," Colley said. "He doesn't just look athletic, he's strong as hell. Found that out the hard way."

"Join us," Jake said.

A pretty blond waitress in khaki shorts, a white T-shirt, and killer legs appeared from the bistro.

"What are you drinking, cowboy?"

"Coors," I said.

"Chilled glass?"

"Keep the glass; just the can," I said. "No lime; no salt. Just Coors."

"I'm Kiley," she said with a wink. 'Be right back with that beer."

Kiley smiled again when I said, "I can hardly wait."

Jake owned a production studio in Tulsa. While shooting in New Orleans, he met Mama Mulate. Now, he had an even larger studio in the Central Business District, and Mama and Jake were inseparable.

"Jake has told me all about you," I said.

Mama glanced at Jake and said, "Has he now?"

"All good," I said. "I've never met a real voodoo mambo."

"Watch yourself," Colley said. "Say the wrong thing and she'll turn you into a frog."

Mama smiled and said, "If I could do that, you'd have been catching flies with your tongue long ago."

"Dr. Mulate isn't only a mambo," Jake said. "She teaches English literature at Tulane University."

"Summer break," Mama said.

"How do you like Tulsa?" I asked.

"People are wonderful and the martinis are cold. What's not to like?"

"Jake says you're a runner," I said.

"Both of us," Mama said. "Every day at dawn, we lace up our running shoes and chase the sunrise. I'm in heaven."

"Mama ran track at the University of South Carolina and almost turned pro," Jake said. "The city is a mecca for sports enthusiasts, with Tulsa's trail system being the heart of the city's outdoor scene."

Kiley rushed out of the nearby café with my beer and fresh drinks for everyone else. After serving us, she set her tray on the table and plopped into my lap.

"This job is killing me," she said. "Mind if I use your lap for a minute?"

I grinned and said, "Anytime, pretty lady."

Kiley's time in my lap was short. After a hug, a kiss, and a smile, she sprang to her feet, grabbed her tray, and hurried back into the café. Jake was shaking his head, Mama smirking.

"Does that happen a lot?" Mama asked.

"Buck's a chick magnet," Colley said.

Mama looked at Jake and said, "You're banned from going to a bar alone with Buck."

"No worries here," Jake said. "You're the only lady in my life."

"Where's Pard?" Colley asked, changing the subject.

"Pard?" Mama said.

"My border collie," I said. "We're both strays, and we adopted each other. I spent the night with a friend who has a house in the Heights. Pard's there."

I smiled when Mama said, "Why don't you call your friend and ask her to join us?"

"Randy's a state trooper. He's at work, Pard in his backyard having fun with his boxer, Bully."

"We'll pick Pard up before we go," Colley said. "You can't go on assignment without him."

"Assignment?" I said. "Maybe you'd better explain."

The sound of geese flying overhead on their way to Lake Skiatook interrupted Jake's explanation.

I nodded when he said, "You're familiar with Picher, Oklahoma?"

"In high school, my class took a field trip there to collect mineral specimens. If there's a creepier place on earth, I'd like to know about it," I said.

"Chernobyl, maybe," Colley said.

"America's most toxic ghost town," Jake said. "Picher sits on

8

top of literally thousands of abandoned mineshafts, making the ground dangerously unstable."

I grinned. "I found some of my best mineral specimens in one of those mineshafts."

"Then you know what I'm talking about," Jake said. "Chat piles, mountains of toxic waste, contaminating the soil, water, and air. Lead exposure so intense it resulted in brain damage, developmental delays, and behavioral problems in children."

Disturbed by the conversation, Mama leaned in. "Colley flew us over the town. I had no idea such a place existed."

"I know it's bad," I said. "The cost to remediate is so enormous that we'll likely never see it happening."

"And that's the problem," Jake said. "The shafts are all full of contaminated water that continues to pollute the creeks and streams. All of northeast Oklahoma is already affected."

"I know you're a billionaire, though all your wealth wouldn't put a dent in the massive amount of money it would take for a complete cleanup," I said.

Jake smiled and said, "The very reason I'm approaching it from a different angle."

"Such as?" I said.

Kiley arrived with more drinks before Jake could answer my question. The curbside business had grown steadily since I had arrived. She was busy and refrained from sitting in my lap. When she was gone, Jake continued his explanation.

"Ever hear of Tsisdetsi's Shadow?" he asked.

He smiled when I said, "Quapaw legend?"

"I forgot you're part Indian," he said.

"It's Oklahoma," I said. "Who isn't?"

"Good point," he said. "Tsisdetsi."

"The Shadow That Watches," I said.

"The legend tells of a spirit arising from the land's suffering —poisoned rivers, scarred earth from mining, and lives lost to greed," Jake said.

"Tsisdetsi is neither flesh nor bone," Mama said. "It's a shadow carrying the weight of every betrayal inflicted on the land."

"It doesn't hunt or kill," Jake said. "It forces you to see what has happened."

Mama and Jake exchanged a knowing glance when I said, "Sounds like a perfect episode of Cryptid Hunter."

"And expand awareness of the underlying problem," Mama said.

"An episode centered in Picher would be mesmerizing," I said. "Most people don't believe it when they see pictures. I can only imagine how creepy it is after dark. Too bad Tsisdetsi's Shadow is only a legend."

When Mama and Jake smiled, I realized I was about to hear something fantastical.

"Sightings of the Picher monster have been reported for years," Jake said. "Mostly by drunks or crackpots wanting attention. That recently changed."

"I'm listening," I said.

"A local news station interviewed a traveling salesman. The old man claimed to have seen the monster beneath a full moon in Picher."

I scoffed. "What was he doing in Picher after dark, and what makes his account any more plausible than any of the others?"

"He took a picture of the monster with his cell phone," Jake said.

He navigated to the pictures file on his cell phone, punched up a picture, and then showed it to me. It was an amorphous figure, dark and foreboding. A human could have created it, except one thing stood out as real: two eyes that glowed red and ghostly.

"Damn!" I said.

"There's a town about ten miles from Picher. Chat Creek is a small community, although it features a café, shops, a bed and breakfast, and a reasonably sized motel located on the highway. Everything my crew needs to set up a shoot and film an episode."

"Picher is in Ottawa County," I said. "There can't be more than thirty thousand people in the entire county."

"And most of those live in Miami, the County seat," Jake said.

"Exactly," I said. "How do people make a living in Chat Creek?"

"Dark tourism," Mama said. "Travel to places historically associated with tragedy and death."

"Not to mention mineral hunters," Jake said. "Crystal specimens taken from the area are valuable and are still sold all over the world. Interested in joining us?"

"You bet I am, but why do you need me?" I asked.

"You're an experienced investigator and quite possibly the best tracker in the state. If money's the problem, I'm prepared to pay top dollar," Jake said.

"I'm not worried about that," I said. "About how long do you think the shoot will take?"

"No more than a week," Jake said.

"Okay," I said. "When do we start?"

"The chopper's ready," Colley said. "As soon as Bossman clears the tab, and I take you to pick up Pard at your friend's house."

Before I could reply, Kiley appeared from the café with another round of drinks. When she returned with Jake's credit card, she sank into my lap and draped an arm around my neck.

"You're my last customer," she said. "I'm off. Want to take me boot scooting tonight, cowboy?"

"Depends," I said.

She grinned and said, "On what?"

"We're on our way to Chat Creek. You can either come with us and go boot scooting there, or take a rain check and wait until I return in about a week."

# CHAPTER 2

The chopper's blades sliced through the Oklahoma air, a rhythmic thrum that vibrated in my chest as we lifted off from Tulsa. Colley Hornbeck, steady as ever, gripped the controls, his eyes scanning the horizon with the calm of a man who'd flown through storms and worse.

Jake Huntington sat upfront, his grin wide as a kid on a rollercoaster, while Mama Mulate and I shared the back with Pard, my border collie, who pressed his nose against the window, tail wagging at the sight of the world shrinking below.

The film crew—cameramen, sound techs, and grips—were already on the road, their transport trucks and cars winding toward Chat Creek with the gear. They'd bunk at the place aptly named Route 69 Motel. Colley, Jake, Mama, and I were headed for The Briar Patch Inn, a bed and breakfast with a landing pad close by.

"Low and slow over Picher, Colley," Jake called over the headset. "Let's give Buck the full ghost-town experience."

Colley nodded, banking the chopper northwest. The Tulsa skyline faded behind us, replaced by a patchwork of green fields, red-dirt roads, and the occasional glint of a creek snaking through the landscape. Below, Route 69 stretched like a scar across the earth, its asphalt cracked and faded, leading toward the ruins of Picher. The air was thick with summer haze, the horizon shimmering under a relentless sun.

As we neared Picher, Colley dropped altitude, the chopper skimming low enough to stir dust from the abandoned streets. The town sprawled beneath us, a skeletal relic of its boom days, its bones laid bare under the harsh light.

Shattered windows gaped like empty eye sockets in the crumbling facades of Main Street—Murphy's Drugs, its sign dangling by a rusted bolt; Lou's Auto & Salvage, choked with the husks of cars long forgotten; Dairy Treats, its faded banner flapping in the breeze. The streets were eerily empty, no cars, no people, just the ghosts of a town hollowed out by greed and poison.

The chat piles loomed on the outskirts, monstrous heaps of mining waste that rose like diseased lungs from the earth. Their surfaces glittered with toxic dust—lead, zinc, cadmium—catching the sunlight in a mockery of beauty.

Some piles were jagged, while others were smoothed by decades of wind and rain, but all were unnatural, their gray and ochre hues stark against the green of the encroaching weeds. From above, they looked like the aftermath of some ancient cataclysm, a warning carved into the land. Tar Creek, sluggish and stained, wound through the scene, its waters carrying the memory of contamination downstream.

"Looks like hell decided to take a vacation here," Mama said, her voice crackling through the headset.

Her eyes were wide, one hand resting on Jake's shoulder as she leaned forward for a better view.

"Creepier than I remember," I said, my high school field trip flashing through my mind—crawling through mineshafts, pocketing galena crystals, oblivious to the poison in the air. Pard whined softly, sensing the wrongness below.

"Imagine it at night," Jake said, turning in his seat. "That's when Tsisdetsi's supposed to show. Red eyes, black shadow, the whole nine yards."

Colley chuckled. "If that thing's real, I'm staying in the chopper."

We circled Picher once more, the chopper's shadow flitting across the chat piles like a fleeting ghost. Then Colley pulled up, pointing us toward Chat Creek, ten miles north. The landscape softened as we flew, the toxic scars of Picher giving way to rolling hills and clusters of oak and hickory. Chat Creek itself appeared as a glint of water first, a narrow ribbon reflecting the sky, before the town came into view.

From above, Chat Creek was a speck of life clinging to the edge of nowhere. Route 69 bisected it, a thin artery lined with a handful of buildings that seemed to huddle together for comfort.

The Chat Creek Café, its red-and-white sign faded but proud, anchored one end of the main drag, its parking lot dotted with pickups and a single Harley. Across the street, a general store with a sagging porch advertised bait, ammo, and "authentic Picher crystals" in hand-painted letters.

A gas station, its pumps ancient but functional, sat next to a small antique shop, its windows crammed with mining relics and dusty trinkets. The motel, a low-slung building with a flickering neon sign, sprawled along the highway's edge, its lot already filling with our crew's vehicles.

Beyond the main strip, a scattering of homes—modest ranches and weathered bungalows—fanned out, their yards dotted with vegetable gardens and rusting swing sets.

The Briar Patch Inn stood apart, perched on a gentle rise just east of town. Its Victorian silhouette was unmistakable, a two-story structure with gingerbread trim and a wraparound porch that gleamed white in the sunlight. The inn's pale yellow siding was accented with green shutters, and a steeply pitched roof sprouted dormer windows like watchful eyes.

A rose garden, meticulously tended, bloomed in vibrant pinks and reds along the front, while a gravel path wound to a small outbuilding—an old carriage house, now a garage. Behind it, Colley's landing pad was a flat circle of packed earth, marked with a faded orange x. The inn looked like a postcard from a gentler time, its charm at odds with the hardscrabble town below and the toxic shadow of Picher looming nearby.

"Home sweet home. At least for a while," Colley said, easing the chopper toward the landing pad.

Dust swirled as we touched down, the blades slowing to a lazy whirl. Pard barked, eager to stretch his legs, and I opened the door, letting the warm Oklahoma air rush in. It carried the scent of roses from the garden, undercut by a faint metallic tang—the ghost of Picher's dust, conveyed on the breeze.

We climbed out, stretching cramped limbs as Colley secured the chopper. The inn's back door swung open, and a woman stepped onto the porch—mid-fifties, with a gray braid, turquoise earrings, and a smile that didn't quite reach her eyes. She wore a floral apron over jeans, her hands dusted with flour.

"Welcome to The Briar Patch," she said, her voice carrying a faint twang. "I'm Clara Hensley. Got your rooms ready and supper in the oven. Hope you like pot roast."

Jake flashed his TV-star grin. "Clara, you're a lifesaver. This is Mama Mulate, Buck McDivit, and you know Colley."

Clara nodded, eyeing Pard. "Dogs are welcome, as long as they're housebroken."

"Pard's a gentleman," I said, ruffling his ears.

He wagged his tail, already sniffing the air for new adventures.

Inside, the Briar Patch was as quaint as its exterior promised. The foyer smelled of lemon polish and fresh bread, its hardwood floors gleaming beneath a crystal chandelier that seemed to belong in a museum. A staircase with a carved mahogany banister spiraled to the second floor, where our rooms waited.

The parlor was a cozy clutter of overstuffed chairs, lace doilies, and sepia-toned photos of Chat Creek's mining days. A fireplace, cold now, dominated one wall, its mantel lined with polished quartz and galena crystals—souvenirs from Picher's past.

Clara led us upstairs, her steps brisk. My room overlooked the rose garden, its four-poster bed draped in a quilt that smelled faintly of lavender. A clawfoot tub gleamed in the attached bathroom, and a small writing desk held a vase of fresh daisies.

Jake and Mama shared a suite across the hall, while Colley's room faced the landing pad. Everything was immaculate, almost too perfect, as if Clara were trying to outshine the ugliness just ten miles south.

"Supper's at six," she said, pausing at the door. "You folks here for the Picher shoot, I take it?"

Jake nodded. "Cryptid Hunter. Ever hear of Tsisdetsi's Shadow?"

Clara's smile faltered, just for a moment. "Quapaw stories. Folks around here talk, especially after a few beers. You be careful out there. Picher's no place to linger after dark."

She turned and departed, her footsteps fading down the stairs. Mama raised an eyebrow, and Jake smirked, but I felt a prickle at the back of my neck. Pard whined, pressing against my leg.

"What's the plan?" I asked.

"Nothing more we can do today. The crew is setting up a staging area at the abandoned high school. We also have another chopper pad there. We'll head that way tomorrow for a briefing and to get started. Right now, Mama and I are going upstairs to clean up, rest a bit, and then make it down for Ms. Hensley's pot roast."

"Sounds like a plan," I said.

The aroma of pot roast, rich with thyme and caramelized onions, pulled me from a dreamless nap. Pard's ears perked, his nose twitching as he leapt off the bed, ready to investigate. I splashed water on my face, tugged on a clean shirt, and followed the scent downstairs, Pard trotting at my heels.

The Briar Patch's dining room was as warm as the foyer promised, its long oak table set with mismatched china and flickering candles. Lace curtains framed windows that looked out on the darkening rose garden, where fireflies were beginning to sparkle.

Clara Hensley bustled in from the kitchen, her apron swapped for a clean one, her gray braid swinging as she set down a steaming platter of pot roast, flanked by bowls of mashed potatoes, green beans, and cornbread that glistened with butter.

Jake and Mama were already seated, their faces glowing in the candlelight, while Colley leaned back in his chair, sipping a glass of sweet tea and looking like he'd just landed in paradise.

"Dig in, folks," Clara said, her smile wide but practiced, like a hostess who'd perfected the art of welcoming strangers. "Hope you're hungry."

We were. The pot roast was tender, falling apart at the touch of a fork, its gravy deep and savory. The green beans snapped with freshness, kissed with bacon grease, and the cornbread was the perfect balance of crumbly and moist. Even Pard, curled up by my chair, got a scrap of meat, which he devoured with a grateful wag.

"Clara, this is a masterpiece," Jake said, raising his glass. "You could open a restaurant in Tulsa and put half the chefs out of business."

Mama nodded, her eyes half-closed in bliss. "This is soul food, Oklahoma style. Where'd you learn to cook like this?"

Clara's laugh was light. "Oh, just years of feeding folks— miners, travelers, family. You pick up a few tricks."

She waved off the compliment, but her hands fidgeted with a napkin, folding and unfolding it. I took a bite of cornbread, watching her. Something was off—not in the food, which was damn near perfect, but in the way Clara moved, the way her gaze darted to the windows when she thought no one was looking. It was like she was waiting for something to step out of the dark.

"Clara," I said, keeping my tone casual, "you've lived here a while, I bet. Ever hear stories about Picher? The shadow thing— Tsisdetsi?"

Her hands stilled, the napkin crumpling in her fist. "Like I said upstairs, Quapaw tales. Folks around here love a good story, especially after a drink or two. Doesn't mean much."

"But you've heard the stories," Mama pressed, her voice gentle but probing. "The Shadow That Watches. People seeing it at night, near the chat piles."

Clara's smile tightened, and she busied herself slicing more cornbread. "People see all sorts of things in Picher. Moonlight on the dust, old buildings creaking—plays tricks on the eyes. You're here for that TV show, so I'm sure you'll find plenty to film."

Colley leaned forward, his grin sly. "What about that salesman? The one who snapped a picture. Said he saw red eyes, a shape that wasn't human. You think he was drunk, too?"

Clara's knife paused mid-slice, then resumed with deliberate care. "I don't know the man. Travelers come through, talk big, then move on. Picher's a place that makes you see what you want to see—or what you're afraid to." She met Colley's eyes, her expression unreadable. "More roast?"

We let it drop, but the air felt heavier, the candles flickering as if stirred by a draft. Clara filled the silence with small talk—Chat Creek's annual fair, the best fishing spots on the creek—but every question about Picher or Tsisdetsi was met with a dodge, a half-answer that led nowhere. She was hiding something, and the way Pard's ears stayed pricked told me he felt it too.

After dinner, we thanked Clara, who waved us off with that same practiced smile and disappeared into the kitchen. Jake and Mama whispered about tomorrow's shoot, while Colley lingered to flirt with a glass of bourbon he'd found in the parlor. I needed air. The dining room felt stifling, as if the walls were holding their breath.

"Ready to hunt a shadow, Buck?" Jake asked, clasping my shoulder.

I glanced out the window, where the distant horizon glowed with the last light of day.

"Let's hope it's just a legend," I said.

But the memory of that cell phone photo—those glowing red eyes—lingered like a bad dream.

"Better hit the sack," Colley said. "Dawn comes early."

Pard and I watched them ascend the stairs. I wasn't sleepy, and Pard needed a walk.

"Come on, Pard," I said, grabbing his leash. "Let's stretch our legs."

# CHAPTER 3

The rose garden was a world apart from Picher's desolation. The night was quintessentially Oklahoma—clear, warm, and with a sky so vast that it seemed to press down on the earth. Fireflies danced among the roses, their blooms heavy with scent, while a soft breeze carried the hum of crickets.

But there was a seclusion here, a stillness that felt unnatural, like the garden existed in a bubble cut off from the rest of the world. I couldn't shake the sense that something was watching, not from the shadows but from the edges of my own thoughts.

Pard led the way down a gravel path, his nose low, sniffing every petal and blade of grass. At the garden's heart was a wrought-iron bench, its paint chipped but sturdy, overlooking a small fountain that gurgled faintly. A figure sat there, half-hidden in the moonlight, its silhouette sharp against the silver glow.

I slowed, my hand tightening on Pard's leash. The figure didn't move, but I felt their attention shift toward me, like a spotlight snapping on. Pard's ears flicked. He didn't growl—just watched, his tail still.

"Evening," I said, stepping closer.

The woman's age was indeterminable, possibly in her early twenties or perhaps a hundred. Her pale skin glowed under the moonlight, her hair long, tangled, and streaked with colors that didn't make sense—blues and greens that shimmered like oil on water.

She wore a loose dress, its fabric patched with patterns that seemed to shift when I blinked. Her eyes were what stopped me

—wide, unblinking, the color of storm clouds, with a depth that made my skin prickle.

"Didn't mean to startle you," she said, her voice soft but carrying a strange cadence, like a song half-remembered. "I'm Sage. Clara's... kin." The pause before "kin" was deliberate, as if the word didn't quite fit.

"Buck McDivit," I said, easing onto the bench, keeping a foot of space between us. Pard sat at my feet, his gaze locked on Sage. "You live here?"

"Sometimes," Sage said, her lips curling into a smile that was both knowing and distant. "The Briar Patch Inn is home, but I wander. The earth calls, you know?"

I didn't, but I nodded. "Nice night for a walk."

"It is," Sage said, tilting her head to study the sky. "The stars are loud tonight. They're talking about you, Buck McDivit."

I laughed, though it came out forced. "That so? What're they saying?"

"They say you're here for the Shadow." Sage's eyes flicked to mine, and for a moment, I swore I saw a glint of red in them, like embers in a storm. "Tsisdetsi. The one that watches."

Though my pulse quickened, I kept my voice steady. "You know about that?"

"Everyone knows," Sage said, plucking a rose petal and twirling it between her fingers. The petal seemed to glow, though it could've been the moonlight. "Picher's full of ghosts. Tsisdetsi's different. It's not a ghost. It's... memory. Pain. The land's own voice."

Leaning forward, I ignored the chill creeping up my spine. "You've seen it?"

Sage's smile faded, her gaze drifting to the fountain. "Seen it, felt it, heard it. It doesn't show itself to everyone. Only those who need to see."

"See what?" I asked.

"What has been done," Sage said, as if explaining the weather. "The rivers, the mines, the children who never grew up right. Tsisdetsi carries it all."

Pard whined, nudging my knee. I scratched his ears, grounding myself. "Sounds like you know more than most. Clara won't talk about it."

"Clara's scared," Sage said, her voice dropping to a whisper. "She's seen things, too. She buries them. Thinks if she feeds folks and smiles, the past stays quiet." She laughed, a sound like wind chimes in a storm. "It doesn't."

The old bench creaked when I shifted. "You're saying Tsisdetsi's real?"

Sage's eyes locked on mine, and I felt like I was falling into them. "Real as the dust in your lungs, Buck. Real as the poison in the creek. Real as me and Clara. You'll see it soon enough."

I wanted to press her, but Sage stood abruptly, her suddenly diaphonous dress swirling like smoke.

"If you want answers, go to the commune. The people of the earth know more than Mama Clara's willing to say."

"Commune?" I asked, standing too. "What people?"

Sage gestured vaguely toward the horizon, where Picher's chat piles would be lurking in the dark.

"Out past the creek, where the land's still wild. They live with the earth, not against it. They listen to Tsisdetsi. At least they once did. They'll tell you what it wants. And Buck, you must go there alone."

I opened my mouth to ask more. Sage was already moving, her bare feet silent on the gravel.

"Wait—" I said.

Sage was gone, slipping into the shadows of the rose garden like she'd never been there. The air felt colder, the crickets quieter. Pard whined again, his nose twitching toward where Sage had vanished. As I stood staring at the empty bench, the rose petals Sage had held now lay on the ground, their edges curling inward.

The stars were bright, but they didn't feel loud to me—just distant, indifferent. I tugged Pard's leash, and we headed back to the inn, the weight of Sage's words settling into my bones like Picher's dust.

Clara Hensley stood on the back porch, gazing at the moon, when Pard and I returned from the rose garden. The light was dim, yet I could see by the shape of her nose and her facial bone structure that the handsome woman was more than just part Native American. She brushed her gray braid off her shoulder, smiling as she saw us.

"Samuel used to take walks in the rose garden after supper," she said.

Clara's smile disappeared when I said, "Your husband?"

"Samuel's gone," she said. "I'm a widow."

"Sorry," I said. "Your garden is epic, like experiencing the delicate aromas in a French perfumery."

Though Clara's arms were clasped tightly around her chest, her sullen expression morphed into something closely resembling a smile.

"Sam and I visited Paris once," she said. "You remind me of him."

Clara's smile grew when I asked, "Are there fairies in your garden?"

"Why do you ask?"

"Except for a single bare spot, it's lush. A circle of mushrooms growing in the center," I said. "A fairy ring."

"My garden is magical," Clara said. "Especially beneath a Strawberry Moon. All sorts of mystical creatures live there."

I glanced at the sky, smiling when I saw the reddish cast of the moon.

"Your garden is truly magical," I said. "Pard and I intend to enjoy it every night we spend here. Right now, your wonderful bed is calling to me."

Clara smiled and said, "Don't miss my country breakfast tomorrow. It'll put some meat on that skinny body of yours."

"I don't recall anyone ever calling me skinny," I said.

"Guess not," she said. "I can see by your shoulders and those tight jeans that you're all muscle."

"I'm looking forward to breakfast," I said as Pard and I walked past her, wondering about her blatant come-on.

I awoke to the scent of bacon curling through the air like a memory you didn't know you missed. Coffee perked somewhere nearby, and a skillet popped and hissed in rhythm with someone humming a slow gospel tune. Pard was already pawing at the door.

In the dining room, Mama Clara was at the stove, wearing a butter-yellow apron and the same braid wrapped over her shoulder. Sunlight slanted through the windows, catching on suspended dust motes like golden fireflies. Jake and Colley were already seated at the heavy oak table, fork-deep in eggs, with thick slabs of cornbread waiting beside bowls of stewed tomatoes.

"Sleep good?" Clara asked, flipping sausage patties with a practiced hand.

"Like a rock," I said, and nodded toward the spread. "This is... extravagant."

"A good day starts with a good meal," she said. "Especially when the land's restless."

Clara's comment gave everyone pause.

Jake set down his fork. "Restless, how?"

She glanced up, smile still warm, but her gaze distant. "Things shift under the surface sometimes. You think the past is buried deep, but now and then, evil claws its way back to the surface. Dreams get louder. Shadows stretch."

Clara shook her head but didn't answer when Mama said, "Evil, you mean Tsisdetsi's Shadow?"

Colley grunted, breaking the impasse. "I swear I heard something last night. Not coyotes. Deeper."

Clara slid a plate in front of me. "Don't give it too much thought. Eat your breakfast before it gets cold."

But her hands trembled slightly as she poured coffee into thick ceramic mugs.

After breakfast, Jake pulled me aside on the gravel walk out front, the chopper already thumping to life in the field.

"What was that bit at breakfast?" he asked. "Clara seemed...

off."

"She hinted something's stirring. Something evil. Like she knows more than she's letting on."

Jake glanced toward the house. "Something unconnected to the Shadow?"

"Don't know," I said. "But I'd like to learn more about her husband. Something about that name—Samuel Hensley—it's digging at me."

Jake nodded. "I'll call Angie. She's good at finding ghosts."

"Who is Angie?" I asked.

"My assistant in New Orleans," Jake said. "She'll find out for us."

Mama and Colley were waiting as we climbed into the chopper, buckling down as the engine roared. I looked back once, catching sight of Clara standing alone on the porch. She wasn't waving, just watching.

# CHAPTER 4

The chopper clawed its way through the heavy Oklahoma air, rotors slicing the late-morning heat with a relentless thwump-thwump. Below, the land sprawled like a fever dream—scarred and hollow, pocked with sinkholes that gaped like open sores.

Skeletal trees, their bark peeled away by years of neglect, stabbed at the sky. My eyes traced the old mining roads, their faded lines snaking through the earth like veins drained of blood, crumbling under the weight of time and the toxic leech of mine waste. Clara's breakfast was already a memory. Chat Creek loomed ahead, a vibrant little town clinging to the edge of oblivion.

Jake leaned forward in his seat, his face pressed close to the chopper's window, squinting against the sun's glare. His voice crackled through the headset, sharp with unease.

"See that?" he said.

I followed his gaze. There it was: Chat Creek High School, a brick relic crouching in a sea of overgrown weeds. Its windows were black voids, reflecting nothing but the desolation around them. The faded lettering on the arch above the entrance—Chat Creek High School—flaked away like dead skin, barely legible.

The roof sagged under the weight of years, and the cracked pavement of the parking lot bled green with moss and thistle, clawing up through the fissures as if the earth itself wanted to swallow the place whole.

"Jesus," Colley muttered into his headset, his voice tight. "It's like the world ended, and nobody told this place."

I stayed silent, my jaw clenched. The building stood, but it was a corpse—hollowed out, abandoned, its pulse long gone. The chopper descended, kicking up a storm of dust and brittle grass as it settled beyond the rusted bleachers, near a goalpost that tilted drunkenly to one side, its paint chipped to bare metal.

The silence that greeted us as the rotors slowed was suffocating. No birds. No hum of life. No echo of what a high school should be—no squeak of sneakers on a gym floor, no laughter spilling from classrooms, no scraps of paper skittering across the lot in the wind. Just the faint moan of a breeze through broken windows, carrying the acrid tang of something chemical, something wrong.

I stepped out first, my boots crunching on the brittle grass, the sound unnaturally loud in the stillness. Jake followed, his face pale, his eyes darting across the lot.

"No kids," he said, almost to himself, his voice barely above a whisper. "Crazy."

Mama shook her head as she stepped onto the ground, her boots sinking slightly into the cracked earth.

"This place..." Her voice was low, heavy with something like grief. "It's dystopian. A graveyard of dreams. Your cameras, Jake —they'll choke on the hopelessness this place breathes."

Colley's fingers twitched. "Something's wrong. It's like the feeling I got in Afghanistan right before making contact."

I felt it too—a weight in my chest, like the land itself was pressing down on me, leeching the warmth from my bones. Pard also felt it, barely sniffing the ground.

A malaise clung to us like damp rot as we trudged toward the staging area at the front of the school. As we rounded the corner, the scene shifted. The desolation gave way to a frenetic pulse of activity, a stark contrast to the dead quiet of the lot.

The staging area buzzed with the clatter of equipment and the sharp voices of workers barking orders. Two semis, their sides emblazoned with bold red and blue Huntington Productions logos, loomed like awaiting soldiers. Crew members swarmed around them, unloading crates of sound gear and cameras, their movements hurried but precise, like ants rebuilding a colony in the ruins.

A man with a clipboard stood near the trucks, his sharp eyes scanning the chaos with a mix of exhaustion and control. His white polo, embroidered with the Huntington logo, was damp with sweat, and his blue chinos were streaked with dust. Well-worn cowboy boots scuffed the pavement as he turned and spotted Jake. A tired smile cracked his weathered face, and he strode over, extending a hand.

"Rod Bloustine," Jake said, clapping the man's shoulder. "Meet Buck McDivit, this episode's chief investigator."

"Pleased to meet you," I said.

"Rod's my production supervisor since day one. Keeps the whole circus running."

Bloustine's handshake was firm, his grip calloused from years of wrangling equipment and egos.

"A hundred forty-two episodes and counting," he said, his voice gravelly but warm. "And this one's already trying to kill us."

He was in his fifties, his dark hair thinning at the crown, his eyes shadowed with the kind of fatigue that came from too many long days and not enough sleep.

Jake's smile faltered. "Everything okay?"

Rod's expression darkened, his jaw tightening. "It was. At least until we rolled into this godforsaken lot."

"Tell me," Jake said.

Rod gestured toward the staging area, where a group of workers was wrestling with a tangled mess of cables.

"Bad luck hit us like a freight train the second we got here."

Jake's brow furrowed. "What happened?"

Rod sighed, rubbing the back of his neck. "Where do I start? One of the transport engines blew on the way in—smoke everywhere, like the damn thing caught fire. Took us an hour to get it limping again. Then we start unloading, and one of our best cameras is dead. Lens cracked, circuits fried, no explanation. Just... kaput."

"Damn!" Jake said, his hands balling into fists.

"That's not the half of it," Rod said, his voice dropping lower, as if he didn't want the crew to overhear. "Jane—one of our camera ops—got sick. Violently sick. Puking her guts out, shaking like a leaf. Doc Hiu took one look at her and called an ambulance. Sent her back to Tulsa."

Jake's face went taut. "A virus?"

Rod nodded grimly. "Doc thinks so. Said it came on fast—too fast. And she's not the only one. One of the grips and an assistant sound tech are showing symptoms now. Fever, nausea, the works. I sent them to the motel to quarantine, but…"

He trailed off, his eyes flicking toward the school, its dark windows staring back like empty sockets.

Jake's voice was sharp. "Anyone else?"

"Not yet," Rod said, but his tone wasn't reassuring. "We're stretched thin as it is. If we lose more equipment and people, this shoot will be a nightmare."

The crew's hustle and bustle felt like a fragile shield against the desolation, and Rod's words hung in the air like a warning. Mama sensed it too and spelled it out in her own words.

"This isn't just bad luck," she said, her voice low and heavy. "We're cursed. You can smell it in the dirt, feel it clawing at your skin. Whatever happened here… It's still alive."

A chill snaked down my spine, prickling the hairs on my neck. Colley shifted beside me, his boots scuffing the cracked pavement as his eyes flicked nervously to the workers milling nearby, then back to the school's shadowed windows.

"Trucks breaking down and cameras fritzing aren't our only problems," he said.

Jake's brow furrowed again. "What now?"

Colley rubbed the back of his neck, his face grim. "Felt a knock in the chopper's engine on the way in this morning."

"Bad?" Jake's voice was sharp, all business.

"Don't know yet. Needs a proper look in Tulsa. Aviation mechanics'll sort it out."

"Is it safe to fly?" Jake asked.

Colley's jaw tightened, but he nodded. "It'll hold. It won't be my first time nursing a wounded bird."

Jake's eyes lingered on him, unconvinced. "You sure?"

"I'll get there," Colley said, his tone final.

"When are you leaving?" Jake asked.

"Now. The sooner I get the chopper fixed, the sooner we'll be back in business," Colley said.

"Damn," I said, watching him go. "And this is the safest town in the area. You think the mine waste's poison stretched this far?"

Mama's lips pressed into a thin line. "Something worse," she said.

Jake shook his head, as if trying to dislodge the unease clinging to him like damp rot. "Like what?"

Her gaze didn't waver from the school. "Don't know, love. We're here to find out."

Rod adjusted his cap and cleared his throat. "What's the plan, Bossman?"

"Take the crew, get footage around town. Then head to Picher. It's a ghost's playground, and the haze today will make it seem like the end of the world. Grab as many atmospheric shots as you can. You know the drill."

"Yes, sir," Rod said, squinting at the school. "What about you?"

"Angie called this morning with leads on Picher's last holdouts. One's holed up right here at the high school."

Rod raised an eyebrow. "Here? The place looks deader than Picher."

Jake's mouth twitched. "There's a sign on the front door. 'Ava's Deli.'"

"A deli in the abandoned school building? The place is a musty coffin," Rod said.

"Free rent's hard to beat," Jake said. "Bikers, truckers, locals, miners—they all know about it. Can you spare a skeleton crew for me? You know what I need."

Rod nodded. "I'll scrape one together."

Jake clapped his shoulder. "Good man."

Rod glanced at the school, its broken windows gaping like empty eye sockets. "Don't know where that deli's located, though we should get a ton of atmospheric footage in that old haunted hulk."

"It's in there," Jake said. "Somewhere in the dark recesses of too many blurred memories. "Get the crew rolling. Mama, Buck, and I will catch up soon."

"Yes, sir," Rod said, turning on his heel and striding off, his boots kicking up dust.

Jake pulled out his phone. "I have calls to make. Mind waiting in the caterer's tent?"

Mama leaned in, her lips brushing his with a warm peck. "Take your time, darling."

As Jake wandered toward the shade of a gnarled oak, the chopper's engine roared to life, a guttural snarl that shattered the oppressive quiet. A lone dove, startled, burst from the grass and skimmed low over a nearby field, its wings a fleeting blur. The helicopter lurched off the old football field, kicking up a storm of grit and dry grass, then climbed unsteadily into the sky, banking toward Tulsa.

Mama nudged me, her eyes glinting with mischief. "You're in for a treat."

"How's that?" I asked, wiping sweat from my brow.

"Jake's catering tent. I need a martini, and I'm betting a cold Coors would hit you just right."

I grinned. "Jake has a bartender on payroll?"

Mama's laugh was low and knowing. "Get used to it, Buck. Jake does everything first class. The food's so good, it's a miracle the crew isn't waddling around fifty pounds heavier."

She wasn't kidding. The catering tent loomed ahead, a circus-style canvas beast decked out in Jake's company colors—red and blue stripes that popped against the dreary landscape. Clear plastic windows ran from the ceiling to the floor, offering a glimpse of the bustling interior. We pushed through the flaps, and a blast of cool air hit us, sharp and welcome, cutting through the day's stifling heat.

Inside, the tent hummed with life. Workers in crisp white smocks and aprons manned a buffet line, their movements quick and practiced. Crew members lounged at portable tables, sipping drinks and picking at plates piled high with food that smelled like roasted herbs, grilled meat, and something sweet, maybe pastries.

At the center, a circular bar gleamed under soft lighting, presided over by an older woman with a warm smile and honey-blond hair swept back to reveal silver hoop earrings.

"This place gets wild after a long shoot," Mama said, steering me toward the bar.

"You've been on location with Jake before?" I asked, sliding onto a stool.

"Oh, yes," she said, her voice rich with memory. "Jake spares no expense to keep his people happy. Spoils us rotten."

"Mama!" the bartender called, her grin wide and genuine. "How the hell are you?"

"Purring like a stray cat in a creamery," Mama shot back, settling beside me. "Norma, meet Buck, our chief investigator on this gig."

Norma leaned over the counter, her handshake firm, her eyes sharp and appraising.

"Love your dog," she said. "What's his name?"

"Pard," I said.

Norma kept a treat jar behind the counter, and Pard quickly snatched it up when she tossed it to him.

"You'll have a friend for life, now," I said.

Norma's eyes twinkled when she smiled. "I know what you're drinking, Mama. And you, cowboy? Let me guess—Coors, ice-cold, no frills."

I blinked. "How'd you know?"

She smirked. "No guess. Bossman's obsessive. Briefs us on every client and crew member's drink of choice."

"Impressive," I said, genuinely taken aback.

A short man with a cookie-duster mustache and a white

beret sidled up, his smock pristine despite the chaos.

"Neil, this is Buck, Jake's newest," Mama said. "Neil's the corporate chef. Used to run the show at Galatoire's."

"Galatoire's?" I whistled. "Jake must be paying you a fortune."

Neil's grin was sly. "Don't ask, don't tell. Pleasure, Buck. Gotta run—the Escargots de Bourgogne won't plate themselves, and the crew'll riot if they're late."

He bustled off, humming.

Norma slid a frosty Coors my way and set a martini in front of Mama, its glass glistening with condensation. She hurried off to serve a straggler waving an empty bottle. Mama tapped my can with her glass, the clink sharp in the tent's hum.

"Cheers," she said, our eyes locking. "You've got something on your mind, Buck. I see it in your face."

I took a long pull from the Coors, the cold biting my throat.

"Last night, Pard and I walked through Clara's rose garden after dinner. Someone was waiting."

Mama's glass paused halfway to her lips. "Go on."

"A woman. Called herself Sage. Young, maybe, or ancient—hard to tell. Her skin... it wasn't right. Pale, almost glowing under the moon, like it was lit from within. Her hair was a wild tangle, streaked with blues and greens, like seaweed caught in a tide."

"Did she say what she was doing in Clara's garden?" Mama asked.

"She implied she was Clara's kin. She never gave me a straight answer when I asked her where she lived. I had the feeling her home was in the garden."

"Clara's kin?" Mama said.

"I know," I said. "It seemed to imply that Clara is as supernatural as Sage."

After a moment of reflection, Mama said, "Go on with your description."

"Sage's dress was patched, with strange patterns stitched together, moving as if they were alive. And her eyes..." I hesitated, the memory tightening my chest. "Storm clouds,

Mama. Not human. She felt... Something other. Supernatural, maybe. Mystical, at the least."

Mama's gaze sharpened, unblinking. "What'd she say?"

"She spoke of a commune. People who know Tsisdetsi's Shadow—more than Clara's letting on. Called them 'People of the Earth.' Gave me vague directions, said I have to go alone."

Mama's fingers tightened around her glass. "Jake won't like that."

"Which is why I'm telling you, not him."

"What else?" Mama asked.

"She was cryptic. Said the stars are loud tonight, and they were talking about me, saying I was here for the Shadow. When I asked her what she meant, she said, "Tsisdetsi. The one that watches."'

"What else did she say?" Mama asked.

"She said, 'Picher's full of ghosts. Tsisdetsi's different. It's not a ghost. It's... memory. Pain. The land's voice. It only shows itself to people who need to see.'"

Mama leaned closer. "See what?"

"'What has been done to the rivers, the mines, the children who never grew up right. Tsisdetsi carries it all.'"

She leaned back, her eyes distant and calculating. After a long moment, she said, "Jake won't like you going alone, and I don't feel right about not telling him."

I nodded and said, "Neither do I. What do you suggest we do?"

"I'll tell him tonight over drinks," she said. "He's been on dozens of these shoots and won't do anything to jeopardize an episode."

"What about Sage?" I asked.

"Tell Jake about her," Mama said. "Her appearance in Cryptid Hunter could be exactly what this episode needs."

# CHAPTER 5

Norma had just served Mama another martini, Pard another treat, and me another frosty can of Coors when she smiled and her eyes lit up.

"Bossman just walked in," she said. "I'd better get his scotch."

Jake joined us at the bar. He wasn't smiling when he reached down and rubbed Pard's head.

"What's up, love?" Mama asked.

"Someone slashed the tires on the film crew's van," he said.

Mama's hand went to her mouth, and she said, "Oh, no!"

Jake's usual smile returned when Norma handed him his cocktail. His mood was even better after a long pull from his tall glass of scotch.

"Whatever Neil cooked smells wonderful," Mama said. "It's past lunch. Shall we get something to eat with our drinks?"

Jake shook his head. "We need to interview Ava and then decide where to go next."

Norma was frowning when she returned to the bar. "The generator's on the fritz. No air conditioning and all the food will spoil in this heat."

"Shit!" Jake said.

"Someone's on their way from Miami to repair it," Norma said. "Hopefully, it won't be down long."

Unlike the city in Florida, the county seat of Ottawa County had a population of only around twelve thousand and was pronounced "Miamuh" by the locals.

"Thanks, Norma," Jake said, chugging the rest of his scotch. "Let's go. We can get something to eat at Ava's Deli."

The day had grown warmer as we left the air-conditioned haven of Jake's catering tent. A breeze blowing from the north helped some, though I felt a chill that had nothing to do with the wind.

By the time we reached the old building, the breeze was gone, the air not just still, but heavy and tainted, as if it carried the memory of the mine's poison. I glanced at the brick walls streaked with rust-colored stains that looked too much like blood. Mama edged closer, her eyes narrowing as if peering through a veil of secrets.

The air around the building was thick with a sour tang, like rusted metal and damp earth mixed with something older, fouler. The doors to the school entrance were slightly ajar. As I stepped inside, the air hit me like a wall—stale and heavy. Dust covered the floors in a smooth layer.

No footprints. There was no sign that anyone had been here for years. I couldn't shake the feeling that the school was watching us. Neither could Pard, his mournful howl echoing down the hall.

"Even Pard thinks this place is creepy," Jake said. "Doesn't surprise me because it smells like a tomb."

The wide hallway was lined with musty old cabinets filled with football trophies from a long-ago past, black-and-white class pictures, track medals, and faded memories. Outside, thunder from a late afternoon storm rumbled as rain peppered the building's flat roof. An old photograph caught my attention, and I gestured for Mama and Jake to take a look.

"What is it?" Mama asked.

"Chat Creek basketball squad, 1945. The young man in the middle is Samuel Hensley," I said.

"He can't be Clara's husband," Mama said. "If he were still alive, he'd be almost a hundred."

"Maybe he's Samuel senior and Clara's husband, Samuel junior."

"Could be," I said.

"Seems quite a coincidence with all the pictures in these

cabinets that you stumbled onto Samuel Hensley's," Mama said.

"Maybe we were meant to see it," I said.

"Let's move and worry about it later," Jake said. "The film crew has been waiting almost an hour for us, and Ava may have already locked up and gone home."

The silence was louder than the clatter of the crew; the only sound the echo of Pard's scratchy steps against the tile floor. When he began sniffing around a locker, Jake investigated.

"Hold up. Pard has found something." Jake pointed at the lockers lining the far hallway. "This is Samuel Hensley's locker."

The metal was rusted, streaked from years of neglect, and the old locker rattled when Jake gave it a pull.

"Is it empty?" Mama asked.

"Hardly," Jake said. "It looks as though someone walked away from it seventy-five years ago and never returned."

A gray jacket emblazoned with a red and black Chat Creek High logo hung inside. Musty old textbooks and lined notepads occupied the shelves. A pair of well-worn basketball shoes rested on the rusting floor of the locker. What caught our attention was a heart scratched on the inside of the old metal door.

"Check out the graffiti heart," I said. "Sam + Clara."

"Impossible," Mama said. "Clara is nowhere near a hundred."

"Maybe this is Sam Junior's locker," Jake said.

"We found the scratched heart, Jake and Clara's heart, and this locker because something wanted us to see them," Mama said.

"For what reason?" Jake asked.

"To tell us something it wants us to know," Mama said.

Jake looked perplexed and said, "The Shadow? What?"

Mama dismissed his question with a shake of her head.

Outside, the wind had picked up, rattling the tiles on the old roof. Somewhere in the building, a door slammed.

"I see a sign at the end of the hallway," I said. "It's Ava's."

Ava's deli was once part of the school cafeteria. A generator rumbled outside the window, providing electricity for the fluorescent lights, air conditioning, a large fan, and the refrigeration. Displayed in the deli cabinets were souvenirs, sandwiches, burritos, and candy bars. Various sodas swam in ice inside a red metal chest, emblazoned with the Coke logo.

The three members of Jake's film crew were anything but bored as they sat at a table with an older woman holding a guitar, singing the protest song, "We Shall Overcome." When they spotted Jake, their accompaniment came to a halt. We walked to the table, applauding when the woman finished the song on her own. The crew's equipment was already set up, and they began filming the scene.

"Thanks," she said. "I performed that song at Woodstock." Winking, she added, "Not on stage. I was an attendee."

"I'm Jake Huntington, and this is Mama Mulate, Buck McDivit, and Buck's dog Pard. Are you Ava?"

The woman nodded as Pard extended his paw and waited for her to shake it. She did, smiling and rubbing his head for good measure.

"Ava Baltimore," she said.

Ava was a petite woman with streaks of henna mixed with gray in her shoulder-length dark hair. Like Clara, she wore silver and turquoise dangling earrings, and her long dress was as black as her eyes. Although she was likely in her eighties, her teeth were full and bright, and her smile was infectious.

"You have a wonderful voice," Jake said. "You should have been performing on the big stage."

"I was lead singer with a group in the seventies," she said. "We toured with the Doors."

"Did you, now?" Jake said. "What was the name of your group?"

"The Pegs. We wrote our own songs, though none of them ever charted." She smiled, reminiscing. "We weren't even one-hit wonders."

"My assistant, Angie, told me you'd been back in Oklahoma for a while and were one of the hold-outs the government couldn't convince to move from Picher," Jake said.

Ava nodded. "My husband was a miner and died when one of

the adits collapsed. Our children moved away to California, but I decided to stay and write songs that would tell Picher's story."

She nodded again when Jake said, "But you finally left."

"Gave up the ghost," she said with a smile. "The Picher-Neosho Tornado in '08. One hundred seventy-five miles per hour beast that was on the ground for an hour and thirty minutes, killing twenty-one people and injuring nearly three hundred more," Ava said. For me, it was the last straw. I accepted the government's offer and moved here to Chat Creek."

"Are any other holdouts still alive?" Jake asked.

"Not many of us left," she said. "Earl Tatum, who everyone calls Grub, Lila Voss, and Toby Redhawk."

Ava nodded when Jake asked, "Do they live in Chat Creek?"

"You can find Grub sitting on his front porch in the town's only neighborhood. He's a little touched in the head, so you might not get much from him."

"And Lila and Toby?" Jake said.

"Toby's a suspicious one," Ava said. "He lives around here, though I'd be surprised if you can get him to talk to you. Lila has a souvenir shop on Main. You'll have a hard time getting her to shut up."

It was clear from Ava's appearance that she was likely full-blooded, or close to it, American Indian. I interrupted Jake's interview to ask a question.

She flashed me one of her inimitable smiles when I said, "Are you part of the Ottawa Tribe?"

"Quapaw," she said.

"Aren't the Ottawas and the Quapaws part of the same tribe?" I asked.

"The Quapaw Nation has a reservation here in Ottawa County, though Quapaw and Ottawa are distinct tribal entities."

Ava's smile disappeared when Jake said, "Then you know about the legend of Tsisdetsi's Shadow?"

"Tsisdetsi's Shadow is no legend," she said. "It's real, an entity that transcends tribal barriers."

"How so?" Jake asked.

"I lived in a commune in Northern California for a while," she said. "A place ripe with Native Americans and people who valued the earth. It was where I first heard of Tsisdetsi's Shadow, not from a Quapaw but from the Yurok, Pomo, and Hupa people living at the commune."

"Have you seen the Shadow?" Jake asked.

"Once," she said. "During a spiritual ceremony, I entered a trance brought on by peyote tea."

"Can you describe it for us?" Jake asked.

Thunder rumbled outside, shaking the old brick building, as if foreshadowing Ava's description.

"Wait," she said. "The Shadow is real and must be treated with reverence."

Ava vanished behind her deli counter and returned with three candles and an eagle feather. After dimming the lights, she lit the candles: one black, one white, and one red. She began to speak while fanning the smoke with the feather.

Jake's crew didn't miss a beat, capturing the suddenly eerie scene that amplified the effects of darkness, thunder, smoke, and Ava's melodious voice.

"The Quapaw language of my ancestors is largely lost. Accept this smoke curling toward the ceiling as my words of reverence."

Thunder shook the building once more, and this time the windows illuminated with the flash of nearby lightning, as if the Shadow had accepted Ava's appeal. When Ava spoke again, her voice had changed from melodious to deep and otherworldly, as scratchy as old vinyl and profound as a preacher's message.

"Time is a river that flows milk and honey from gentle earth blessed by the Great Spirit. Evil has damaged the bounty, infecting the river, poisoning the land, and killing its people. I am but the messenger of the madness. Take heed."

The candles flickered and then died. Ava's eyes shut, her long hair splayed across the table as if she had fainted. The air had become stuffy, prompting one of Jake's crew to rush behind the counter to turn on the lights and air conditioning.

Pard whined as Mama grabbed a soda from the red metal Coke chest, popped the top, and lifted Ava off the table until she opened her eyes and could take a sip. When she finally came around, it was clear she was either unable or unwilling to continue the interview.

"Thank you, Ava," Jake said. "You've provided lots of grist for our mill."

"I love Cryptid Hunter and was happy to oblige," she said. "Not to mention, I'll probably have an influx of tourists detouring off the beaten path."

Jake grinned. "Prepare to sign lots of autographs. I noticed your souvenir T-shirts."

"I'll get you one," she said with a smile.

"Not just one. I'll take all you have."

Ava's T-shirts were colorful and featured Native American-inspired art. The back said Ava's Deli, Chat Creek, Oklahoma."

"They're twenty bucks apiece," she said.

"I'll give you fifty apiece if you'll autograph them for me," Jake said.

"That's a lot of money," she said.

Jake opened his wallet, showing his wad of cash, and said, "No problem. "

Her smile returned after she autographed and handed the T-shirts to us.

"Thank you. It's my first big sale of the year. Even in Chat Creek, Social Security only goes so far."

"You'll have a hard time keeping them in stock once the episode airs," Jake said.

"Jake," she said. "There's someone else you need to talk to: **Nadie Red Eagle, a Quapaw medicine woman who lives in Bone Hollow.**"

"How do I find her?" Jake asked.

Ava shook her head and said, "You won't unless she wants you to. It would help if you were an Indian."

The film crew had stowed their equipment, everyone smiling as we trekked back down the long hallway.

The crew began high-fiving when Jake said, "Good work, gang. Now I know why I pay you so much. Drinks and autographed T-shirts are on me."

We were halfway down the long hall when I said, "I forgot something in the deli. Meet you at the catering tent."

Pard and I found Ava standing almost comatose near her deli stand. When Pard extended a paw, she smiled, knelt, and shook it.

"I have another question I didn't want to share with the rest of the crew, and I thought you might tell another Indian."

"What tribe are you?" she asked.

"Cherokee," I said.

"Who are your parents?" she asked.

"Don't have any," I said. "Raised mostly in Indian schools and with a couple of benevolent foster parents."

Ava clutched my hand and said, "I'm so sorry."

"I survived," I said. "We all have our crosses to bear and PTSD to overcome."

"What's your question?" she asked.

"You mentioned you lived in a commune in Northern California. Are you familiar with "The People of the Earth," a commune here in Ottawa County?"

"Protectors of the old ways, Indians and like-minded people. I'm not a member. Sorry."

"Any idea who might know something about them?" I asked.

"Amos would know," Ava said.

"Amos?"

"Amos Callahan," she said. "Ottawa County Sheriff."

"You know him?"

Ava grinned. "Everyone in the county knows Fry. He has a café in Miami, home of the best chicken fry in Oklahoma."

I returned Ava's grin and said, "Hell, he sounds like someone I need to visit even if he knows nothing about the commune."

"Fry knows," Ava said. "He's the resident expert on all things supernatural: crop circles, cattle mutilations, pagans. You'll have a hard time shutting him up."

"You're a lifesaver. Thank you," I said. Pard and I started for the door. I stopped, turning before reaching it. "Ava, when I was in Indian school, they played your songs on the intercom. Your song, "Time," was one of them. It was wonderful and evocative, and I'll never forget it."

"You just made my day." She walked behind her counter, returning with a vinyl record whose cover said, "Time by Ava Baltimore and the Pegs."

I took the record, squeezed her hand, and said, "Thank you, Ava."

# CHAPTER 6

Rain hammered the catering tent, the wind howling through the flaps as if Tsisdetsi's Shadow itself was trying to claw its way inside. The air was cool, the generator humming steadily now that the repairman from Miami had worked his magic.

The catering tent's appearance changed dramatically after dark, with a heavy canvas covering the plastic sides to protect it from unusually intense weather conditions, such as the thunderstorm that night. The lights were dimmed, and the atmosphere was cozy.

The aroma of Neil's gourmet spread—roasted quail with wild mushroom risotto and a hint of truffle oil—pierced through the persistent metallic tang of the storm. The film crew, fresh from their successful shoot in Picher, gathered around the long table, their chatter loud and lively, a stark contrast to the somber weather outside.

The vibrant Native American designs of the souvenir T-shirts stood out against the tent's muted canvas walls, lighting up the crew's eyes. Hands shot out, eager for their own. I passed them around, the bold "Ava's Deli, Chat Creek, Oklahoma" text on the back earning nods of approval.

"Jake, as usual, you're a hero," Neil said, trying on his T-shirt.

"Glad everyone likes them," Jake said, scratching Pard's ears as he nosed around for scraps.

He leaned back on his barstool, a fresh scotch in hand. His eyes, though, were sharp, scanning the crew with that calculating look he got when he was piecing things together. Mama sat beside him, her martini glass half-empty, her gaze distant as if still processing Ava's trance and the cryptic warning about the poisoned land. Pard, sensing the shift in mood, settled at my feet with a low whine.

"All right, folks," Jake said, clapping his hands to quiet the crew's banter. "Great work in Picher today. You got some killer footage, and I'm proud of you."

"The company transport is at the front door," Norma said.

"Daylight comes early," Jake said.

The crew headed for the front flap, an overhang protecting them from the rain as they entered the bus. Neil tapped Jake's shoulder.

"Plenty of snacks," he said. "Your ride is waiting outside when you're ready for it."

Except for Norma, we were soon alone in the tent. She smiled as she mixed Jake and Mama more drinks and presented me with a cold Coors.

"The interview went great, love," Mama said.

"It did, but while poignant interviews make for good episodes, only one thing makes them great," Jake said.

"What?" Mama asked.

"In this case, we need footage of Tsisdetsi's Shadow, and I don't mean the blurred footage taken by a drunk with a cell phone," he said.

I knew better than to ask Jake if he believed in the supernatural.

Instead, I said, "And that's why you're paying me the big bucks?"

Jake's smile indicated that I'd hit the nail on the proverbial head. The weight of my all-but-impossible task began to settle in, and I didn't like the thought of being set up for failure. The idea faded to the back of my mind when he changed the subject.

"Clara's not expecting us for dinner," he said. "She baked an apple pie and said to feel free to raid the refrigerator if we get hungry later tonight."

"My favorite," I said.

Something else has you excited," Mama said, "What's up?"

"When I returned down the hall to see Ava, she gave me the name of someone who might help us."

"Who?" Jake asked.

"Amos Callahan, the county sheriff. Ava says there's not much about Ottawa County he doesn't know," I said.

"But will he tell us?" Mama asked.

"His nickname is Fry, and he owns a café in Miami named Fry's Chicken Shack. Ava said once we get him started, we'll have a hard time shutting him up. His specialty is chicken-fried steak."

Mama glanced at Jake, smiled, and said, "Oh Lord!"

"What?" I said.

"I gain five pounds every time I see one. I'm not as lucky as you and Jake, who can eat anything they want and never gain a pound."

"Then maybe I should challenge you to a little foot race when we return to Chat Creek," Jake said.

"Don't you dare," Mama said.

"Might be the only way I'll ever beat you," he said.

"You love it," she said. "Quit whining."

Jake was smiling when he said, "You think the sheriff knows about Tsisdetsi's Shadow?"

"Ava said if our questions involve the supernatural, Sheriff Callahan is the man to ask," I said.

Jake smiled. "Perfect. We'll make his interview the first scene of the episode. I need to talk to Angie and have her arrange it. Will you and Buck be okay while I call her?"

Mama laughed. "Take your time, love. Buck and I will be fine."

After kissing Mama, Jake left the barstool and strolled to a table at the rear of the catering tent. Thunder shook the large canvas structure as Norma served another round.

"I talked with Jake about your meeting with Sage," Mama said. "He's intrigued."

"Ava believes Sheriff Callahan knows all about the commune. Maybe he can help us arrange a photo shoot," I said. "Something else."

"What?" Mama said.

"After my walk last night, Clara was waiting for me on the back porch."

"And?" she said.

"I had the distinct feeling she was coming on to me."

Mama laughed. "You're a handsome man. Women must hit on you all the time."

"My Indian intuition tells me it was something other than that," I said.

"Like what?"

I shook my head and said, "Don't know, but I have a feeling I'm going to find out."

Thunder shook the tent before Mama could reply. Jake was smiling as he rejoined us.

"What's up, love?" she asked.

"Angie has been researching Sam and Clara Hensley," he said. "What she learned will blow your mind."

"Tell us," Mama said.

"First, I need another scotch."

Norma had seen Jake returning to the bar and smiled when she presented him with a fresh drink.

"You looked as if you needed another," she said.

"Mama, remind me to put Norma in for a raise," Jake said.

Mama was grinning and shaking her head as Jake took a drink from the chilled beverage.

"Now, tell us what Angie told you."

"There's only one Samuel Hensley. That was his locker we saw. If he were alive, he'd be nearly a hundred."

Jake shook his head when Mama said, "Then Clara was either very young when she married him or is way older than she looks."

"There's no record of Clara's existence; no birth certificate, no high school diploma, and no driver's license. No records at all."

Neither Mama nor I replied, allowing Jake's words to sink in.

"Tsistedsi's Shadow is more than a legend," Mama said. "Its presence permeates everything and everybody in Ottawa County."

"Even Clara?" I asked.

"Why not? Ava saw it. Felt it. And that school... It's like it wanted us to find that locker, that heart. Sam and Clara's story is tied to this. I'd bet my last dollar."

I nodded, the image of the rusted locker and the scratched heart still vivid.

"I have the feeling Ava didn't tell us everything she knows," I said.

Mama set her glass down, her voice low but firm. "Ava wasn't just spinning stories. That trance, those words about the river and the madness—they're no coincidence. Something's guiding us, and it's not just intuition."

"Maybe," Jake said. "I have other news. Angie called Sheriff Callahan while I waited. He loves Cryptid Hunter, as does everyone in Miami, and is over the moon."

"And?"

"We're taking a crew to Fry's Chicken Shack tomorrow, and let's keep our fingers crossed that the entire town doesn't show up."

"My stomach's already growling," I said.

"Sorry, Buck. You aren't invited?"

"I'm crushed," I said with a smile.

"I have another assignment for you," Jake said.

"I'm all in," I said. "Hit me."

"Bone Hollow," Jake said. "Angie wasn't able to locate it on any map. Think you can find it?"

"Maybe," I said.

"We need to make contact with Nadie Red Eagle," Jake said. "The sooner we find her, the better."

"I'll need a horse," I said.

"Our ATV is better. It can go anywhere a horse can, and you'll be able to haul more equipment."

"What kind of equipment are you talking about?" I asked.

"Video equipment," he said.

"Why can't I use the camera on my phone?"

"That would work in a pinch. This isn't a pinch, and I'm sending a professional with you; someone who can handle a camera and sound equipment. You'll meet Tessie tomorrow morning before you leave," Jake said.

"Tessie?" I said.

"Tess Hawthorne. You'll like her."

"I'm sure of it, but will she be able to handle the wilds of northeast Oklahoma?" I said, leaning back in my chair, arms crossed.

Hearing my frustration, Jake smiled and motioned for Norma to bring me another Coors. He waited until I'd taken a drink before addressing my concerns.

"Hard to pack an ice chest on a horse," he said. "No problem with the ATV, and there's plenty of room for two."

Still unconvinced, I said, "Bone Hollow's no picnic, Jake. It's likely deep in the Ozarks, miles from anything resembling a road. We're talking triple-digit heat, humidity that'll drown you, mosquitoes the size of sparrows, and copperheads that don't give a damn about your boots. Not to mention the blackberry brambles that'll tear your skin to ribbons if you're not careful. And that's just the warm-up. You sure this Tess is up for it?"

Jake raised an eyebrow, unimpressed. "She's a pro, Buck. Shot documentaries in the Amazon and the Outback. I think she can handle some Oklahoma brush."

"Amazon's got guides and crews," I said. "Out here, it's just me, her, and whatever's lurking in the hollow. If she's never dealt with chiggers or pissed off a wild hog, she might not be as ready as you think."

Jake leaned forward, his voice steady. "You're the best tracker I have, Buck. You'll figure out how to make it work. Keep Tessie safe, get her to Nadie Red Eagle, and let her perform her magic. That's the deal."

I sighed, running a hand through my hair. "All right, but if she faints from heatstroke or runs screaming from a rattlesnake, don't say I didn't warn you."

I'd been so busy venting my spleen that I hadn't noticed my words were upsetting Mama. When I looked at her, I quickly realized my mistake. Her arms were crossed tightly over her chest, and her toes were tapping the floor.

"Maybe Buck would be more comfortable with a male videographer," she said.

Realizing I'd crossed a line in the sand, I grinned and said, "Guess my little rant sounded sexist."

"A bit," Mama said. "It wasn't that long ago women weren't allowed to run marathons because certain people, all men, questioned their fitness."

"I apologize," I said. "I know lots of women who are stronger, faster, and smarter than me. If Tess is ready, then so am I. Forgive me?"

"Maybe," she said. "If you keep your big mouth shut, that is."

I grinned and said, "Yes, ma'am."

Mama smiled, glanced at Jake, and uncrossed her arms.

"Guess you have some good qualities that offset the bad ones," she said.

"I keep trying," I said.

Jake tapped my shoulder with his palm. "I'll give you a driving lesson on the way back to the inn."

"The storm has let up," Mama said. "Let's go now."

"You got it, my dear," Jake said.

We left Norma a hefty tip and stepped into the drizzle. The Polaris Xpedition gleamed under the floodlights, fully enclosed with heat, AC, and all the bells and whistles. My jaw dropped.

"How much did this baby set you back?" I asked.

Jake grinned. "If you have to ask, you can't afford it. Want to drive?"

"For sure," I said, sliding behind the wheel.

The ride to Clara's Briar Patch Inn was a blast, the Xpedition eating up the muddy road. A light glowed in the hallway and kitchen as we pulled up.

"Keep the keys," Jake said. "Tess'll meet you at the tent at dawn. Mama and I are turning in early for our chicken fry adventure. The bus is picking us up."

"Eat one for me," I said.

Pard and I followed them upstairs, but Clara's apple pie kept calling my name. The cuckoo clock chimed two a.m. as I crept downstairs, barefoot and shirtless, expecting a quiet kitchen raid. I was wrong.

Clara was waiting at the foot of the stairs, her baby blue peignoir appearing ghostly in the dim light, her Cheshire cat grin sharp as a blade.

"See something you like, cowboy?" she said, her voice low and teasing.

"Ms. Hensley," I said, heart pounding, "are you trying to seduce me?"

The attractive older woman's dark eyes sparkled. For a split second, I could swear I saw something flicker in them—something older, darker, like the Shadow we were chasing.

# CHAPTER 7

The sun beat down on the cracked asphalt of Route 66, its late June heat shimmering off the highway as the Cryptid Hunter bus roared toward Miami, Oklahoma.

The bus, a gleaming beast painted in bold red and blue, sliced through the flatlands of Ottawa County like a rockstar's chariot, with the words Cryptid Hunter emblazoned in jagged white letters across its side.

Inside, Jake Huntington, all lean muscle and weathered charisma, lounged in a plush leather seat. Beside him, Mama, his love interest, filed her vividly painted nails. The film crew, a scrappy group of camera operators and sound techs, fiddled with equipment in the back, the hum of anticipation filling the air.

As the bus crested a low hill, Miami, pronounced Miamuh by the locals, came into view—a modest grid of brick buildings and neon signs, the county seat and the closest thing to a metropolis in the region.

Fry's Chicken Shack stood proudly on the edge of town, a low-slung diner with a faded sign promising "Best Chicken-Fried Steak in Ottawa County." Its gravel parking lot was already a zoo, packed with pickups and a growing crowd of locals clutching phones and homemade signs scrawled with "We Love Jake!" and "Hunt the Unknown!"

When the bus hissed to a stop, the doors swung open. Mama was the first to step down, followed by Jake, his boots crunching on the gravel, a grin spreading across his face as the crowd erupted.

"Cryptid! Hunter!" they chanted, kids waving, teens snapping selfies, and old-timers squinting curiously at the rockstar cryptozoologist. Fans spilled out of trucks and sedans, phone cameras held high like offerings. A group of teens raised a poster that read "Sasquatching With Jake!"

Somewhere in the crowd, someone had brought a papier-mâché Mothman. Jake smiled, his signature aviators reflecting the chaos, and Mama—calm, grounded, and somehow larger than life in her African sandals and wraparound turquoise sunglasses—cut a path through the crowd with practiced grace.

Mama signed a few autographs as Jake worked the audience like a pro, shaking hands and tossing winks, his deep Oklahoma drawl cutting through the noise.

"Holding up in this heat? Stay cool, now!"

Inside Fry's, the air was thick with the smell of sizzling grease and fresh coffee. The diner was a time capsule of small-town Americana—red vinyl booths, checkered linoleum, and a jukebox in the corner.

Sheriff Amos "Fry" Callahan held court at his usual spot, a large round table by the window. His khaki sheriff's uniform was crisp despite the humidity, and his badge gleamed. His handlebar mustache twitched as he leaned back, one arm draped over the chair.

Next to the sheriff sat Deputy Roy Hill, a wiry man with a buzzcut and a permanent grin, nodding eagerly as Fry spun a yarn about a '98 crop circle out by Quapaw that "was no prank, I'm telling you."

The door jingled as Jake and Mama pushed through, the crowd's noise fading behind them. Fry stood, all six-foot-three of him, and waved them over with a meaty hand.

"Well, if it ain't the Cryptid Hunter himself!" he boomed, his voice carrying over the clatter of plates. "And Mama, looking fiercer than a chupacabra in a henhouse!"

"Happy to meet you, Sheriff," Jake said.

Callahan paused, peering over his iced tea at the famed Cryptid Hunter like a man eyeing a rival storyteller. Then he grinned, wide as the Grand Lake horizon.

"Well," he said in a drawl, "I'll be plucked and fried. You

*do* look like the kind of fella who's talked face-to-face with a wampus cat."

"Only once," Jake said, deadpan. "He owed me money."

The few locals permitted inside—Fry's buddies from the VFW and a couple of old farmers—chuckled as they sipped iced tea and eyed the newcomers.

In his element, Jake grinned, his crew already filming.

The wood-paneled walls were cluttered with old sheriff's badges, signed photographs, and framed news clippings featuring headlines like *"Local Boy Finds Crop Circle in Cow Pasture Again"* and *"Chupacabra? Callahan Thinks So."* The old jukebox crooned Patsy Cline softly in the background.

"Sheriff, heard your chicken fries are as legendary as your stories."

Mama took a seat, her sharp eyes scanning the room, the crew sizing up angles as they set up cameras nearby.

"Damn right," Fry said, settling back down.

Deputy Hill piped up, "Ain't nobody tells a tale or cooks a steak like Sheriff Callahan. Man's a living legend!"

The sheriff puffed up, clearly pleased, as Roy launched into a story about the time he "single-handedly chased off a pack of coyotes with nothing but a flashlight and grit."

A waitress, young and freckled with a nametag reading Tammy, swung by with a tray of plates piled high with golden chicken-fried steak, creamy mashed potatoes, and green beans swimming in bacon fat. A basket of biscuits landed in the center, steam rising, and Tammy flashed a shy smile at Jake.

"On the house for the Cryptid Hunter," she said, blushing.

Jake leaned forward, cutting into the steak as Fry launched into his spiel.

"Now, Jake, you want to hear about something real strange? Back in '03, we had a rash of cattle cuttings out near Devil's Hollow. Clean cuts, no blood, like something from a surgical procedure. Folks blamed witches, maybe pagans from over in Joplin." His eyes gleamed, relishing the tale. "I'm telling you, there are things in these hills that don't show up on no trail cam."

Mama raised an eyebrow. "Witches, huh? That's new. Got any evidence, Sheriff?"

Fry grinned, undeterred, as Roy chimed in, "Oh, Sheriff Fry's got stories that'll curl your hair!"

The clatter of plates and the low hum of conversation in Fry's Chicken Shack faded as Jake leaned forward, his hands clasped on the table, his usual roguish grin replaced by a serious gaze.

The camera crew adjusted their lenses, feeling the shift in mood. Mama folded her arms, her sharp eyes fixed on Sheriff Amos "Fry" Callahan.

The large round table, littered with half-eaten plates of chicken-fried steak and mashed potatoes, seemed to shrink under the weight of the moment. Deputy Hill, usually quick with a quip, sat silent, his grin faltering. Outside, the crowd's chatter was a distant murmur, the Miami noon sun glaring through the diner's windows.

"Sheriff," Jake said, his voice low but clear, "tell us about Picher. The mines. What happened there?"

Fry's weathered face, typically animated with stories of crop circles and witches, grew still. His handlebar mustache drooped as the twinkle in his eyes faded. Setting his fork down, he wiped his hands on a napkin and leaned back in his chair, the creak of the wood echoing in the sudden quiet.

Gone was the cornpone drawl he wielded like a showman; his voice turned gravelly, deliberate, carrying the weight of a man who'd seen too much.

"Picher," he said, staring at a spot on the table like it held the town's ghosts. "Was a boomtown once. Lead and zinc were the biggest deposits in the world back in the day. In the early 1900s, companies arrived, tore up the land, and made fortunes.

"Folks built lives around those mines—homes, schools, churches. My granddaddy worked the Eagle-Picher shafts. Hard work, but it paid. Kept the lights on."

He paused, his jaw tightening. The café had gone stone-cold quiet. Hearing the sheriff's voice begin to crack, Jake motioned for Tammy to refill his tea.

"Please," Jake said. "We need to hear what you have to say."

Sheriff Callahan took a sip of tea and nodded.

"As the mines began playing out, the companies got greedy. Cut corners. Didn't care what they left behind." He leaned forward, his sheriff's badge catching the light. "They dug too deep, too fast. Left piles of waste—chat, they called it—mountains of it, full of lead."

The money for the jukebox had run out, leaving the only sound in the café as the click of Sheriff Callahan's glass and the swish of the overhead fans. Mama started to say something, but fell silent when Jake shot her a glance and shook his head. The sheriff began again.

"Tar Creek ran orange for years, like something out of a nightmare. Kids got sick. Folks started leaving. By the 1980s, the EPA designated it a Superfund site, one of the worst in the country. Promised a cleanup." He snorted, a bitter edge to it. "That was forty years ago, Jake. They're not even halfway done."

Mama shifted, her voice soft but probing.

"The government just... left it like that?" she said.

Fry's eyes flicked to her, then back to the table.

"Left us to rot. They bought out some folks, relocated them, but the money dried up. Picher's a ghost town now—empty houses, sinkholes from collapsed mine shafts."

"And the people who remained?" Jake asked as Sheriff Callahan's pause became prolonged.

"Folks who stayed, they were mad as hell. Felt abandoned. You drive through, you'll see it: land's scarred, water's bad, and the people of Ottawa County..." He shook his head. "They're tough, but they're tired. Tired of promises, tired of waiting for help that's never going to come."

Deputy Roy nodded slowly, his usual flattery absent. The crew's cameras whirred, capturing the sheriff's clenched fists, the way his broad shoulders sagged as he spoke.

Jake's face was unreadable, but his eyes held a flicker of anger, maybe at the story, maybe at the helplessness of it all. The waitress, Tammy, hovered nearby, her tray forgotten, caught in the gravity of Fry's words.

"Corporate greed did this," Fry said, his voice barely above a whisper now. "They took the wealth, left us the poison. And the government? They look the other way. That's the real monster in Ottawa County, Jake. Ain't no cryptid."

He sat back, the weight of his words settling over the table like dust. The café's usual warmth felt stifled, the jukebox silent. Outside, the crowd waited, unaware of the somber turn that had taken place inside.

Jake exchanged a glance with Mama, who gave a slight nod, signaling the crew to keep rolling. Leaning back in his chair, he met Callahan's gaze, the crew's cameras capturing every somber pause. Jake's voice pierced the silence, steady and respectful.

"Sheriff, that's a brutal but honest take on Picher. Thanks for laying it out like it is." He paused, then leaned forward, a spark of purpose in his eyes. "We're here because of that grainy video —the one shot by that drunken salesman from Tulsa. Tsisdetsi's Shadow. What can you tell us about it?"

Fry's weathered face softened, the lines around his eyes crinkling as his somber demeanor cracked like the sun breaking through clouds. A slow grin spread beneath his handlebar mustache, and the old showman's twinkle returned.

"Well, now, Jake," he said, his cornpone drawl creeping back. "That's a story I'm happy to spin. But first—" He raised a hand, snapping his fingers with a flourish toward the counter. "Tammy! Let's treat these fine folks to what Fry's is really famous for. Bring out the peach cobbler, darling!"

Tammy, who'd been lingering near the pass-through, broke into a smile and rushed to the kitchen, her sneakers squeaking on the checkered linoleum. The mood in the rural café shifted like a breeze through an open window.

Deputy Roy perked up, slapping the table with a chuckle.

"Oh, you're in for a real treat, Jake! Ain't nobody does cobbler like Fry's!"

The crew, sensing a break, lowered their cameras, grins

spreading as the promise of dessert lightened the room. Mama raised an eyebrow but couldn't hide a grin.

Moments later, Tammy returned, balancing a tray filled with bubbling dishes of peach cobbler, the golden crust shimmering beneath a scoop of vanilla ice cream that melted into sweet rivulets.

The scent of cinnamon and caramelized peaches filled the air, chasing away the lingering weight of Picher's tragedy. She set a dish in front of each person at the table—Jake, Mama, Fry, Roy, and even the crew, who eagerly pulled up chairs, their gear temporarily forgotten.

"On the house," Tammy said with a wink, her freckled cheeks flushed with pride.

Fry dug in first, his spoon breaking the crust with a satisfying crunch.

"This is my mama's recipe," he said, his voice warm with nostalgia. "Peaches from right here in Ottawa County, picked ripe and baked with a touch of magic."

He took a bite, closing his eyes as if savoring a memory. Jake followed suit, the first spoonful hitting his tongue with a burst of sweet-tart warmth, the ice cream's creaminess balancing the flaky crust. He let out a low whistle.

"Sheriff, you weren't kidding. This is worth the trip alone."

Mama took a bite and gave a nod of approval. "Damn fine cobbler, Amos."

The crew laughed, digging in with gusto, their spoons clinking as they swapped stories of road food disasters. Even the locals at nearby tables, Fry's select friends, leaned in, drawn by the infectious lightness.

The jukebox kicked on, Roy Acuff's soft drawl weaving through the chatter, and the diner felt alive again, the somber fog lifted by shared dessert and the promise of a wild tale.

Fry leaned back, wiping a bit of ice cream from his mustache, his grin wide.

"All right, Jake, you want Tsisdetsi's Shadow? I'll tell you what I know about that spooky ol' thing skulking around our hills."

His eyes gleamed with mischief, the cobbler-fueled warmth setting the stage for the next chapter of the Cryptid Hunter's quest. The cameras rolled again, capturing the sheriff's renewed energy, the crew's laughter, and the sticky joy of a perfect Oklahoma peach cobbler.

# CHAPTER 8

The first light of dawn had barely crested the Oklahoma horizon as I eased out of the Briar Patch Inn, the gravel crunching under my boots. The air was already thick with June heat, a faint mist clinging to the fields around Chat Creek.

I climbed into the Xpedition, Jake's custom beast—a matte-black, rugged off-road vehicle tricked out with reinforced shocks, all-terrain tires, and a climate-controlled cabin that felt like a sanctuary.

Pard jumped into the front seat next to me, his tail thumping against the leather seats. I held back a yawn, my eyes feeling gritty from a strange night spent with Clara Hensley that seemed more like a dream than reality.

I pulled up to the catering tent just outside of town, where Tess Hawthorne waited, her silhouette sharp against the rising sun. She was a vision of restless energy—five foot six, lean and athletic, her chestnut hair woven into a loose braid that caught the morning light. I was instantly attracted to her.

Tess's hazel eyes, flecked with green and gold, sparkled with a mix of curiosity and guarded intensity. Freckles dusted her face, and her outfit—cargo pants, a faded flannel, and a worn leather jacket—exuded practicality and coolness, as if she were born for road trips and late-night edits. With her camera bag slung over one shoulder, she flashed me a quick grin when I rolled to a stop.

"Morning," she said, climbing into the passenger seat, her voice carrying a playful edge. "I'm Tess Hawthorne."

"Buck McDivit," I said with a smile.

Tess had a load of heavy equipment. When I got out to put it into the vehicle, two of Jake's workmen motioned to me that they didn't need my help. I returned to the driver's seat while they loaded the back of the Xpedition.

Hearing Tess's voice, Pard immediately perked up, shoving his curious nose over the console to sniff her. She laughed, scratching his ears.

"Who's this charmer?"

"Pard," I said as I watched my best friend melt under Tess's touch, tail wagging like a metronome. "Traitor," I muttered under my breath.

Tess grinned, catching my comment but letting it slide.

I'd missed breakfast, and my stomach was growling. The main street of downtown Chat Creek lay ahead, and I decided to cruise it and take a look.

Chat Creek resembled many rural towns dotting Oklahoma's countryside: a bank, a five-and-dime, a vacant lot, and a tiny café with pickups parked outside.

"You hungry?" I asked.

"Not really," Tess said.

"Pard and I missed breakfast," I said.

"Pull in. I can always use another cup of coffee."

Downtown Chat Creek was coming to life. Farmers in worn overalls leaned against storefronts, swapping stories about the weather and crop prices. A couple of kids zipped by on bikes, their laughter cutting through the morning silence. The aroma of hot biscuits and sizzling bacon wafted out of the kitchen, hooking me like a fish.

Inside, the café was a hive of noise and warmth. Ceiling fans spun lazily overhead, stirring the air thick with grease and the scent of coffee. Every table was packed—ranchers with calloused hands, old-timers nursing mugs, a few women in scrubs fresh off the night shift at the clinic.

Waitresses in gingham aprons wove through the crowd, balancing plates of eggs and hashbrowns. The jukebox in the corner hummed with a twangy Merle Haggard tune. Tess and I snagged the last table, a wobbly one by the window, just as a harried waitress slapped down menus.

"Coffee?"

Tess and I both laughed out loud when we said, "black," at the same time.

We'd barely ordered biscuits and gravy for me, oatmeal for Tess, when the bell above the door jingled. A woman stepped in, scanning the room with sharp eyes. She was maybe late fifties, with a tangle of auburn hair pinned loosely at her neck.

Her denim skirt and embroidered blouse screamed local, but her restless energy set her apart. She sighed, seeing no empty seats, and turned to leave when she bumped our table, nearly toppling Tess's coffee.

"Sorry," she said, her voice bright but frayed. "Guess I'll wait for breakfast."

Tess glanced up, her spoon paused mid-bite. "We have room. Join us."

The woman hesitated, then slid into the chair with a grateful grin.

"Name's Lila Voss. Run the souvenir shop down the street—mugs, keychains, all that junk tourists buy." She waved a hand, her silver bangles clinking. "You aren't tourists, though. Buck, right? And you're Tess. Heard you're headed to Bone Hollow."

I raised an eyebrow. "News travels fast."

Lila laughed, sharp and knowing. "Chat Creek's small. I make it my business to know folks."

"Do you?" I said. "What do you know about Nadie Red Eagle?"

She pulled a small notebook from her purse, its pages dog-eared and crammed with scribbles. A pencil was tucked behind her ear, and she plucked it out, tapping it against the table.

Tess stood from the table and said, "Wait! Mind if I get my camera?"

"You want to interview me for Cryptid Hunter?" Lila asked.

I nodded my approval when Tess glanced at me and said, "We have time, and I'm sensing we should film this."

Everyone in the little café took notice when Tess returned from the Xpedition with her camera and recording equipment.

"We're from Cryptid Hunter," she said to the crowd. "I want to film the café and everyone here. Is everyone in?"

From the tumult and smiles of approval Tess's question caused, it was apparent they were. She handed a clipboard and a pen to our waitress.

"What's this?" she asked.

"Release forms," Tess said. "Please have everyone sign one."

Lila eagerly signed a form when Tess placed it in front of her. When Tess gave her a thumbs up, Lila began talking as if she'd never paused.

"Old Indian woman living alone with her chickens in the middle of nowhere. What's got you chasing Nadie Red Eagle?"

I shrugged, guarded. "Just curious."

Lila's eyes gleamed. "Mmm-hmm. Well, Nadie's a strange one. Lives out there with those goats and chickens like they're family." She leaned in, voice dropping. "You think she'll tell you about the Shadow?"

"Maybe," I said. "How did you know that we're looking for the Shadow?"

"I'm not blind. Everyone knows the Cryptid Hunter is in town and what he's looking for," she said. "You both work for him, so you already know what I'm talking about."

Lila grinned and gave me a knowing smile when I asked, "You know Clara Hensley?"

"No one in my high school class remembers her. She just appeared from nowhere. Why do you ask?"

Lila grinned again, and Tess gave me a look when I said, "I'm staying at the Briar Patch."

"I don't see a ring on your finger. Are you married?"

"Single," I said. "Why?"

"Clara has a bad reputation in town, you know?"

I shook my head and said, "Because?"

"She and the mayor, James Pressley, had an affair. Almost got him divorced. To say Patsy was pissed is an understatement."

When I stifled a yawn, Tess gave me an appraising glance.

Lila nodded when I said, "Patsy is the mayor's wife?"

"The mayor's not the only one. Rumor has it she banged a state senator in a room at the Route 69 Motel." She winked and said, "I can see why Clara might be attracted to you, and you know the Cryptid Hunter's plans."

"Jake Huntington, the Cryptid Hunter himself, is staying at the Briar Patch. If Clara were digging for information about his show, why wouldn't she have come on to him instead of me?"

"Maybe because Clara's afraid of the voodoo woman with him."

"That wasn't where I was going when I asked about Ms. Hensley," I said.

Tess continued filming but was tapping her toe and rolling her eyes at me. Her look made my gut twist. Lila was a gossip, the kind who'd know your shoe size before you stepped into town.

"What, you think she's supernatural?"

"The thought crossed my mind," I said.

Lila's laugh was too loud, drawing eyes from nearby tables.

"Wouldn't put it past Chat Creek. This town's got secrets older than the chat piles." She flipped open her notebook, revealing pages of cramped handwriting—names, dates, numbers. "See this? I track everything: horse races, jukebox songs, even Shadow sightings. I have a system. Numbers don't lie."

Tess raised an eyebrow. "You bet on horses?"

"Online, mostly," Lila said, scribbling something new. "Drive to Sallisaw's casino for off-track betting when I'm feeling lucky. Last week, I called 'Dusty Trail' to win at 12-1 odds. Nailed it. You two bet?"

"Not me," I said.

"Me either," Tess said. "My money's too tight to throw away."

Lila grinned. "I'm betting Johnny Cash comes up next on the jukebox. Five bucks says I'm right."

I shook my head, half-amused, half-skeptical, though thankful the conversation had changed from Clara Hensley.

"And the Shadow? Have you seen it?" I asked.

Cash's song "Ring of Fire" began playing on the jukebox.

"Told you so," Lila said with a grin.

"You are good," I said.

"Though I've never seen the Shadow, I have it figured," she said. "Next sighting's soon, out by Picher's old smelter."

"Thanks for all the info, Lila," I said. "Is there anyone else in town we should speak with?"

"Toby Red Hawk, the man sitting over there, can probably tell you a few things."

"Toby Red Hawk?" I responded, recognizing the familiar name.

"Yes," she said.

She nodded toward a man hunched in the corner, picking at a plate of eggs. He was lean, his black hair streaked with gray, his face carved with lines deep as arroyos.

"What's Toby Red Hawk's story?" I asked.

"Quapaw. Lives by a chat pile near Picher. Folks call him an outcast, but he sees things others don't."

She smiled when I asked, "How do you know so much about him?"

"Word gets around," she said.

I glanced at Toby, who seemed to sense the attention and stiffened. Before I could say more, Lila was off again, chattering about the time she bet on a thunderstorm's exact start time and won twenty bucks from the barber.

Tess caught my eye, her look clear: She's a crackpot. I nodded. Lila was lonely, spinning tales to feel important. Still, her words about Clara gnawed at me. A waitress appeared with a fresh pot of coffee and refilled our cups.

After thanking the waitress, it suddenly dawned on me why Toby Red Hawk's name sounded familiar. Lila and Toby Red Hawk were two of the holdouts Ava Baltimore had mentioned during her interview.

"You moved here from Picher, didn't you?"

My question came out sounding almost like an accusation,

and I regretted not addressing the subject more subtly as soon as it escaped my lips.

"The government had no right to take our land," she said.

"They had their reasons," I said.

"Who told you I was a holdout?" she asked.

"Ava Baltimore. You know her?"

Lila's smile returned. "Ava and the Pegs," she said. "Chat Creek's resident would-be rock star. The system abused me. Ava and her kind take advantage of it."

Tess had quit filming, our food was gone, and the café's bustle was slowing. I stood, tossing cash on the table.

"I'm going to talk to Toby."

As I neared his table, Red Hawk's eyes flicked up—wary, almost hunted. When I opened my mouth to speak, he was already moving, shoving past a waitress to our table, where Tess was pointing her camera at him.

Shoving it angrily aside, he said, "No pictures; I didn't sign your damn release."

He ran out the door without paying his tab, the bell jingling sharply in his wake.

Back at the table, Tess was stowing her gear, Lila still talking, her pencil dancing across her notebook. Tess grabbed the clipboard with the signed releases and motioned to the door.

"We have to hurry, Lila," she said. "Nice meeting you."

I hurried after Tess as she dashed out the door and got into the Xpedition, the scent of biscuits lingering on my shirt. When I started the engine, I felt Tess's eyes on me and realized she wasn't smiling.

# CHAPTER 9

The Xpedition purred as I pulled onto the rural highway, the air-conditioned cabin a crisp contrast to the sticky heat outside. The dashboard glowed with navigation screens and climate controls, the seats cradling us in plush comfort as the vehicle glided over the cracked asphalt of Route 10. I could still feel Tess's eyes focused on me.

"What?" I finally asked.

"That was almost a good interview back there," she said. "Almost."

"Maybe because I wasn't hired to interview people," I said.

"We're on our way to Bone Hollow to interview Nadie Red Eagle. You're the interviewer; I'm the cameraman."

"That's different," I said.

"Tell me how," Tess said.

By this time, Pard was sitting in Tess's lap, and it made me wonder what else she intended to take from me.

"What exactly did I do wrong?" I asked.

"For one thing, you were lying. Everyone in America will recognize your complicity. Luckily for you, most of that part will be edited out because of Lila's blatant accusations concerning the Chat Creek mayor and the unnamed state senator."

"I didn't lie," I said.

"You didn't exactly tell the truth, either," she said. "Did you?"

"We only just met," I said. "I'm not comfortable telling you what happened."

"Hell, Buck," she said. "That's lame. You need to do better than that?"

"Am I on trial here?" I asked.

"You tell me," Tess said. "Did you fuck Clara Hensley last night, or not?"

"I'm single and so is Clara. What if I did?" I said.

"I'm not your girlfriend. We're trying to accomplish the same thing here. Tell me what the hell you did. Trust me and start a dialogue."

Tess smiled when I said, "The only female I've ever had a dialogue with is my quarterhorse, Lady."

"Not even your mother?"

"Never had a mother, or a father," I said.

"Then it's stretch time," she said. "Turn off your defences and tell me what happened with Clara. It's important."

"Why is it important?" I asked.

"Because I sense you're hiding something from me. Something that could affect our shoot."

The Xpedition's hum filled the silence as Tess's words hung between us, sharp and expectant. Pard, sprawled across her lap, flicked his ears, like he was waiting for my answer. I gripped the wheel, the road stretching toward Bone Hollow, its cracked asphalt shimmering in the Oklahoma heat.

My mind churned, Clara's face flickering behind my eyes— her dark eyes, her voice like a song you can't unhear. I didn't want to tell Tess, but the truth was clawing its way out, wild and impossible.

"Fine," I said, my voice low, like I was afraid the Xpedition itself might hear.

"I'm listening," she said with folded arms.

"I didn't... we didn't sleep together. Not like you're thinking. Something else happened. Something I can't explain."

Tess raised an eyebrow, stroking Pard's fur. "Spit it out, Buck. What does that mean?"

I exhaled, the memory rushing back like a dam breaking. "I had... an out-of-body experience. I was there, with Clara, in her house. Then I wasn't. I was... flying. Over Picher. Over everything."

Tess's hand froze on Pard's back. "Flying? Like, what, a

dream?"

"No dream," I said, my knuckles whitening on the wheel. "It was real. Too real."

The words spilled out, and I was back in Clara's dim living room, her sage-scented candles flickering. She'd poured me wine, her fingers brushing mine, and then—nothing.

My body stayed slumped on her couch, but I was gone, untethered, soaring into the night sky. The air was cold, electric, the stars above Picher sharp as shattered glass. I wasn't me anymore, not exactly—just a consciousness, weightless, streaking over the ruined landscape.

Below, Picher sprawled like a wound. Chat piles loomed, jagged pyramids of toxic earth glowing faintly under the moon, their shadows twisting into shapes that weren't natural—faces, maybe, or claws reaching for the sky.

I saw the old smelter, its rusted skeleton pulsing with a sickly green light, as if it were breathing. Rivers ran red, not with mud but with something thicker, alive, coiling through the ground like veins.

And then there was the shadow—Tsisdetsi's Shadow, it had to be. It wasn't just a shape but a presence, a darkness that moved with purpose, weaving through the chat piles, whispering in a language I couldn't grasp but felt in my bones. It wanted me to see.

I flew lower, pulled by some invisible thread. The air thrummed with voices—cries of miners long dead, their echoes trapped in the earth; children laughing, then screaming, their voices swallowed by the wind.

I saw Clara's house from above, its roof glowing faintly, sage smoke curling upward like a signal. Inside, I glimpsed her, standing over my body, her lips moving in a chant, her hands tracing symbols in the air. Was she guiding me? Or was I her puppet?

The Shadow led me further, to a clearing near Picher's edge. There, the ground split open, a jagged maw revealing a cavern glittering with crystals that pulsed like heartbeats. Shapes moved inside—human, but not. Their eyes glowed, their limbs too long, their voices a chorus of static and sorrow.

They were digging, clawing at the earth, unearthing something ancient, something that burned my mind to look at. The Shadow hovered, watching, and I felt its command: Witness. Remember.

Then, a jolt. I was yanked back, slamming into my body on Clara's couch.

"Her face was close, her breath warm, saying, "You saw, didn't you?"

"I couldn't speak, my head spinning, the room tilting. She'd smiled, handed me my keys, and sent me stumbling into the dawn."

Tess was staring at me now, her mouth half-open. "Buck, that's... insane. You're saying you flew? Saw ghosts? Some glowing cave?"

"I know how it sounds," I said, my voice tight. "But it happened. I saw Picher as if it were alive, Tess. Like it was... angry. And Clara—she's tied to it. Her and the Shadow. Hell, maybe she is the Shadow."

Tess leaned back, her eyes narrowing. "You think she did this to you? Like, what, witchcraft?"

"I don't know," I said. "But Lila said Clara appeared from nowhere. And that Shadow—it isn't just a ghost story. It's real, and it has a purpose. Something about fixing what we broke. The mines, the land, all of it."

Pard whined softly, sensing the tension. Tess chewed her lip, processing.

"So, what, you think Clara's some... spirit? And you just happened to stumble into her supernatural field trip?"

"I don't know what she is," I said. "I'm starting to think nobody in Chat Creek does."

The Xpedition rolled on, the horizon swallowing the road. Tess was quiet, though I could feel her mind working, piecing together Lila's notebook, Toby's silence, my story. I didn't tell her the worst part—the feeling that the Shadow wasn't done with me, that it had marked me, its whispers still echoing in my skull.

What was Clara? Was she guiding me to the truth, or luring me into something darker? And that cave—what the hell was down there, pulsing under Picher's skin?

I pressed the gas, the truck surging toward Bone Hollow. Nadie Red Eagle better have answers, because the questions were piling up, and they were heavier than the chat piles themselves.

Tess fiddled with her camera, checking lenses, her movements precise.

"So, let's forget what you just told me. Where are we headed?" she asked, glancing at me. "Bone Hollow's not exactly on Google Maps."

I kept my eyes on the road, one hand on the wheel, the other resting on the gearshift.

"I found an old 1913 topography map in the online county archives. It showed a spot called Bone Creek, tucked deep in the northeast hills. I cross-referenced it with Google Earth and drew a mental path through the brush and gullies. It isn't exactly a Sunday drive, but the Xpedition can handle it."

Tess raised an eyebrow, impressed but skeptical. "You just... drew a path in your head? No GPS?"

"I'm half Cherokee. Seems I was born with a GPS already in my head," I said.

"Cherokee, huh? What's the other half?"

Tess smiled when I said, "A bit of wolf, a touch of owl, and a lot of coyote."

"You have a horse?" she asked.

"Miss Lady," I said. "Wish she were here with me now. You like horses?"

"Love horses," she said. "My baby's named Rio. Back home in Texas. Wish we were on our horses instead of in Jake's absolutely crazy vehicle."

Tess's eyes flashed when I said, "Want to drive? This baby's a dream."

I pulled over and swapped seats with her. We were in a dry arroyo, and I had barely fastened my seat belt when she slammed the gas and started cutting figure eights in the dry dirt. Grabbing the seat rest, I held on as we spun around.

"Damn, girl! Are you getting your rocks off?"

"Hell, yes! This is more fun than bull riding," she said.

"You've never ridden a bull," I said.

"In my dreams," she said.

"You like rodeos?" I asked.

"Love rodeos." She slid the car to a stop and said, "This ride is fucking amazing. I love it!"

"Yeah, well, don't crash us or we'll be walking back to Chat Creek," I said.

"Want to drive?" she said.

"Hell no," I said. "You're doing great. I'll guide you."

I caught her staring and stifled another yawn, my jaw cracking. Tess tilted her head, her hazel eyes narrowing.

"Need a nap?" she asked, her tone teasing but sharp.

I shrugged, keeping my gaze forward. "Just... planning the route."

Tess smirked again, letting it go, and turned to pet Pard, who was now sprawled across the back seat, drooling happily.

We'd long left the highway behind, the Xpedition's tires biting into a dirt track that snaked into the wilds of Ottawa County. The terrain turned rugged fast—red clay ruts, overgrown sumac, and tangled blackjack oaks closing in on the narrow path.

The vehicle rocked over uneven ground, its suspension absorbing the jolts with ease, the cabin staying cool and quiet despite the chaos outside. Tess navigated a sharp dip where a dry creek bed cut through, the Xpedition's off-road prowess making light work of the obstacle.

I braced myself, one hand on the dash, but my grin betrayed my thrill.

"This thing's an off-road Ferrari," I said, glancing at the high-clearance undercarriage through the window as we climbed a rocky incline.

"Jake doesn't skimp," Tess said, swerving to avoid a fallen

branch.

The path twisted through a thicket, thorns scraping the Xpedition's reinforced sides. Inside, the air stayed crisp, the hum of the AC drowning out the cicadas' drone. Pard whined softly, shifting as the vehicle tilted, but Tess reached back to pat him, her voice soothing.

"Easy, boy. Mama has this."

I shot her a look, half-irritated, half-amused.

"He likes you better than me," I said.

"Jealous?" she asked.

"Yes," I said.

Tess's laugh—bright, unguarded—filled the cabin, cutting through the tension I hadn't realized I was carrying.

The trail grew wilder, forcing her to slow as we forded a shallow stream, the water splashing against the Xpedition's grille. She leaned forward, her eyes scanning the dense underbrush.

"This is it, huh? Bone Hollow. Feels like we're driving into a ghost story."

"Hope so," I said, my voice low. "Nadie Red Eagle's out here for a reason. Quapaw medicine women don't live alone in the middle of nowhere without one."

I glanced at Tess, catching the way her eyes lit up at the mention of a story. There was something about her—grit, curiosity, a guarded heart that matched my own—that stirred a flicker of something I wasn't ready to name.

Another yawn slipped out. Smiling, I said, "That nap's calling my name."

Tess slowed, almost to a stop. "Want me to pull over?"

"I'll make it," I said.

"Let's take a break," she said. "With all the coffee we drank, I need to take a trip behind the bushes."

"Me too," I said.

Tess pulled to a stop, pointing out a hawk circling overhead as she opened the door. While I napped in the front seat, she raided the ice chest for a soda for herself and water for Pard.

Considering the position of the sun, it was well past noon when she finally woke me.

"Can't believe you let me sleep so long," I said.

"You needed it. Pard and I took a walk, and I got some dynamite footage. I've never seen terrain as rugged as this, not even in the Outback. Look what I found."

Something in Tess's hand flashed silver.

She smiled when I said, "What the hell?"

"A galena crystal," she said. "Pard and I found a mineralized quartz vein exposed in the dry creek bed. If mining companies knew about it, we'd be in for Picher 2."

"You're right about that," I said, studying the beautiful crystal. Unless I miss my guess, this sample is flecked with pure silver."

# CHAPTER 10

The air in Fry's Chicken Shack hung thick with the sweet aftermath of peach cobbler, the scent of cinnamon and melted ice cream blending with the faint tang of grease from the fryer. The jukebox crooned a lonesome Hank Williams tune, its notes weaving through the clatter of spoons and the low hum of conversation.

At the large round table by the window, Jake Huntington leaned forward, his aviators pushed up into his dark hair, his eyes locked on Sheriff Amos "Fry" Callahan. Mama sat beside him, her turquoise sunglasses resting on the table, her sharp gaze flicking between the sheriff and the camera crew, who'd repositioned their lenses to catch every word.

Deputy Roy Hill, still nursing his cobbler, grinned like a kid at a campfire, eager for the tale to come. The locals—Fry's handpicked crew of buddies—leaned in from nearby tables, their murmurs fading as the sheriff cleared his throat.

"All right, Jake," Fry said, his drawl thick with showman's flair, though a shadow lingered in his eyes from the earlier talk of Picher's scars. "You want Tsisdetsi's Shadow? Well, buckle up, 'cause this ain't no campfire yarn for the faint of heart."

Jake nodded, his face serious but curious, the kind of look he wore when the hunt was on.

"Lay it on us, Sheriff. That grainy video's got folks buzzing from Boston to Los Angeles. What's the deal with this thing?"

Fry took a slow sip of iced tea, letting the moment stretch, his mustache twitching as he savored the attention. The café was quieter now, the weight of the story pulling everyone in. Tammy, the freckled waitress, lingered by the counter, her tray forgotten, caught in the sheriff's orbit.

"Tsisdetsi's Shadow," Fry began, his voice dropping low, "ain't just some boogeyman locals whisper about to scare kids. It's been seen, Jake, by folks you wouldn't expect. Regular folks, sure—farmers out by Tar Creek, truckers pulling late-night hauls on Route 66. But important people, too. Hell, even the governor of Oklahoma caught a glimpse."

Mama raised an eyebrow, her spoon pausing mid-air. "The governor? You're pulling our leg, Amos."

Fry chuckled, but his eyes stayed steady. "No ma'am, I ain't. Happened a couple of years back, during a campaign swing through Miami."

"We're all ears," Mama said.

"The governor was campaigning for a local candidate running for state senate, one of his friends. After a speech here in town, they took a late drive out to Picher—wanted to see the old mines, maybe drum up some votes with a photo op. It was late winter, dark by five o'clock, and pitch-black when they rolled into that ghost town."

He leaned forward, his badge glinting in the diner's fluorescent light.

"Spooky," Jake said.

"Yes. They're out there, idling by one of them chat piles—those mountains of lead waste—when something moves in the dark. Big, taller than a man, all wrong angles and shadow, like it's part of the night itself. Governor's people start hollering, driver floors it, and they peel out of Picher faster than a jackrabbit with a coyote on its tail. No pictures, no proof—just a car full of city folks scared witless."

Jake leaned back, arms crossed, a spark of excitement in his eyes. "And the governor never went public with it?"

"Nope," Fry said, shaking his head. "Man's no fool. A story like that? Press would have a field day, call it a stunt or worse, say he's lost his marbles. Word got back to me through a trooper friend who was on the detail. Swore up and down that the governor's face was white as a sheet, muttering about 'something unholy' out there."

Deputy Roy nodded eagerly, his buzz cut bobbing. "Heard it from my cousin, too, who works highway patrol. Said the whole entourage was shook. Ain't been back to Picher since."

The crew's cameras whirred, capturing the tension, the way Fry's hands moved as he spun the tale. Mama tapped her fingers on the table, her voice cutting through the hush.

"So, this Shadow—it's tied to Picher's mines? The poison in the land?"

Fry's grin faded, his eyes narrowing. "Could be. Folks say Tsisdetsi's Shadow's been around as long as the mines, maybe longer. Some reckon it's a spirit, angry at what we've done to the earth. Others say it's something... older. Something that don't like us poking around where we don't belong."

Jake's jaw tightened, his mind turning. "I was told about a commune. The 'People of the Earth.' What's their deal? They know something about this Shadow?"

The air in the diner shifted, like a cold draft slipping through a crack. Fry's face hardened, and even Roy's grin faltered. The locals at nearby tables exchanged glances, their forks still. Tammy stepped back, busying herself with a coffee pot, as if the mention of the commune carried a weight she didn't want to touch.

Fry leaned back, his chair creaking, and ran a hand over his mustache.

"The commune," he said, his voice low, deliberate, like he was choosing every word with care. "They're a peculiar bunch, Jake. Tucked deep in the wilds of Ottawa County, where the roads turn to dirt and the trees close in. Ain't nobody finds them unless they want to be found."

He paused, glancing at the crew's cameras, then back at Jake. "Call themselves the 'People of the Earth.' Indians, outcasts, outlaws—folks who've turned their backs on the modern world. No taxes, no government, no grid. They got their own laws, their own way. Pagans, every last one of them."

Mama tilted her head, her voice sharp but curious. "Pagans?

Come on, Sheriff, that's a broad brush. What do you mean?"

Fry's eyes flicked to her, a glimmer of respect in them. "Before Christianity swept through, Mama, everybody was pagan. Easter and Christmas—those holidays have roots in ancient rituals, solstices, and harvests."

When Sheriff Callahan turned and signaled Tammy, she nodded and brought a fresh pot of coffee and a pitcher of iced tea. The café had grown quiet. Outside, the crowd stirred.

"Pagans, huh?" Jake said.

The sheriff grinned. "These folks, they lean into that. No churches, no crosses. They worship the land, the stars, maybe something else we don't understand. Word is, they've got ways of pulling energy straight from the earth itself—stuff Tesla figured out, then got buried by the big energy boys and the powers that be."

Jake's brow furrowed, his voice steady. "Tesla? That's a leap, Sheriff. You saying they're off the grid with some secret tech?"

Fry shrugged, a wry smile tugging at his lips.

"I'm just saying what I hear, Jake. They don't have power lines running to that place, but they have light, heat, and whatever else they need. Folks whisper it's more than solar or wind—something deeper, tied to the land. Could be hogwash, could be truth. Ain't nobody getting close enough to find out."

Deputy Roy piped up, his voice hushed, as if he were sharing a secret. "Heard Timothy McVeigh himself visited them, back before he blew up the Murrah Building. Looking for advice, they say. The feds went sniffing around afterward. The commune shut them out. Ain't been an outsider there since."

The cameras caught the shift in Jake's expression—a mix of intrigue and caution.

"Who's running the show out there?" he asked. "Sounds like they have a tight grip."

Fry's face darkened, his voice dropping to a near-whisper. "Charismatic fella, name's David. Think Jim Jones, maybe a touch of Manson, but sharper. Got a way of talking that makes you believe the sky's green if he says so. Everyone is loyal to him like he's the second coming. They're tied to the land, Jake."

Fry shook his head when Jake asked, "What's David's last name?"

"Ain't got no last name," he said.

Mama leaned forward, her eyes narrowing.

"And you think they're connected to it? This Shadow?" she asked.

Fry met her gaze, unflinching. "I think they know more than they let on. They're protective and suspicious of outsiders."

"Dangerous?" Jake said.

The sheriff nodded. "You roll up with cameras, they won't just turn you away—they'll make sure you regret it. No one is filming or interviewing the 'People of the Earth,' unless they're invited. And they don't invite."

Fry's Chicken Shack had gone dead silent, the jukebox's last notes fading into the hum of the overhead fans. The crew's cameras lingered on Fry's face, capturing the weight of his words. Jake sat back, his fingers drumming on the table, his mind racing. Mama's lips pressed into a thin line, her eyes darting to Jake, a silent question passing between them.

"Sounds like a challenge," Jake said.

Fry nodded, his expression grim. "Careful ain't enough, Jake. You go poking around that commune, you better have more than cameras and charm."

The cameras panned to Jake, his face lit with determination, the weight of the hunt settling over him.

"That's a wrap," he said with a grin. "Thanks, Sheriff. Better think about adding an addition. When this episode airs, you're going to need it, not to mention another cook to make that wonderful cobbler of yours."

"Mind if we take a few pictures to hang on the wall?" Sheriff Callahan asked.

"Not at all," Jake said, still smiling.

Outside, the Miami sun blazed high in the sky, but inside Fry's Chicken Shack, a chill lingered in the air, carrying the promise of secrets and shadows lying in the wilds of Ottawa

County.

Pictures were taken, and more coffee and tea consumed as the crew packed up their gear. The crowd outside the café had only grown larger, screaming, chanting, and animated as Jake, Mama, and the crew returned to the tour bus. Jake's production supervisor, Rod Bloustine, joined them.

"Great shoot," he said. "Want me to contact the governor's office and see if he's available to comment?"

Jake snickered. "That would be a hoot. He'd have a hard time spinning his way out of this one."

"He'd find a way. Well?" Rod said.

"Waste of time," Jake said. "Sheriff Callahan's hilarious description of the event is better than the governor's explanation, and we already have almost enough footage for an episode."

"Except we're still missing one important thing," Mama said.

Jake nodded. "Footage of the Shadow."

"We can use the salesman's cell phone vid in a bind," Rod said.

"That would be a giant cop out," Jake said. "The commune may be our only answer."

"You don't know that," Mama said. "Buck and Tess are interviewing Nadie Red Eagle. We need to wait and see what they come up with."

"What if their shoot turns out to be a bust?" Jake asked. "We already have more than enough atmospheric footage for two shoots."

"Mama's right, Bossman," Rod said. "The commune sounds like a dangerous place. Even the sheriff seemed afraid to go there."

"How can we show the Sheriff's interview and then not visit the commune?"

"Hell, Bossman, we'll just edit it out," Rod said.

Jake shook his head. "There must be a better way. I can't get over the feeling that the commune is our key."

Mama rested her hand on Jake's knee and said, "Something I

need to tell you."

"Sounds serious," he said.

"When I shared the story of Buck meeting Sage, the spirit-like person in Clara's garden, I didn't tell you everything."

"Oh?"

"Sage advised Buck to visit the commune alone," Mama said. "Buck didn't want to tell you about the 'People of the Earth' because he knew you would want to be there, and he realized how dangerous the place is."

"It's no more dangerous for me than it would be for Buck," Jake said. "I've never asked one of my people to do anything I wouldn't do myself."

"That's the point," Mama said. "Sage told Buck to go alone. She must have a reason."

Jake clasped her hand in his. "It's going to take a while to be hungry enough to eat again after Sheriff Callahan's chicken fries. I'll call Clara and ask her to make dinner later. Afterward, you and I will take a walk in Clara's rose garden and consult with Sage."

# CHAPTER 11

The dry creek bed stretched into the distance, surrounded by tall cottonwood trees and blackberry bushes filled with ripe fruit. I picked one and ate it.

"Spit that out," Tess said, disturbed.

"Why?" I said.

"It's contaminated," she said

"It isn't," I said.

"You don't know that."

A pool of water filled a sandstone cavity in the middle of the creek, and the water was crystal clear. I stuck my finger in the water and tasted it.

"No poison here," I said.

Pard believed me, lapping water happily from the clear pool.

"Don't let him drink that water. He'll get sick," she said.

"Too late," I said. "The water's fine."

"What about the vein? There's ore here. It's dangerous," Tess said.

"Not processed ore," I said. "It's in its natural state. No more dangerous than the blackberries. Try one."

"I'll pass," she said, arms folded.

When a voice spoke behind us, Pard barked, and we both wheeled around. On the bank of the creek, towering over us, was a woman.

She stood with an aura of quiet authority, her presence shimmering against the backdrop of the cottonwoods. Her raven-black hair flowed over her shoulders, streaked with silver strands that caught the sunlight like the galena Tess had discovered.

Her eyes, deep and wise, held a spark of something ancient, as if they perceived not just the world before her but the very fabric of time itself. Detailed beadwork decorated her earth-toned dress, and a leather pouch hung at her waist, likely filled with her tools—herbs, stones, or whatever a medicine woman might carry.

Her skin, weathered yet glowing, reflected the years she had spent under open skies, connecting with the land. At her side stood a massive wolf-dog, its fur a mottled blend of gray and white, with eyes that mirrored its mistress's—piercing and wise.

The animal's gaze fixed on us, not with threat but with curiosity, its tail giving a single wag. He stepped closer to his mistress as if tethered to her by an invisible bond. The big animal moved with a grace that belied his size.

"You've reached Bone Hollow," she said, her voice low and melodic, carrying the cadence of someone who spoke with purpose. "I am Nadie Red Eagle. And this," she gestured to the wolf-dog, "is Ahanu. You needn't fear him—or this place. Nothing here is polluted. The earth in this hollow is clean, as it has always been. The water, the berries, the stone beneath your feet... they hold no poison."

Tess's arms remained crossed, her skepticism plain, but I could see her eyes darting between Nadie and the crystal-clear pool in the creek bed.

"How can you be sure?" Tess asked, her voice sharp but wavering. "Everything around Picher's tainted. The mines—"

"The mines are not here," Nadie interrupted gently, her gaze softening. "Bone Hollow is apart, protected. The spirits of this land keep it whole." She looked at me, a faint smile tugging at her lips. "You've tasted the water and the berries. You feel no harm, do you?"

I shook my head, wiping stained fingers on my jeans. "Told you, Tess. It's fine," I said.

Nadie stepped closer, her moccasins silent on the creek bank, Ahanu shadowing her every move.

"You've come far to find me," she said, her eyes searching

ours. "Why?"

Nadie smiled when I said, "To learn from your wisdom."

"My encampment is near," she said. "We'll talk."

"I need to get my camera," Tess said.

When she wheeled around, she stepped into a hole, a sharp rock cutting her leg to the bone. She winced in pain and almost fainted as I helped her out. Though my bandanna was damp with sweat, I had nothing else to stop the bleeding, so I stuffed it into the wound. Nadie and Ahanu scurried down the creek bank and joined us.

Pard and Ahanu touched noses as Nadie examined the deep cut on Tess's leg.

"What about her wound?" I said. "She needs stitches. I'm taking her to the nearest ER."

Nadie shook her head and said, "Bring her to me. Ahanu and I are just over the rise. I'll doctor Tess's leg."

I nodded, my gut twisting with worry for Tess, who was pale and leaning heavily on me.

"All right," I said, hoisting her up, careful not to jostle her leg. "Hold on, Tess. We're going to get you fixed up."

Pard trotted beside us, sensing the urgency, while Nadie and Ahanu led the way, moving with a quiet grace over the rise.

The trail wove through an ancient grove of cottonwoods, their leaves whispering in the breeze as they cast dappled sunlight onto the ground. The air felt different here—cleaner, charged with something I couldn't quite name.

As we crested the hill, Nadie's encampment came into view, nestled in a clearing that seemed to glow with an otherworldly light. It was like stepping into a dream, every detail vivid and alive, as if the land itself were breathing.

Towering trees ringed the encampment—cottonwoods and oaks, their branches forming a natural canopy that swayed gently overhead. At the center stood a sturdy wigwam, its frame of bent saplings covered in woven mats and hides, smoke curling lazily from a small opening at the top.

Painted symbols—spirals and stars—that seemed to

shimmer when the light hit them just right, adorned the structure. Nearby, a loom held an unfinished blanket, its vibrant threads of red, blue, and gold woven into a pattern that suggested a shadowy figure, perhaps Tsisdetsi itself. The design pulsed with a quiet energy, as if it were more than mere fabric.

Goats bleated, their eyes curious as they watched us approach. A grizzled donkey stood among them, ears twitching, its presence a quiet sentinel against coyotes. Free-range chickens clucked and scratched in the dirt, their feathers catching the light like tiny prisms.

To one side, an artesian spring bubbled up from the earth, feeding a rock-bottom pool that reflected the sky like a polished mirror. The water's surface rippled with a silvery glow, and I swore I could feel its purity just by looking at it.

Nadie gestured to a soft bed of hides near the wigwam.

"Lay her here," she said, her voice calm but commanding.

I eased Tess onto the bed, her face tight with pain, blood seeping through my bandanna.

"I'm fine, Buck," she said, her voice weak.

I wasn't convinced.

Nadie knelt beside Tess, Ahanu settling nearby, his eyes never leaving his mistress. From her leather pouch, she drew a small bundle of dried herbs, a stone bowl, and a vial of clear liquid that shimmered like the spring water.

Working with practiced hands, she ground the herbs into a paste, her lips moving in a soft chant that seemed to weave itself into the air. The words were unfamiliar, but they carried a weight that made the hairs on my neck stand up. The encampment felt alive, the trees and animals seeming to lean in, as if drawn to her magic. She peeled back the bandanna, revealing the deep gash.

"This will sting, but only for a moment," Nadie said.

She cleaned the wound with spring water, then applied the herbal paste, her fingers moving with almost ceremonial precision. The air around us grew warm, and I noticed a faint glow—perhaps just a trick of the light—around her hands as she pressed them over the wound. Tess gasped, her face tense, then relaxed, her features softening.

"Better?" Nadie asked, her eyes meeting Tess's.

Tess nodded, stunned. "It… it doesn't hurt anymore." She flexed her leg, the wound already looking less angry, and the bleeding stopped. "How did you—?"

Nadie smiled, a knowing glint in her eyes. "The land gives what we need, if we listen." She rose, brushing her hands on her dress. "Rest now. We'll talk when you're ready."

I sat back, my worry easing, though my mind reeled. The encampment hummed with a mystical energy—the spring's glow, the blanket's shadowy design, the quiet watchfulness of Ahanu and the animals.

The color had returned to Tess's face, along with a faint smile. Pard snuggled close to her.

"You okay?" I asked.

"I thought I was going to pass out when I stepped in that hole and cut my leg," she said. "Whatever Nadie put on the wound is working; the pain gone."

"You had me worried," I said.

Tess smiled. "We're here. Can you go get the Xpedition? I need my gear."

"You bet," I said.

Pard reluctantly came with me as I trekked back to Jake's sleek off-road vehicle. Finding it where we'd left it, I cranked the engine and turned the beast toward Nadie's encampment.

The Xpedition's cabin was a cool oasis, with the leather seats soft against my back and the dashboard's easy glow steady. Pard snored lightly now, sprawled across the back. I hummed to myself, my fingers tapping Tess's camera bag.

Curious, Nadie's donkey and a couple of the goats trotted over to see what metallic beast was invading their domain. Nadie, smiling, joined them to have a look, Ahanu by her side.

Glancing at the donkey, she said, "Her name is Kwanita. In some Native American languages, it suggests 'guardian' or 'spirit.' It aligns with her purpose of keeping coyotes at bay."

"I have a donkey at home," I said. "His name is Grit; He's old, grizzled, and not afraid of anything."

"Like you, Buck McDivit," she said.

"How do you know my name?" I asked.

"These hills whisper secrets," she said. "There isn't much I don't know."

"You know about Tsisdetsi's Shadow?" I asked.

"If I didn't, you wouldn't be here," she said. "Grab Tess's equipment. I'll tell you both about the Shadow later, when the sun begins to set and the stars and moon align in the sky above."

"We weren't planning on spending the night," I said.

"Plans change," she said.

Darkness settled over Nadie's encampment like a velvet cloak, the sky ablaze with a vivid tapestry of stars and a full moon glowing untainted by city lights.

"Strawberry Moon," Nadie said.

I could see the same red glow as the moon I'd seen in Clara's garden the previous night.

"It's sitting so low in the sky," Tess said.

"The summer solstice is the longest day of the year in the Northern Hemisphere, with the sun at its highest point in the sky. Because the full moon is always opposite the sun, it appears at its lowest point," Nadie said.

The air was warm and humid, heavy with the sweet perfume of night-blooming jasmine and honeysuckle. Frogs sang in a rhythmic chorus from a nearby pond, their voices blending with the soft rustle of cottonwood leaves.

Fireflies danced in the clearing, their tiny lights flickering like scattered embers, casting a magical glow over the scene. The encampment felt alive, as if it were holding its breath, waiting for something extraordinary.

Nadie had prepared a meal in a large cast-iron pot, suspended over a crackling fire on a tripod that sent sparks spiraling upward into the night. The rich aroma of stew—wild herbs, root vegetables, and tender meat—filled the air, mingling with the earthy scent of the surrounding trees.

Tess, Pard, and I sat comfortably on a colorful Indian blanket spread across the ground, its intricate patterns echoing the unfinished weave on Nadie's loom. We ate from clay bowls with large wooden spoons, the stew warm and savory, its flavors deep and comforting.

From the ice chest, we drank cold Coors from cans, the crisp taste of the beer cutting through the humid night. Nadie smiled and nodded when I handed her a fresh can, as if the beer was some ancient Indian intoxicant.

Tess's leg, now free of pain, rested easily as she leaned back, her eyes reflecting the firelight. I sat cross-legged, Pard curled beside me, his ears twitching at the occasional hoot of an owl.

Nadie sat across from us, her presence serene yet commanding, Ahanu lying at her side, his eyes glinting like twin moons. Kwanita, the donkey, stood watchfully near the goats, her silhouette a quiet guardian in the darkness.

"This is the first day of summer," Nadie said, her voice low and resonant, carrying the weight of ancient knowledge. "The summer solstice, when the sun stands still and the earth hums with power."

"It's so beautiful," Tess said, smiling. "I've never seen a full moon so crimson and vivid. It's..."

"Magical?" Nadie said.

"Exactly," Tess said.

Nadie gestured to the sky, her beaded bracelet catching the moonlight.

"It is a time of balance, when the veil between worlds thins, and the spirits speak clearly to those who listen. Tonight, the stars and moon align to show us truths hidden in the daylight."

She raised her hands, palms upward, and the air seemed to shimmer. A soft chant escaped her lips, words that felt older than the hills, weaving into the night like threads of silver.

The fire flared briefly, and a strange stillness fell over the encampment—the frogs went silent, the fireflies froze mid-flight. Tess and I exchanged a glance, our breaths catching as the sky above began to shift.

"Oh, my God!" she said, pointing upward. "Look, Buck."

"I see it," I said.

A mirage had formed, spreading across the moon and stars like a veil of rippling light. It glowed with an otherworldly greenish hue, eerie and mesmerizing, unlike anything I had ever seen.

The vision took shape, revealing the skeletal remains of Picher—crumbling buildings, rusted machinery, and barren earth scarred by decades of mining. The scene panned slowly, drifting over heaps of tailings and poisoned streams, the devastation stark and haunting.

Then, a shadow emerged, vast and indistinct, its edges flickering like smoke. It spread across the mirage, a winged silhouette that seemed to pulse with life—Tsisdetsi's Shadow.

My heart pounded, and Tess gripped my hand, her eyes wide. The Shadow didn't feel malevolent, though its presence seemed overwhelming, heavy with purpose. Nadie's voice cut through the silence.

"Tsisdetsi's Shadow is not here to harm," she said, her eyes fixed on the sky. "It is a messenger, born of the earth's pain. It rises to show us the true evil—the poison men have sown in the soil, the water, the air. It begs us to see, to act, before the land is lost forever."

The mirage shimmered, then faded, the stars and moon reappearing as if nothing had happened. The frogs resumed their song, and the fireflies flickered back to life.

My head felt heavy, my thoughts sluggish, as if the stew—or something in it—had woven a spell over me. I glanced at Tess, whose eyelids were drooping, her bowl slipping from her hands. Pard yawned, already asleep beside us.

"Nadie…" I said, my voice thick. "What was…"

"Rest now," Nadie said softly, her smile enigmatic. "The solstice has spoken. You'll understand in time."

Tess slumped onto the blanket, her camera forgotten, her breathing slow and steady. I tried to fight the drowsiness, but the warmth of the fire and the weight of Nadie's words pulled me under.

# CHAPTER 12

The dining room of the Briar Patch Inn radiated the warmth of Clara Hensley's hospitality, with the air filled with the smell of roasted chicken, fresh-baked cornbread, and a tangy blackberry cobbler steaming in the middle of the oak table.

Candlelight flickered across the lace tablecloth, casting delicate shadows on the walls, where old photographs of Chat Creek's mining days hung in silent vigil. Clara moved with practiced ease, setting down a pitcher of sweet tea; her gray braid swayed as she smiled at Jake and Mama Mulate.

The meal was a masterpiece of comfort, each bite laced with the kind of care that could make you forget the world's troubles —but not the questions simmering beneath the surface.

Jake leaned back in his chair, wiping his mouth with a napkin, his TV-star charm dialed low but still present.

"Clara, you've outdone yourself again. I'd hire you for the Cryptid Hunter crew just for this cobbler."

Mama nodded, her eyes warm but sharp, studying Clara over the rim of her tea glass.

"You have a gift, Clara. This feels like more than food—it's like a spell for the soul."

Clara's laugh was soft, but her hands paused, fidgeting with a spoon.

"Good ingredients and a hot oven. Nothing magical about it."

"I don't think so," Jake said. "I have both of those things, and I can barely boil water."

Clara's smile was practiced, and her gaze flicked to the window, where the moon hung low, casting a silvery glow over the rose garden.

"You folks must be tired after your day with Sheriff Callahan."

Jake's grin tightened. "Fry's a character. Had a lot to say about that commune—the 'People of the Earth.' Sounded like he thinks they're trouble."

Clara's fingers tightened around the spoon, though her expression didn't shift.

"Those folks keep to themselves. They're... different. Not much for outsiders. But dangerous?" She shrugged, her voice careful. "I wouldn't know. Chat Creek has enough stories without borrowing theirs."

Mama leaned forward, her voice gentle but probing. "What about Tsisdetsi's Shadow? You've lived here a long time. Surely you've heard more than barroom tales."

Clara set the spoon down, her smile thinning. "Like I said before, it's just talk. Picher's a sad place—makes people see things that aren't there. Shadows, lights, whatever you want to call it. I don't put stock in it." She stood, gathering plates with a briskness that felt like a shield. "More cobbler?"

Jake and Mama exchanged a glance, then let the topic go. The conversation shifted to lighter subjects—the town's annual fair, the best fishing spots on Chat Creek—but the atmosphere grew heavier, as if Clara's words were a curtain covering something unspoken.

After dinner, she vanished into the kitchen, leaving Jake and Mama alone with the flickering candles and the distant hum of crickets outside.

"Let's take that walk," Mama said, rising from the table. "The rose garden's calling. Maybe Sage will show herself."

Jake nodded, his jaw set. "I want to hear about the commune directly from her. If it's as dangerous as Fry says, I'm not letting Buck go alone, no matter what she told him."

They stepped into the night, the air warm and thick with the scent of roses and earth. The moon hung full and luminous, its light bathing the garden in a silvery glow that made the blooms seem to pulse with life. Fireflies drifted lazily, their soft lights weaving through the air like tiny stars fallen to earth.

The gravel path crunched underfoot as Jake and Mama wandered deeper into the garden, the world beyond the inn fading into a hush of cricket songs and rustling leaves. The rosebushes, heavy with pink and red blossoms, seemed to lean in, their thorns glinting like secrets in the moonlight.

They reached the heart of the garden, where the wrought-iron bench sat beside the gurgling fountain. The water reflected the moon in fractured ripples, and a faint breeze carried the heady scent of night-blooming jasmine. Jake scanned the shadows, his hand resting on the phone in his pocket, ready to call Buck if needed. Mama stood still, her eyes half-closed, as if listening to something beyond the crickets.

"Thought she'd be here," Jake said, his voice low.

Mama's lips curved into a knowing smile. "Patience. This garden has its own rhythm. Sage'll come when she's ready."

They waited, the silence stretching, the air growing heavier, as if the garden itself were holding its breath. Just as Jake opened his mouth to suggest heading back, a figure stepped from the shadows near a cluster of roses, her movements fluid, like water flowing over stone.

Sage's pale skin shimmered under the moonlight, her hair a tangle of blues and greens that seemed to shift with each step. Her dress, patched with patterns that danced in the dim light, clung to her like a second skin, and her storm-cloud eyes locked onto Jake and Mama with a weight that made the air feel electric.

"You're looking for me," she said, her voice a soft melody that seemed to weave into the night. "The stars told me you'd come."

Jake straightened, his charm replaced by a wary edge. "I'm Jake Huntington. This is Mama Mulate. We need to talk about the commune—the 'People of the Earth.' Buck said you told him to go there alone, for answers about Tsisdetsi's Shadow. Sheriff Callahan says it's dangerous. What's the truth?"

Sage's smile was enigmatic, her gaze drifting to the fountain before returning to Jake.

"The commune is a place of truth, but truth can be sharp, like a thorn. the 'People of the Earth' listen to the land, to Tsisdetsi's voice."

"And?" Jake said.

"They understand the pain and anger, but they guard their knowledge closely. For you, Jake, or you, Mama, going there would bring danger."

"What makes it any different for Buck?" Jake asked.

"The land trusts him. He's walked its wounds, tasted its berries, felt its pulse. He must go alone, or perhaps with the woman who carries the camera, Tess Hawthorne. She sees with clear eyes."

Mama's brow furrowed. "How do you know about Tess?"

"How does the rain know to fall from the sky?" Sage asked.

There was no answer to Sage's question. When Jake started to reply, Mama clutched his hand and shook her head.

"Why just them? What makes Buck so special?" Mama asked.

Sage tilted her head, her eyes glinting with an ember-like red.

"Buck carries no greed in his heart. The land knows him, even if he doesn't know it yet. Tess seeks truth, not glory. The commune will open to them, but not to you. You carry too much... noise."

Jake's jaw tightened, though he didn't argue. "And the danger? Fry made it sound like a cult out there."

Sage's laugh was like wind chimes in a storm. "Danger is everywhere, Jake Huntington. In Picher's dust, in the creek's poison, in the shadows you chase for your show. But the commune's danger is not what you think. It's not knives or guns —it's knowledge that cuts deeper. Buck will find what he needs there, but only if he goes alone."

Mama stepped closer, her voice firm. "And Tsisdetsi? What does it want with Buck?"

Sage's gaze lifted to the moon, her expression softening. "Tsisdetsi is the land's cry, its memory of betrayal. It watches Buck because he listens, even if he doesn't know it yet. The commune will show him why."

"Even if he goes alone," Jake said. "How will he find it? The county sheriff doesn't know exactly where it's located."

"Buck is with Nadie Red Eagle as we speak, sitting beneath the same moon as we are. She will tell him how to reach the commune."

Sage nodded when Jake asked, "Is Tess with him?"

"She was hurt," Sage said.

"Hurt? How?" Jake asked, disturbed.

"Nadie doctored her wound. She is in good hands," Sage said.

Jake glanced at Mama. "I tried to call them earlier but got no signal," he said.

Sage's eyes flicked back to them. "Stay here, in the garden, under the moon. It's safer."

Before Jake could press further, Sage stepped back, her form blending into the shadows of the roses. The air shivered, and she was gone, leaving only the faint scent of jasmine and a single rose petal on the bench, its edges curling inward.

The garden felt alive again, the crickets resuming their song, but Jake and Mama stood frozen, the weight of Sage's words settling over them like moonlight on the earth.

§⌒〜⅝

Jake paced the upstairs bedroom of The Briar Patch Inn, his boots scuffing the polished hardwood as moonlight spilled through the open window, casting long shadows across the quilted bed. Mama Mulate sat in a wicker chair by the dresser, her arms crossed, her face a mix of concern and exasperation.

The rose garden's encounter with Sage lingered like a chill in the air, her supernatural presence and cryptic warnings about the commune gnawing at Jake's nerves. He clutched his phone, thumb hovering over Buck's contact, but the screen mocked him with a single bar that flickered and died.

"No signal," Jake said, tossing the phone onto the bed. "Buck's out there with Tess, and I can't even check on them. I'm the 'Cryptid Hunter,' Mama. I'm supposed to have answers, not be stuck here feeling like a damn bystander."

Mama's voice was soft but firm, cutting through his frustration.

"You're human. You can only do so much. Chasing shadows doesn't mean you control them."

Jake stopped pacing, his jaw tight. "I've never asked my crew to do anything I wouldn't do myself. I can't let Buck and Tess walk into that commune alone, not after what Sheriff Callahan said about those 'People of the Earth.' Dangerous, he called them. And Sage—whatever she is—she's not human. Those eyes, that voice... she's something else. Why should I trust her?"

Mama leaned forward, her eyes narrowing. "Because she's more than us. Sage sees what we can't. She said Buck and Tess are the ones the land trusts. You heard her—your 'noise' would only stir up trouble. Listen to her, or you'll be the one putting them in danger."

Jake ran a hand through his hair, his voice dropping to a raw whisper. "I feel responsible for Tess. She cut her leg badly out there, Mama. What if it gets infected? What if she dies? I sent her with Buck to find Nadie Red Eagle, and now they're off the grid. I should've gone with them."

Mama's expression softened, but her tone held steady. "Sage said Nadie healed Tess. You have to trust that. Nadie's a medicine woman, and Bone Hollow's a protected place. Buck's not answering because he's where he's meant to be. You can't carry the weight of every choice they make."

Jake sank onto the edge of the bed, his shoulders slumping. "I tried calling Angie. No answer. I'm supposed to lead this team, but I'm helpless. I hate this."

A sudden breeze wafted through the room, stirring the lace curtains and sending a shiver down Jake's spine. The air carried a faint scent of roses, as if the garden itself were listening. Before he could speak, his phone buzzed, the screen lighting up with Colley Hornbeck's name. Jake snatched it, his voice sharp with hope.

"Colley? You get the bird fixed?"

"Yessir, Bossman," Colley's voice crackled through, cheerful as ever. "Chopper's purring like a kitten. I'll be back in Chat Creek by noon tomorrow. Hey, you catch the game tonight?"

Jake blinked, thrown by the shift. "What game?"

"Thunder and Pacers, man! Pacers pulled it out, 108-105. Sets up a do-or-die Game 7 in OKC. I got tickets, Jake—prime seats, the best in the house."

Jake's eyes flicked to Mama, who was now glaring at him, her lips pursed. She was a die-hard Pelicans fan, her loyalty to New Orleans sports running as deep as her love for the Saints. Basketball was their shared passion, but their team allegiances were a constant source of contention. Jake felt the tension spike, a new kind of unease settling in his gut.

"How many tickets did you get?" he asked, his voice cautious.

"Just two," Colley said, oblivious to the storm brewing. "It's the game of the century. We have to be there."

Mama's frown deepened, her arms tightening across her chest.

"You aren't seriously thinking about ditching me for a Thunder game, are you?" she said, her voice low but laced with fire. "You know I'd sell my best gris-gris bag to see the Pelicans take down OKC any day."

Jake held up a hand, trying to defuse her. "Hold on, Mama. Colley, I can't go without her. She's family, and you know she's got a meaner courtside yell than me."

Mama's eyes narrowed, but a flicker of amusement crossed her face. "Don't try to sweet-talk me, Jake Huntington. You're a Thunder fanatic, and I'm not sitting home while you cheer for those overrated flashers in OKC. If Colley has tickets, you'd better find a third, or I'm hexing your whole season."

Colley laughed through the phone, catching the edge in her voice.

"Damn, Mama. All right, Bossman, I'll see what I can do, but these tickets are gold dust. Game 7's gonna be wild—Shai versus Halliburton, winner takes it all. I'll call you tomorrow."

"Make it three, Colley," Jake said, his tone half-pleading.

"Don't let me down."

The call ended, the room falling into a charged silence. Mama's glare softened, but her competitive spark didn't fade.

"You're lucky I love you," she said, pointing a finger at him. "But if you sneak off to that game without me, I'll root for the Pacers just to spite you."

Jake managed a half-smile, the weight of Sage's words and Buck's silence still heavy but momentarily eased by their familiar banter.

"Deal," he said. "But if we get those tickets, you're wearing a Thunder jersey for one quarter. Just to see how it feels."

Mama snorted, standing too close to the window, shutting out the rose-scented breeze.

"Over my dead body. Now get some sleep. Tomorrow, we figure out how to keep Buck and Tess safe, commune or no commune."

Jake nodded, but as he lay back on the bed, staring at the ceiling, his mind began to churn. The Thunder game loomed like a distant escape, a chance to reclaim some control in a world slipping through his fingers. For now, though, the night held its secrets, and the stars outside burned cold and silent.

# CHAPTER 13

Morning sun filtered through the cottonwood canopy, casting golden flecks across Nadie Red Eagle's encampment in Bone Hollow. A gentle breeze stirred the air, carrying the savory aroma of something extraordinary simmering in Nadie's cast-iron pot, suspended over a low fire.

The scent—wild herbs, smoked meat, and a hint of sweet corn—woke me from a dreamless sleep. I blinked awake on the colorful Indian blanket, the stars and moon of the previous night's solstice vision still lingering in my mind like a half-remembered song.

Beside me, Tess stirred, her face peaceful, the lines of pain from her injury gone. Pard, my border collie, lay sprawled nearby, his tail thumping lazily as he sniffed the air. I sat up, rubbing my eyes, the memory of Tsisdetsi's Shadow and its eerie greenish mirage over Picher flashing through my thoughts. Tess was frowning.

"What's the matter?" I asked.

"That was Tsisdetsi's Shadow we saw last night," she said.

"Yes," I said.

"My camera was right beside me," she said. "I never thought to film the Shadow, and it's what we came for."

"Nadie put something in our food," I said. "We were drugged."

"Still…"

"You'll get another chance," I said.

The encampment hummed with life: Kwanita, Nadie's donkey, munched on a patch of clover, her ears flicking at the clucking of free-range chickens scratching in the dirt. Ahanu,

Nadie's wolf-dog, sat regally near the artesian spring, his gray-white fur catching the sunlight, his piercing eyes watching me and Tess with quiet curiosity.

The spring's lowest pool shimmered, reflecting the bright blue sky, and the unfinished blanket on Nadie's loom swayed softly, its shadowy pattern seeming to pulse in the morning sunlight.

Nadie stood by the fire, stirring the pot with a wooden spoon, her raven-black hair streaked with silver shimmering as she moved. Her earth-toned dress swayed with her motions, the beadwork catching the sunlight like tiny stars. She glanced over, her knowing eyes meeting mine.

"Morning," I said, my voice hoarse from sleep.

Tess sat up, stretching with a surprised ease and a smile returning to her face.

"Smells like heaven out here, Nadie. What's cooking?"

"Venison stew with sage and cornbread dumplings," Nadie said. "The land provides. You both need nourishment after last night's vision."

Tess touched her leg, her fingers tracing the spot where the gash had been. The wound was nearly gone, reduced to a faint pink line, as if days of healing had passed in hours.

"Nadie, this... It's a miracle," she said. "I don't know how to thank you."

Nadie waved a hand, dismissing the gratitude. "The earth heals those who respect it. You're welcome here, Tess."

She ladled steaming stew into bowls and handed them to us along with spoons carved from polished cedar. I took a bite, the flavors bursting with warmth and depth, grounding me in the moment, though the weight of last night pressed on me.

"Nadie, that mirage... Tsisdetsi's Shadow. It felt real. And I don't remember falling asleep. Did you put something in the stew?"

Though Nadie's smile didn't falter, her eyes held a glint of mischief.

"You needed rest. The solstice is heavy with power—it opens

the mind but taxes the body. A few herbs to ease you into sleep, nothing more. You're awake now, stronger for it."

Tess raised an eyebrow, her attention shifting to her camera bag, as if itching to capture the morning's magic. I let it go, sensing Nadie's truth, though the idea of being guided so subtly by her medicine unsettled me. Ahanu tilted his head, as if amused by the exchange. Nadie sat across from us on a woven mat, her gaze turning serious.

"You came for answers about Tsisdetsi's Shadow, and last night showed you its purpose. I can help you find the shadow. In exchange, I need your help."

"Doing what?" I asked.

"The commune—the 'People of the Earth'—has answers to help us all."

"Sage told me about the commune," I said. "What do they know about the Shadow that you don't know?" I asked.

Nadie's answer was cryptic. "How to make it go away," she said.

"If the Shadow is here to shed light on the damage done to Picher, isn't it counterproductive to make it go away?" I asked.

Nadie smiled. "If the Shadow is gone, then maybe so is the pollution," she said,

"How is that possible?" I asked.

"The 'People of the Earth' have the answer to that question," Nadie said. "They just don't know it yet."

"Jake, my boss, wants an interview. Sounds as if you have other plans," I said. "Can you get me into the compound?"

"I can get you in," Nadie said. "Once you're there, you are on your own. Can you handle it?"

"Where is the commune?"

It isn't far, just beyond the next ridge, where the creek forks and the pines grow dense."

"It seems you know a lot about the commune," I said. "What's your connection?"

"My granddaughter lives there, and she has big ideas."

"Your granddaughter?" I said.

"Avini. Her name means 'the Earth.' Her father, David, is the leader of the commune."

"Is David your son?" I asked.

"Estranged son," Nadie said.

I leaned in, listening for answers to the subtle nuances in Nadie's voice.

"Because?"

"David's wife, Little Bird, died during childbirth. David blames me."

"For what?" I asked.

"I wasn't there to save her," Nadie said.

"That's so sad," Tess said. "I'm so sorry."

"I'm sorry also," I said. "It sounds, though, as if you are very proud of Avini."

Nadie smiled. "Very proud. She has a double PhD in math and physics from OU. Her specialty is artificial intelligence."

"Oh, my!" Tess said. "She's a smart one."

"Her grandfather was John Kane, who apprenticed with Nikola Tesla. He founded the commune, dropping out of society due to persecution, whether real or perceived. Many like-minded people joined him."

Nadie nodded when I said, "Then you were John Kane's wife?"

"Why didn't David take the family name?" Tess asked.

Nadie's smile disappeared, her expression darkening.

"When the commune was formed, the emphasis was on science and technology. David took over leadership following his father's death. Now, he rails against science and has become a religious zealot."

"But he didn't stop Avini from pursuing a science degree," I said.

John took Avini under his wing, sharing all of Tesla's secrets with her. He was quite old when he died, much older than even I. Avini was already a college graduate when he died.

"Okay," I said. "I'm unsure exactly where we're going with this, though I'm good at ad-libbing."

"You'll have to be," Nadie said. "David is no longer the wonderful son I raised. Under his leadership, the 'People of the Earth' practice human sacrifice. If he determines your true purpose for visiting the commune, he will have your head on a platter."

The weight of Nadie's words hung in the air, heavier than the morning mist rising from the artesian spring. Human sacrifice? My spoon froze halfway to my mouth, the stew's warmth no longer comforting.

Tess's eyes widened, her fingers tightening around her bowl as she glanced at me, searching for a reaction. Pard sensed the shift, his ears perking up, his gaze darting between us.

"Human sacrifice?" I said, my voice low, hoping I'd misheard. "You're saying David's gone that far?"

Nadie's face remained steady, her eyes unyielding as polished obsidian.

"Not in the way you're imagining, perhaps. Not yet. But his zeal has twisted the commune's purpose. They offer 'sacrifices' to the earth—rituals to appease what they believe is its wrath. Blood has been spilled, though they claim it's symbolic. For now."

"For now?" Tess's voice cracked, her usual bravado faltering. "Nadie, you're asking us to walk into a cult compound led by a man who might kill us if he doesn't like our questions?"

Nadie leaned forward, her voice soft but firm. "You've seen Tsisdetsi's Shadow. You know its power, its warning. Picher's poison runs deeper than the lead in its soil—it's in the hearts of those who ignore it. Avini is the key to cleansing this land, but she's trapped in her father's shadow, unaware of her own strength. You, Buck, can reach her. You're an outsider, a truth-seeker. She'll listen to you where she won't hear me."

I set my bowl down, my appetite gone. "And what about David? You think I can just waltz in, dodge his suspicions, and convince Avini to... what, exactly? Fix Picher's pollution? How does that even work?"

Nadie's gaze drifted to the loom, its unfinished blanket

swaying in the breeze, the shadowy pattern seeming to writhe.

"Avini's work builds on her grandfather's legacy—Tesla's dreams of harnessing the earth's energy. She's developed a model, a kind of artificial intelligence, that can map and neutralize the toxins in Picher's soil and water."

"Impossible," I said.

"No, it isn't," Nadie said. "It's not just science; it's a bridge between the physical and the spiritual, a way to heal the land's wounds."

"Why do you need us?" Tess asked.

"Avini doesn't yet know her own powers. She's buried it in academic papers, thinking it's theoretical. You'll show her it's real."

Tess frowned, her journalist instincts kicking in.

"Wait. You're saying Avini has the knowledge to clean up decades of mining waste? That's... incredible, if it's true. Why do you need Buck? Why not go to her yourself?"

Nadie's shoulders sagged, a rare crack in her composed exterior. "David has forbidden me from entering the commune. He blames me for Little Bird's death, for abandoning them when they needed me most. I wasn't there because I was here in Bone Hollow, seeking answers from the earth about Picher's curse."

Nadie nodded when I asked, "Your son cast you out when you returned?"

"Little Bird had passed, and David's heart had hardened. Avini loves her father, but she's caught between his dogma and her own truth. She won't leave the commune—not yet. But an outsider, someone like you, Buck, can plant the seed."

I rubbed my jaw, the stubble rough under my fingers.

"So, let me get this straight. You want me to infiltrate a cult, convince your granddaughter to use her knowledge to de-pollute Picher, and somehow not get my head on a platter. Meanwhile, you're hoping this mends your family rift and gets you back into the commune?"

Nadie's lips curved into a faint smile. "You're quick," she said. "Yes. And more. If Avini succeeds, Tsisdetsi's Shadow will fade—not because we banish it, but because its purpose will be fulfilled. The land will heal, and the commune's need for rituals, for sacrifices, will end. David may find his way back to the son I knew."

Tess shook her head, her voice sharp when she glanced at me.

"This is insane. You can't seriously be considering this. I'm a journalist, not an eco-warrior or a family therapist."

"And the plan needs your journalism," Nadie said.

"You want me to accompany Buck?"

Nadie's gaze softened. "You're part of this. Your camera, your eye for truth, will document what happens. The world needs to see Picher's redemption, not just its ruin."

"Don't know about Tess, but I'm in on the plan. One question, though," I said. "Why me?"

Nadie's eyes locked onto mine, piercing through my doubts.

"Because you've seen the Shadow. It chose you last night, in the solstice vision. You carry its truth now, whether you want to or not. And because you're stubborn enough to see this through, even when it scares you."

Pard whined softly, nudging my hand, as if urging me to listen. I looked at Tess, her face a mix of fear and determination, then back at Nadie, her quiet certainty anchoring the moment. The spring bubbled nearby, its rhythm steady, like a heartbeat.

"I need more than a cryptic plan," I said. "How do I get past David?"

Nadie crossed to the loom, pulling a small leather pouch from a basket. She handed it to me, its contents shifting softly —herbs, stones, something metallic. The beaded message said, John, Nadie, and David."

"John made this and gave it to me when David was born. He'll recognize it and know you're trustworthy."

"And then?" I asked.

"Tell David his father's spirit has ordained you to document the commune's mission and share their truth with the world. His superstition and ego will open the gate, though his suspicion will test you. Speak plainly, but guard your purpose."

I tucked the pouch into my pocket, its weight grounding me. "When do we go?"

"I'll let you know when the time is right," Nadie said. "Rest today, gather your strength. You'll need every piece of this puzzle."

Tess sighed, slinging her camera bag over her shoulder. "I'm getting some shots of this place before we dive into this madness. Nadie, you mind?"

Nadie nodded, a spark of approval in her eyes. "Capture the truth, Tess. It's your gift."

As Tess wandered toward the spring, camera in hand, I looked at Nadie, the enormity of her vision settling over me.

The cottonwoods whispered above, their leaves dancing in the breeze, as if the land itself was watching. What happened next shook me to my core.

# CHAPTER 14

A sharp crack split the air, like glass shattering deep underground. Pard barked, lunging to his feet. Ahanu snarled, his fur bristling as he wheeled around and faced the spring. The ground shook, knocking me on my ass.

The water's shimmer dulled, a sickly green haze rising from its depths, curling like smoke. The cottonwoods trembled, their leaves rattling despite the still air.

"What the hell?" I said, my heart pounding.

I didn't have to ask; I knew we were in the throes of a massive earthquake. One like none other I had ever experienced. Unlike the small earthquakes that had become common in Oklahoma, this one was different; the ground continued to shake.

Nadie's face hardened, her hand gripping the wooden spoon like a weapon.

"Tsisdetsi's Shadow. It's here," she said.

The dark haze thickened, forming tendrils that snaked toward the encampment. Kwanita brayed, rearing as the chickens scattered, their clucks turning to panicked shrieks. The air grew heavy, acrid, like Picher's mine dust. Tess grabbed her camera, instinctively raising it to her shoulder. Her hands shook, and the wildly trembling ground prevented her from standing. On her knees, she began panning the camera, catching the action.

"Stay back!" Nadie shouted, darting to her loom and snatching a bundle of dried herbs from a basket. She tossed them into the fire, sending up a plume of sharp smoke.

The Shadow's tendrils coiled closer, brushing Kwanita's flank. The donkey screamed, her eyes rolling, a faint green sheen spreading across her fur. I lunged forward, grabbing her halter, pulling her away from the spreading haze and toward the fire's smoke.

"Nadie, Kwanita's hurt!"

"Hold her steady!" Nadie called, her voice cutting through the chaos. She sprinkled more herbs into the flames, the smoke thickening, pushing back the tendrils. "Buck, the spring—throw this into it!" She tossed me a small vial, its contents glowing faintly blue.

I caught it, sprinting to the spring's edge. The green haze stung my eyes, my lungs burning as I uncorked the vial and poured its liquid into the water. A pulse of light flared, the spring bubbling violently, driving the haze upward. The tendrils recoiled, but one lashed out, grazing my arm. Pain seared through me, cold and toxic, like lead in my veins.

Tess shouted my name, her camera flashing as she documented the madness. The Shadow writhed, its form destabilizing, but it didn't retreat. Ahanu leaped, snapping at a tendril, his teeth tearing through it like mist.

"Buck, get back!" Nadie yelled. She stepped forward, her hands raised, a final chant ringing out. The fire roared, its smoke enveloping the Shadow, forcing it skyward. With a sound like a dying wind, the haze dissipated, and the ground stopped shaking, leaving the spring clear and the air clean.

I stumbled back to the fire, clutching my arm, the pain fading but leaving a faint green mark. Kwanita calmed, her fur looking normal again. Pard pressed against my leg, whining. Tess lowered her camera, her face ashen.

"What... what was that?"

Nadie sank to her knees, exhaustion etching her features. "The Shadow," she said. "It grows bolder. Your vision last night drew it here. It's a warning—we're running out of time."

I caught my breath, the empty vial still in my hand. "Time for what?"

"For Avini to act," Nadie said, her voice hoarse. "For you to reach her. This land is dying, Buck, and the Shadow won't wait."

Tess knelt beside me, her hand on my shoulder. "You okay?"

I nodded, though my arm throbbed like hell.

Nadie was off tending to Kwanita and her chickens.

"Was that really Tsisdetsi's Shadow?" Tess asked.

"An earthquake," I said. "A big one."

"We don't have earthquakes in Texas," Tess said.

"Oklahoma has always had earthquakes," I said. "They started in earnest a few years back. Environmentalists said it was because of fracking."

I shook my head when she said, "It isn't?"

"Waste water disposal," I said. "When the industry began horizontal drilling, they started having to dispose of massive amounts of water."

"How does that cause an earthquake?" Tess asked.

"Most shallow disposal zones won't take the amounts of water being produced as a byproduct of horizontal drilling, so operators began drilling disposal wells deep, often to the highly fractured basement rock. The influx of fluids causes the faults and fractures to slip."

"And?" Tess said.

"Even a little movement deep down can result in a big quake at the surface," I said. "There's a problem in this county, though."

"What problem?" Tess asked.

"There's no oil production in Ottawa County. Something else caused the quake."

"Tsisdetsi's Shadow?" Tess asked.

"Nadie thinks so," I said.

"What do you think?"

"Logic says it was an earthquake." I touched the throbbing green mark on my arm. "I have no clue what caused the toxic cloud."

Bone Hollow wasn't the only place in Ottawa County shaking. As Mama and Jake strolled along the sidewalk bordering the old abandoned Chat Creek High School, the ground began to tremble, and a deep groan rose from the earth like a wounded beast. In the parking lot, where Jake's film crew had set up their staging area, chaos broke out.

Cracks began spiderwebbing across the asphalt, jagged and sudden, some wide enough to swallow a tire. A pickup truck lurched forward, its front end plunging into a gaping fissure with a sickening crunch of metal. Nearby, a catering van tilted precariously, its rear wheels dangling over another crack, trays of sandwiches and coffee cups spilling out in a cascade of debris.

"Get back! Move!" Jake bellowed, his voice barely cutting through the screams and the roar of the earth. His film crew scattered, tripping over cables and equipment. A lighting rig toppled, its glass shattering in a spray of sparks. One of the grips froze, staring as the ground beneath his feet split open. A sound recordist yanked him back just as the crack widened, swallowing a tripod and a camera bag.

A deafening explosion rocked the lot, like a bomb detonating deep underground. The crew ducked instinctively, hands over their heads, as a massive dust cloud billowed up from the east, blotting out the afternoon sun. It rolled over the staging area, choking the air with grit and the sharp tang of pulverized stone.

Birds erupted from the trees lining the lot, a frantic mass of wings and screeches, while dogs howled and bolted, their tails tucked. Squirrels and rabbits darted from the nearby brush, scrambling in every direction, driven mad by the trembling earth. Even the snakes were in retreat, causing a script tech to drop her burden, throw up her hands, and scream.

"Everybody, stay calm!" Jake shouted, though his own face was pale. He grabbed a megaphone from a folding table, its legs wobbling on the unsteady ground. "Head for the open field! Away from the cracks!"

The shaking subsided, but the dust cloud lingered, coating everything in a fine gray haze. Crew members coughed, pulling shirts over their faces, their eyes wide with panic. A few clutched each other, muttering prayers or curses. One of the PAs, a young woman with a clipboard, sat on the ground, sobbing, her papers scattered around her like fallen leaves. When he spotted Jake and Mama, Rod Bloustine came running.

"What the hell was that?" he said, his voice shaking as he stared at the wrecked parking lot. "I thought we were all going to die."

"Earthquake," said one of the electricians, spitting dust from his mouth. "Had to be. But... Jesus, that explosion. Sounded like the whole damn town blew up."

"Northeast Oklahoma is laced with subsurface faults," Jake said. "A powder keg ready to explode if one of them shifts."

"Knocked me on my butt," Rod said, rubbing his rear end.

Jake scanned the chaos, his jaw tight, though thinking ahead. "Did anybody get any footage?"

"Don't know," Rod said. "I'll find out."

Behind them, in the Chat Creek football field, Jake's helicopter was landing, blowing up dust and grass.

"There's your Thunder tickets," Mama said, drily.

Jake raised his palms, shaking his head and not bothering to answer.

"Is anybody hurt?" he said, his voice echoing across the broken parking lot.

The sound of approaching sirens answered his question.

"Hopefully, no more than minor injuries," Rod said.

"I hope the hell that's all we had," Jake said.

The shaking had ended, and the toxic cloud had dissipated. Still, the Chat Creek parking lot resembled the aftermath of an aerial strafing attack, with smoking vehicles displaying broken wheels and bent fenders, their remains scattered in the gaping maws left in the wake of the earthquake.

"Rod, start a damage report," Jake said.

An ambulance, its siren still screaming, screeched to a halt on the edge of the parking lot, the incisions left by the earthquake too deep to circumvent. Three EMTs hurried out of the pulsating ambulance.

"How many casualties do you have?" the head EMT asked.

"At least a dozen. We're going to need more ambulances," Jake said.

"No can do," the EMT said. "We have 9-1-1 calls from all over Ottawa County. The quake caused damage all the way to Tulsa."

"Damn!" Jake said. "What about St. Louis, Louisville, or Nashville?"

The EMT shook his head and then hurried off to help people lying on their backs in the parking lot.

"Why did you ask him about those cities?" Mama asked.

"They surround New Madrid, Missouri, the sight of the largest earthquake in U.S. history," Jake said.

"An earthquake in Missouri bigger than the ones in California?" Mama said.

"You kidding me?" Jake asked. "The quake formed Reelfoot Lake in Tennessee and Caddo Lake in Louisiana. It caused the Mississippi River to run backward for three days. If it had happened in modern times, it would have killed millions."

"Damn!" Mama said.

"Affected an area of thirty to fifty thousand miles," Jake said. "By comparison, the San Francisco earthquake affected less than fifteen thousand."

"Never heard of it," Mama said. "When was this earthquake?"

"1811," Jake said. "It has been dormant since then, but it's a tectonic ticking time bomb."

The earthquake had caused a sudden temperature change, and Mama shivered in her colorful blouse as the temperature hovered in the seventies. Light rain started to fall. She and Jake continued across the parking lot, assessing the damage and checking on the health of their crew.

"We're not filming a disaster movie, people," Jake said. "Get it together. Check for injuries, secure the gear that's left, and let's figure out what's still standing."

The crew moved sluggishly, still dazed, as the ground gave a final tremble. The dust began to settle, revealing the extent of the damage: vehicles half-swallowed by cracks, equipment strewn like toys after a tantrum, and the catering tent sagging on one side, its poles bent but holding.

"We need to get the injured into a cool tent until Doc Hiu can assess their injuries," Mama said.

"Good idea," Jake said, waving for Rod to join them.

"The supply tent is undamaged and the air conditioning is still working," he said. "I'll get the injured heading in that direction."

"Good man," Jake said. "What about the catering tent. Everyone's going to need a drink, and that includes me."

"I'm on it, Bossman," Rod said. "It sustained minimal damage. Head over, I'll take care of everything."

"You sure?" Jake said.

"I used to work for FEMA. I can handle it," Rod said.

"Thanks, Rod," Jake said. "I know you can."

Mama and Jake turned toward the catering tent, Colley Hornbeck hurrying toward them.

"Good God almighty," he said when he reached them. "Glad I was in the air. You can't believe the turbulence I fought."

"Any report yet on the quake?" Jake asked.

"A big one," Colley said. "Picher was the epicenter. I can only imagine what's left there?"

"Any damage in Tulsa?"

"Nothing major," Colley said. "Our building is still standing. What's the damage here?"

"A few injuries; maybe a few broken bones. We're going to survive," Jake said.

"Good," Colley said. "I don't know about you two, but I need a drink."

# CHAPTER 15

Tess and I pulled into the high school parking lot, navigating around chunks of broken asphalt. The scene was a mess—cracks everywhere, a van teetering over a fissure, and Jake's crew milling about like shell-shocked soldiers. Dust hung in the air, catching the late sun in a gritty haze. Pard woofed in the backseat, his ears flat.

"Looks like a war zone," Tess said, her camera resting on her lap, lens cap off. "Let me out."

She'd continued filming, even after the earthquake. Hopping out of the Xpedition, she raised the camera to her shoulder and began documenting the aftermath in Chat Creek. I parked near the catering tent, its canvas flapping in the faint breeze. The air was cooler inside, a relief from the dut-choked lot.

Jake, Mama, and Colley sat at the bar, a bottle of scotch between them and plastic cups in their hands. Candy wrappers littered the table.

"Well, look who survived the apocalypse," Jake drawled, raising his cup. His eyes were glassy, his grin a little too wide. "Grab a stool. We're toasting to the end of the world."

Mama scoffed, her braid loose and dusted with grit. "Not the end of the world. Just another day in Chat Creek." She took a swig, wincing at the burn. "Though I've never heard the ground scream like that."

Norma came out of the back, shaking her head and brushing dust from her blouse.

"Sorry, folks," she said. "A falling can of sauer kraut knocked Neil silly. I just got him loaded on the ambulance."

"Is he okay?" Jake asked.

"Cracking jokes when the EMTs loaded him. He didn't want to go to the hospital, but they were insistent. Said he probably has a concussion but would be okay."

"That's good," Jake said.

"This place is about to get busy," she said. "If you want to take the

113

big table by the window, you'll have plenty of room."

"Good idea," Jake said.

"I'll bring your drinks," she said.

Jake turned his attention back to me and asked, "Where's Tess?"

"In the parking lot. She hasn't stopped filming since the earthquake began," I said.

"Tess got footage of the quake?" Jake asked.

"You bet. She previewed it for me. It's awesome," I said.

"Outstanding," Jake said.

Mama put her arms around his shoulders. "I told you someone would catch the earthquake on camera," she said.

"And you were right, my dear," Jake said.

"I was nearing Chat Creek when the earthquake occurred," Colley said. "I swear I could feel it from up there."

"Good thing you weren't on the ground," I said.

Ava Baltimore came through the tent's flap, her apron covered in flour and coffee stains, with her old guitar under one arm and a sackful of something in the other. Jake was the first to see her.

"Ava, over here," he said.

With an expression of relief, she said, "I was worried sick. Is everyone okay?"

"We survived," Mama said. "How did you fare?"

"Not so good," Ava said. "The roof collapsed on the old high school, Ava's Deli gone in a heartbeat."

Mama stood and grabbed Ava's hand, pulling her to the empty chair beside her.

"Were you hurt?" she asked.

Ava shook her head, "I grabbed my guitar and ran like hell."

"What's in the sack?" Jake asked.

"Subs and burritos. I managed to salvage my inventory."

Jake's crew had cleaned up following the aftermath of the earthquake and were beginning to fill the catering tent.

"You came to the right place," Jake said. "Neil, my chef, is in the hospital with a concussion. I have a bunch of hungry crew members, not much to feed them, and no cooks."

Ava handed them to Jake and said, "Happy to donate to the cause."

"Jake Huntington doesn't take or need charity," Colley said with a grin.

"Colley's right," Jake said. "I'll have Norma cut you a check."

"There aren't enough sandwiches or burritos in my sack," Ava said. "Where's your kitchen? I'll start cooking."

Norma heard Ava as she arrived with drinks. After handing her a frozen Margarita, she pointed behind the bar.

"Thank God!" she said. "I'm Norma. Ava. Sure you don't mind?"

"The only thing I like doing more than cooking is playing my guitar." She thumped it. "Glad I saved it."

"You're a godsend," Norma said. "I'll be in to help soon as I deliver these drinks."

Ava smiled, licked the salt on the frosty drink, and headed for the kitchen.

Tess followed some of the crew into the tent and slid into a chair beside me. Pard flopped at my feet, still edgy.

"Everybody okay?" she asked.

"Bumps and bruises," Jake said, waving a hand. "Lost some gear, but we're alive. Crew's shaken up, though."

"Earthquake," I said, echoing my earlier words to Tess. "Big one. Felt it out at the spring, too."

"Buck said you have film," Jake said.

Tess shot me a look, her fingers tightening on her cup. I knew she was thinking of Nadie's words, of Tsisdetsi's Shadow.

"Want to see?" she asked. "I can preview it for you on my camera."

Mama leaned forward, her voice low but steady as she watched the film. "Awesome," she said. "Whatever it was, it isn't done with us. This part of Oklahoma has secrets, and they're waking up."

Jake leaned closer, his eyes glued to the tiny screen on Tess's camera as she played back the footage. The images were raw, visceral —trees swaying like drunken giants, the ground splitting open like a wound, dust clouds swallowing the spring at Bone Hollow.

Tess had captured it all: the chaos, the fear, the surreal beauty of destruction. Her lens lingered on a cracked street sign dangling by a single bolt, then panned to a group of locals pulling a dazed shopkeeper from a collapsed storefront. The footage was shaky in places, but that only added to its immediacy and authenticity.

Jake let out a low whistle, his scotch forgotten. "Tess, this is *Pulitzer quality*. I'm serious. You've got an eye for the real stuff, the heart of it." He turned to Mama, his grin wide but genuine. "You were right, darling. She's our secret weapon."

Tess flushed, brushing a strand of hair behind her ear. "Just doing my job."

"Your job?" He laughed, clapping her on the shoulder. "This is more than a job. This is history. We're including this in the episode. Front and center."

Mama nodded, her eyes still on the footage looping on the camera. "It's like the earth's telling us something."

"We talked with Nadie Red Eagle and were with her when the quake hit," I said. "She said the ground holds stories. It screamed one today."

Colley, quieter than usual, swirled his drink. "Screaming's right. From the air, it looked like the whole damn world was going to split open."

The tent began filling with the aroma of sizzling spices, pulling everyone's attention to the kitchen. Ava was at the stove, her guitar propped against a counter, as she worked with a kind of frenetic grace. She'd found a stash of ingredients in the catering tent's pantry —chiles, tomatoes, onions, and some ground beef—and was whipping up a spread of Mexican dishes. The crew, drawn by the smell, started drifting closer, their shell-shocked expressions softening.

Norma poked her head out from behind the bar, a tray of frosty margaritas in hand.

"Ava has enchiladas and tacos going. Might be the best thing to happen all day."

"Better than my scotch?" Jake said.

Ava emerged, wiping her hands on her stained apron, a faint smile breaking through her weary expression. Behind her, Norma carried a steaming tray of enchiladas, the sauce bubbling red and fragrant, and set it on the big table by the window. Another tray followed— crispy tacos stuffed with seasoned beef, topped with fresh cilantro and crumbled queso fresco. The crew descended like a pack of wolves, their earlier gloom replaced by murmurs of appreciation.

"Damn, Ava," Colley said through a mouthful of taco. "You're hired. Neil's gonna have to fight for his spot when he's back."

Ava laughed, brushing off the compliment. "Just glad to feed folks. Keeps my mind off... everything." Her eyes flickered, and I caught a glimpse of the weight she was carrying—her deli gone, her life upended in a single shake.

Jake watched her, his usual swagger softened by something else— admiration, maybe. He leaned toward me, voice low. "She's something else, huh? Tough as nails and cooks like a dream."

"Colley may be right about her taking Neil's job," I said.

Jake shook his head but didn't deny it.

Dinner passed in a blur of laughter and clinking cups, the crew's spirits lifted by Ava's food and the shared relief of being alive.

"Best tacos and enchiladas I've ever eaten," Jake said. "Can I impose on you to do something else for us?"

"Name it," Ava said with a smile.

"My crew has been through hell today. Will you sing for us?"

As plates emptied, Jake stood, tapping his cup with a spoon to get everyone's attention.

"Folks," he said, his voice carrying over the chatter. "We've had a hell of a day. This quake shook us up, but we're still here, still standing."

Drink glasses and beer bottles clinked, and someone said, "Here, here!"

"That's not all," Jake said. "We have someone special with us tonight. Ava Baltimore—not only does she save our stomachs with her cooking, but she's got a voice that'll knock your socks off."

I looked at Ava and saw from her smile that she was in her element, enjoying the moment before she took the stage to perform. Jake continued.

"Some of you might not know, but she sang with a group called the Pegs back in the day. Even opened for the Doors once. How's that for a resume?"

The crew cheered, raising their cups. Ava grabbed her guitar, bowed once, waved, shook her head, and flashed a genuine smile.

"So," Jake said, "I've asked her to play for us. Figure we could use a little music to soothe our souls. Ava, you up for it?"

She hesitated, then nodded, hoisting her guitar over her head. The crew cleared a space near the bar, and Tess, ever the opportunist, set up her camera, adjusting the lens for the dim light. Ava settled on a stool, her fingers brushing the strings, testing the tuning. The tent went quiet, the only sound the faint hum of the generator outside.

Ava started with a soft chord, her voice low and husky, weaving through the opening bars of a song I didn't recognize at first. Then the melody took shape—"Time," her signature song, a raw, haunting ballad of loss and resilience that felt like it was written for this very moment.

Ava's voice rose, clear and powerful, cutting through the dust and despair of the earthquake. The crew was transfixed, some swaying, others closing their eyes, letting the music wash over them.

Tess moved quickly, kneeling with her camera, capturing every angle—the way Ava's fingers danced on the strings, the flicker of emotion in her eyes, the crew's rapt faces. I glanced at Jake, who stood with his arms crossed, a rare stillness in him.

When the final note faded, the tent erupted. The crew leapt to their feet, clapping and whistling, a standing ovation that echoed into the night. Ava blinked, surprised, then laughed, her cheeks flushed.

"You are too kind," she said as the crew kept cheering.

Jake stepped forward, raising his cup. "To Ava, for reminding us what it means to keep going."

"To Ava!" the crew echoed, their voices a defiant roar against the day's chaos.

Tess lowered her camera, her eyes bright. "Got it all," she whispered to me. "Every second."

I nodded, my gaze drifting back to Ava, who was already strumming a new tune, something lighter, pulling the crew into a sing-along. The ground might've screamed today, but tonight, Ava's music was the louder voice. And somehow, it felt like Chat Creek was listening.

# CHAPTER 16

The catering tent hummed with the murmur of conversation, its canvas walls faintly glowing under the amber string lights stretched across the ceiling. Outside, the Oklahoma night felt close, stars piercing the velvet sky above Chat Creek, their light unchanged by the faint dust still lingering from the day's chaos.

The distant croak of frogs and the occasional hoot of an owl wove through the chatter, grounding the scene in the wild pulse of the land. I leaned against the bar, my boots scuffing the plank floor, a cold bottle of Coors sweating in my hand. Beside me, Tess swirled a glass of bourbon, her camera resting on the counter, its lens cap off as if she might spring into action at any moment.

Mama Mulate sat on a stool beside me, a colorful shawl draped over her shoulders. Colley Hornbeck sprawled in a chair nearby, his lanky frame relaxed, but his fingers tapping a nervous rhythm on his beer bottle, his aviator's tipped back on his head.

The tent felt like a bubble, a fleeting sanctuary from the strangeness that had dogged us since Picher's quake and the Shadow's eerie haze. The crowd had dispersed, most of Jake's crew piling into the shuttle back to the motel on Highway 69.

Jake pushed through the tent flap, his phone pressed to his ear, his voice low but urgent. The TV-star polish was gone, replaced by a taut energy that made his jaw clench as he ended the call and slipped the phone into his pocket.

"Chat Creek took a hit," he said. "Nothing catastrophic—some cracked foundations, a few busted windows. Everything's under control. Briar Patch Inn, and Clara are fine, not a scratch."

"Sounds as if we all dodged a bullet," I said.

Jake leaned against the bar, his gaze sharpening.

"All right, you two. I've been out of the loop. What happened with Nadie Red Eagle? You said Bone Hollow was... something else. Spill it."

I set my bottle down, the condensation cool against my fingers, and exchanged a glance with Tess. Her lips trembled, a mix of skepticism and wonder, as if she were still processing the memory of Nadie's encampment.

The light caught the faint scar on her leg, a reminder of the gash Nadie had healed with herbs and chants that felt like magic. My arm itched where the Shadow's mark lingered, a faint green trace under my sleeve.

"Nadie's place is like stepping into a dream," I said. "Cottonwoods, a spring that glows like it's alive, and a wolf-dog named Ahanu who looks like he could read your soul. Nadie has this... presence. She knew things she shouldn't, like my name, like what we're chasing."

"What did she say about the commune?" Jake asked.

"She said the 'People of the Earth' have answers about Tsisdetsi's Shadow. Her son, David, runs it."

"Interesting," Jake said. "Then there should be no problem gaining entry."

"Not so simple," I said. "She and her son are estranged. David's wife died during childbirth. Nadie wasn't there to help. There's more."

"Tell me," Jake said.

"David's... intense. Religious. Maybe dangerous."

Tess leaned forward, the ice in her bourbon clinking when she set her glass on the bar.

"Nadie thinks her granddaughter, Avini, can fix Picher's poison."

Tess's words caught Jake's attention. "Sounds impossible. Did she tell you how she intended to go about it?"

"Nadie didn't explain, though she did tell us Avini has a double Phd, in math and physics," I said.

"Smart woman," Mama said.

Tess's eyes flicked to my arm, then back to Jake. "The Shadow showed up. Not just a vision this time. It came with an earthquake, a green haze that burned like acid. Nadie fought it off with herbs and some glowing water, but it marked Buck. Show them your arm."

I pushed up my shirt sleeve, revealing the mark left by the green cloud's touch on my arm.

Mama and Jake shared a look when I said, "Tess and I will visit the commune when Nadie thinks the time is right."

"Jake and I took a walk in Clara's rose garden last night," Mama said. "We spoke with Sage."

"Sheriff Callahan called that commune a cult," Jake said.

"He's right," I said. "Nadie told us her son has the members of the commune practicing blood rituals."

"Blood rituals?" Colley said. "What the hell are you talking about?"

"Nadie says the commune has stopped short of human sacrifice, at least so far," I said.

Jake looked at Mama and said, "I know what we agreed on, but we can't let Buck and Tess walk into a hornet's nest."

Nadie gave us a way to gain David's trust," I said.

I pulled the beaded pouch from my pocket and placed it on the bar.

"What is it?" Jake asked.

Mama didn't ask, clutching the pouch. "Looks like an American Indian form of the voodoo gris gris," she said.

"David's father, John Kane, gave it to Nadie when David was born," I said. "His name is on it and he'll recognize its significance."

"John Kane?" Jake said.

"The commune's founder," I said. "He was an apprentice of Nikola Tesla. He felt persecuted and dropped out of regular society."

"The sheriff insinuated the commune has electricity, even though they're off the grid," Jake said.

"That confirms what Nadie told us," I said. "Nadie said Kane passed all his knowledge to Avini before he died."

Rod Bloustine burst into the tent. Seeing Jake, he hurried to the bar.

"What's up, Rod?" Jake asked.

"More vandalism," he said. "Someone spray-painted the bus. Ruined the logo."

"Damn it!" Jake said. "Did you call the sheriff?"

"I did," Rod said. "He laughed at me and said, 'Is that all you got?' I had to admit it wasn't much after today's earthquake."

Jake and Rod looked at me when I said, "I have an idea who might be behind the vandalism."

"Who?" Jake and Rod said at once.

"Tess and I had breakfast at a little café on Main Street in Chat Creek yesterday before heading to Bone Hollow," I said.

"And?" Jake said.

"We met an interesting woman named Lila Voss who owns a souvenir shop in town. She agreed to an interview. Tess and I filmed it."

"Outstanding," Jake said.

"Tess got releases from everyone in the café except for one person."

Jake's gaze was intense. "I'm listening," he said.

"A man named Toby Red Hawk," I said.

"Why does that sound familiar?" Jake asked.

"Because Ava mentioned him as one of the last people to leave Picher. He returned."

"What do you know about him?" Jake asked.

"When I approached him in the café, he hurried away without paying his bill. On his way out the door, he got in Tess's face when she tried to film him." I got up and started for the door. "I'm going to Picher."

"Now?" Mama said.

"No time like the present," I said.

Tess grabbed her camera and said, "You're going nowhere

without me."

Tess and Pard followed me out the door.

The Xpedition's headlights sliced through the darkness as we rumbled toward Picher, the full moon hanging low and heavy, casting an eerie silver glow over the abandoned town.

The road was a cracked ribbon of asphalt, flanked by skeletal trees and heaps of mine tailings that loomed like forgotten graves. Picher after dark felt like a place the world had left behind, its silence broken only by the hum of the engine and the occasional rustle of something moving in the shadows.

Pard sat alert in the back, his ears pricked, his nose twitching as if he could smell the ghosts that clung to this place.

Tess gripped her camera, her knuckles pale in the dashboard's glow.

"How are we supposed to find Toby Red Hawk?" she asked, her voice tight, eyes scanning the desolate streets. "This place is creepy as hell. It's like the town's watching us."

"Don't know," I said, my hands steady on the wheel, though my gut churned with unease. "Look for a light. If he's squatting here, he's got to have something—a lantern, a fire. People don't live in the dark."

We crept through Picher's main drag, past crumbling storefronts with shattered windows and faded signs that whispered of better days. The moon painted everything in stark contrasts—black shadows pooling in doorways, rusted machinery glinting like bones.

A chill ran through me, the green mark on my arm throbbing faintly, as if the Shadow itself lingered nearby, watching.

"There," Tess said, pointing. A flickering light glowed from a sagging house at the end of a dirt lane, its windows boarded but for one where the glow seeped through. "That's got to be him. Or something worse."

I parked the Xpedition a block away, not wanting to spook whoever—or whatever was inside.

"Stay sharp," I said, grabbing a flashlight from the glovebox.

"Pard, you're with us. Tess, keep that camera ready, but don't flash it in his face. He's already twitchy."

She nodded, slinging the camera strap over her shoulder, her bourbon-fueled bravado replaced by a journalist's focus. Pard hopped out, his tail low but steady, his eyes glinting in the moonlight.

We moved quietly, the crunch of gravel under our boots too loud in the stillness. The house loomed closer, its warped siding peeling like dead skin, the porch sagging under years of neglect. The air smelled of dust and decay, with a faint whiff of something sour—unwashed flesh, maybe, or rot.

Inside, the flicker of light came from a single kerosene lantern on a splintered table, casting jagged shadows across the room. Toby Red Hawk sat slumped in a rickety chair, his clothes ragged, his hair a matted tangle streaked with gray.

His face was gaunt, eyes sunken but wild, darting like a cornered animal's. Mice skittered across the floor, their claws scratching on warped boards, while bats clung to the bare rafters above, their wings twitching in the dim light. The place was a wreck—piles of trash, broken furniture, and a stench that made my stomach turn.

"Who's there?" Toby's voice rasped, sharp with paranoia. "You with them? The ones who watch from the shafts?"

I raised a hand, keeping my tone calm. "Just us, Toby. Buck McDivit and Tess Hawthorne. We met you at the café in Chat Creek. You ran off before we could talk."

His eyes narrowed, flicking to Tess's camera. "No pictures. No damn pictures. You think I don't know what you're after? You want my secrets, same as them."

Tess lowered the camera, her voice soft but firm. "We're not here to hurt you. We only want to talk. About Picher, about what you've seen." She pulled a small flask from her jacket, unscrewed the cap, and offered it. "Bourbon. Good stuff. Want a sip?"

Toby's gaze locked on the flask, his hands trembling as he snatched it. He took a long swig, coughing as the liquor hit his throat, then leaned back, the wildness in his eyes dulling slightly.

"You're not with the ghosts. They don't drink. They... whisper."

I crouched near him, keeping my distance from a pile of moldy rags. "What ghosts, Toby? What's going on in Picher?"

He laughed, a jagged sound that echoed in the hollow room. "You think you know this place? Picher's dead, but it ain't empty. Down in the mines, under the dirt, they're still here. Miners, kids, whole damn families—trapped in the shafts. They talk to me at night, tell me things. Say the earth's angry, say it's waking up."

Tess shot me a glance, her eyebrow raised, but she kept her camera rolling, the red light steady.

"The earth's angry?" I asked. "You mean the quakes? The Shadow?"

Toby's head snapped up, his eyes blazing. "You seen it, ain't you? Tsisdetsi's Shadow. It ain't no ghost—it's the land itself, spitting back what we done to it. Lead, zinc, cadmium, all that poison we dug up. It's in the air, in the water, in them." He pointed a shaky finger at the floor, toward the unseen mines below. "They show me. Every night, they show me."

"Show you what?" I asked, my voice low, the mark on my arm pulsing like a heartbeat.

Toby leaned forward, his breath sour with whiskey and neglect. "The truth. The shafts ain't empty. They glow green, like your arm, boy. I seen them—shadows moving, not human, not anymore. They guard something down there, something old. Older than the mines, older than us. They want out."

Pard whined, pressing against my leg, his hackles up. The bats above stirred, their wings rustling like dry leaves. Tess's camera zoomed in, her hands steady despite the tension in her jaw.

"Toby," she said, "can you take us there? To the mines? If we see it ourselves, we can tell the world. Make them listen."

He cackled, the sound unhinged, and drained the flask. "You want to see? You think you're ready? They'll smell that mark on you, boy. They'll know you're one of theirs now. But fine. I'll show you. Ain't far—just under our feet."

He staggered up, grabbing the lantern, its light swaying as he shuffled toward a back door half-hanging on its hinges. I exchanged a look with Tess, her eyes wide but resolute.

"You sure about this?" I asked in a whisper.

"No," she said, gripping her camera. "But we're not turning back now. Let's go."

Toby led us into the backyard, where a rusted hatch jutted from the ground, half-buried in weeds. He yanked it open, revealing a black maw that swallowed the moonlight. The air rising from it was cold, heavy with the metallic tang of damp earth and something sharper—poison, maybe, or fear. Pard growled low, his ears flat, but he stayed by my side.

"Down here," Toby said, his voice a mix of glee and dread. "They're waiting."

I clicked on my flashlight, its beam cutting through the dark as we descended a rickety ladder into the mine shaft. The walls were rough, streaked with veins of ore that glinted dully, the air growing thicker with every step.

Tess followed, her camera's light casting stark shadows, while Pard's claws clicked on the stone floor. The shaft sloped downward, branching into narrow tunnels that seemed to pulse with a faint green glow, just as Toby had said.

"Keep close," I told Tess, my voice echoing. The mark on my arm burned now, a cold fire that made my skin crawl. "Toby, how far?"

"Not far," he said, his lantern swaying. "They'll find us first."

The tunnel opened into a wider chamber, its ceiling braced with rotting timbers. The green glow was stronger here, pulsing from a pool of stagnant water at the center, its surface shimmering like liquid jade. Shapes moved in the shadows—indistinct, flickering, like smoke given form. My heart pounded, the mark on my arm searing as if answering a call.

"Tess," I said. "You seeing this?"

Tess's camera whirred, capturing the glow, the shapes, the

impossible weight of the air.

"Yeah," she said, her voice barely audible. "It's real."

Toby turned, his eyes gleaming in the lantern's light. "Told you. They're here. Tsisdetsi's Shadow ain't just one thing—it's all of them, all the pain we left behind. You wanted the truth, here it is."

A low rumble shook the chamber, dust sifting from the ceiling. The shapes in the shadows grew sharper, their edges winged and vast, like the mirage from Nadie's encampment. Pard barked, sharp and urgent, as the green glow flared, tendrils snaking toward us. My hand went to the vial Nadie had given me, its faint blue light a fragile shield in my pocket.

"Tess, stay back!" I shouted, uncorking the vial and splashing its contents into the pool. The water hissed, the glow dimming, but the shapes didn't retreat—they surged closer, their whispers filling my head with words I couldn't understand but felt in my bones.

Toby laughed, a mad sound that echoed off the walls. "They know you now! You're marked, same as me!"

Tess grabbed my arm, her camera still rolling. "We need to go. Now."

I nodded, pulling Pard close as we backed toward the tunnel, the shapes swirling behind us. The vial's effect was fading, the green haze thickening again. Toby didn't follow, his lantern a lone beacon as he stood by the pool, muttering to the shadows like old friends.

We scrambled up the ladder, the hatch slamming shut behind us as we stumbled into the night. The moon was still full, its light cold and unyielding, but Picher felt alive now, the ground thrumming faintly beneath our feet. Tess clutched her camera, her breath ragged, while Pard pressed against me, his growl a low warning.

"What the hell was that?" Tess said, her voice shaking but her eyes fierce. "Those weren't ghosts. That was... something else."

I touched the mark on my arm, still burning. "Tsisdetsi's

Shadow. Toby's not crazy—he's seen it too. Whatever's down there, it's tied to the commune, to Avini's tech, to all of this."

Tess checked her camera, her hands trembling but steady enough to review the footage.

"I got it. The glow, the shapes, everything. This is proof. But what do we do with it?"

"Take it to Nadie," I said, starting the Xpedition's engine. "She needs to know the Shadow's not just in visions anymore. It's here, and it's not waiting."

As we drove away, Picher's ruins fading in the rearview, the mark on my arm pulsed like a second heartbeat.

The commune was our next stop, but the mines had shown us something worse than David's rituals—a truth that could swallow us whole if we weren't ready.

# CHAPTER 17

The Xpedition's engine growled as we reached Bone Hollow, the full moon casting a silver sheen over Nadie Red Eagle's encampment. Giant cottonwoods stood guard, their leaves whispering in the warm night breeze, while the artesian spring bubbled softly, its surface reflecting the sky like a mirror.

The air carried an earthy scent of sage and cedar, mingling with the faint sweetness of night-blooming jasmine. Fireflies danced in the clearing, their flickering lights weaving through the darkness, imparting an otherworldly glow that felt both welcoming and charged with secrets. Overhead, a solitary owl hooted, its call echoing through the hollow, as if the land itself were speaking, warning us of truths yet to unfold.

Nadie stood by a crackling fire, stirring a cast-iron pot suspended over the flames, the rich aroma of roasted vegetables and wild herbs wafting toward us. Ahanu, her wolf-dog, lounged nearby, his gray-white fur catching the moonlight, his piercing eyes tracking our approach with quiet curiosity. Kwanita, Nadie's donkey, flicked her ears from her post among the grazing goats, while free-range chickens clucked softly, their feathers glinting like prisms in the firelight.

The unfinished blanket on Nadie's loom swayed gently, its shadowy pattern seeming to pulse under the moon's gaze. The intricate weave, half-formed, revealed a story—lines of ochre and indigo twisting like rivers and veins, hinting at something hidden.

Pard leaped out of the Xpedition, his tail wagging but his posture alert, still on edge from our encounter in Picher's mines.

Tess slung her camera bag over her shoulder, her face pale but her eyes sharp, the memory of the green-glowing shapes and Toby Red Hawk's mad laughter clinging to her like dust.

My arm throbbed where the Shadow's mark lingered, a faint green tracery that felt alive under my skin. Each pulse whispered a faint echo of the mines' hum, as if the Shadow itself was testing my resolve, probing for weakness.

Nadie's raven-black hair, streaked with silver, shimmered as she ladled steaming stew into wooden bowls.

"Welcome back," she said, her voice low and melodic, carrying the weight of someone who'd been expecting us. "You've seen something tonight. It's in your eyes. Sit, eat. The land's strength will steady you."

Nadie's words felt like a ritual, a blessing woven into the night. She handed us bowls of stew—chunks of venison, sweet corn, and herbs that burst with flavor on the tongue—along with cornbread dumplings still warm from the fire. Pard settled beside me, his nose twitching as I slipped him a piece of cornbread.

Tess took a bite, her shoulders relaxing, though her gaze kept darting to the shadows beyond the firelight. Nadie reached into a woven basket and pulled out a clay jug, pouring a deep amber liquid into carved wooden cups.

Symbols—spirals and feathers, remnants of stories older than the mines, older than all of us, etched the cups.

"Herbal wine," she said, handing one to each of us. "Sage, elderberry, and a touch of moonflower. It'll clear your minds, open your hearts to the truth." She paused, her eyes lingering on me, as if she could see the mark's pulse beneath my sleeve. "Drink slowly. The land's gifts demand respect."

I sipped the wine, warm and sharp, with a floral bite that tingled on my tongue. It hit like a slow wave, loosening the knot in my chest, though the mark on my arm pulsed in rhythm with my heartbeat.

Tess drank deeply, her eyes half-closing as the firelight played across her face. The wine seemed to hum with the land's energy, each sip pulling me deeper into Bone Hollow's pulse, as if the spring, the cottonwoods, and the fire were all conspiring to draw me in.

"Careful," I said, half-joking. "Last time you drank Nadie's brew, we slept through a solstice vision."

Tess grinned, but her voice was tight. "After what we saw in Picher, I'll take all the courage this jug can give."

Nadie sat across from us on a woven mat, Ahanu curling beside her, his eyes glinting like twin moons. The fire crackled, sending sparks spiraling into the intoxicating night, the full moon bathing the encampment in a glow that made every leaf, every stone, feel alive.

Nadie's beaded dress caught the light, with patterns shimmering like stars, and her gaze fixed on us with quiet intensity. Above, a nighthawk's wings fluttered, and the air seemed to thicken, as if the hollow itself was holding its breath, waiting for the weight of Nadie's words to fall.

"You found Toby Red Hawk," she said. "What did he show you?"

I set my cup down, feeling the wine's warmth spread through me, and glanced up at the moon.

"He's living in a wreck of a house in Picher, half-mad, talking about ghosts in the mine shafts," I said.

Nadie grinned at my description. "What else?" she said.

"He took us down into a chamber glowing green, like the haze at your spring. Shadows moved—big, winged, like Tsisdetsi. They weren't human. Toby said they're the miners and their families, trapped down there. Said they guard something old, angry. The ground shook, and they came for us."

As I fell silent, a cool breeze wafted up the creek bed, disturbing the wind chimes hanging from the branches and triggering a midnight symphony. Nadie remained quiet, pulling the colorful shawl she wore up over her shoulders. The chimes' notes were haunting, each one seeming to carry a fragment of the land's memory, of promises broken and secrets buried.

Tess gripped her camera, her voice low. "I got it on film—the glow, the shapes. It's real. But Toby... he's not right. He laughed like he was one of them, said they know Buck because of his mark."

She nodded at my arm, her eyes flicking to the green tracery.

Nadie's expression darkened, her fingers brushing the beads at her wrist. The gesture felt deliberate, like a ward against the shadows creeping closer in my mind.

"Toby Red Hawk was once a keeper of stories. He stayed in Picher when others fled, listening to the land's pain. But the mines... they broke him."

"No kidding," I said. "He's nutty as a fruitcake."

"The ghosts aren't just spirits—they're the echoes of Picher's betrayal, the lives lost to greed, the poison left behind. Tsisdetsi's Shadow feeds on that pain, and it's driven Toby to the edge of his mind."

I leaned forward, the wine making my thoughts sharp but heavy.

"He said the shadows guard something. Something older than the mines. What is it? And why's it after me?"

Nadie stared into the fire, its flames reflecting in her eyes like a vision. For a moment, she seemed to age, the lines on her face deepening, as if the weight of her secret pressed against her very bones.

"The mines contain more than just lead and zinc. Deep beneath Picher, there's a vein of silver running through sacred ground—a place the old ones honored long before the miners arrived."

"How did the miners miss it?" Tess asked.

"They weren't searching for silver, and sometimes, as the old saying goes, you can't see the forest for the trees."

Remembering the vein of silver-laced ore Tess had found, I glanced at her. She nodded.

"I found an ore vein nearby," she said. "According to Buck, the lead and zinc were flecked with silver. Is it true?"

As if listening for an answer in the windchimes, Nadie hesitated a moment before answering.

"Toby and I were the only two humans aware of the silver. No one would believe Toby, and knowing about its existence has been a heavy burden for me to carry," she said. "Now, you and Buck know."

"And the mine we visited?" I said.

"The Shadow was born there, a guardian of the earth's heart, awakened by the wounds we carved into it. It marked you, Buck, because you've seen its truth, tasted its water, its berries. You're part of its story now."

"Now I understand why you live alone here," I said. "You're the protector of the land that remains pure and guarding a secret that, if revealed, would ruin it."

She smiled and said, "Like Kwanita guarding her goats, and even her hide brushed by the green cloud."

"I'm beginning to sense the weight of your burden," I said.

Her smile faded, and she leaned closer, her voice dropping to a whisper.

"The silver is more than wealth. It's the land's blood, sacred to those who came before. If the mining companies knew, they'd tear this place apart, poison the spring, the air, the earth itself. I've carried this alone for years, and now it binds us all."

"How will Avini's power clean up Picher without revealing the untapped riches and triggering the cycle of pollution again?" Tess asked.

"That's the Gordian Knot I have yet to sever," she said.

Tess set her cup down, her journalist's edge cutting through the wine's haze.

"So, those shadows we saw—they're real, tied to this... sacred vein?" she said.

Nadie nodded. "Miners plundered the land's bounty, leaving behind poison and death. I've had to live with the fear that they'll return once they realize what they left behind. Now, you and Buck share my secret."

I touched the green mark on my arm. "And the Shadow thinks I'll tell? What about Tess?"

"Tess will never share the secret; you will," Nadie said.

"I'm no Judas and have no intention of telling anyone," I said.

"Intentions are like raindrops. They don't intend to fall, they just do," Nadie said.

Nadie's words cut deep, and I felt the mark flare, as if the Shadow itself were listening, doubting me. I thought of Toby's wild eyes, his laughter echoing in the mines, and wondered if the Shadow had whispered the same doubts to him before he broke.

"And what does any of this have to do with Avini and the commune?"

Nadie's gaze lifted to the moon, its light bathing her face in silver. The air grew heavier, the fire's crackle softening as if the hollow itself were leaning in to hear her.

"Toby's mind is fractured, but he perceives what others cannot. The Shadow speaks to him, just as it did to you. Like her grandmother, Avini can heal, even if she isn't yet aware of it."

I nodded. "And that's where I come in?"

"Avini's work—her grandfather's legacy—can heal the land by neutralizing the toxins without disturbing what is sacred," Nadie said. "Someone needs to prod her into action, and I can't be that person."

She looked at me and smiled when I said, "Bingo!"

"I knew you would accept the challenge," she said. "But the Shadow grows restless, and David's rituals are stirring it further. You are in grave danger and must proceed with great caution."

"Because?" I asked.

"Toby wandered too close to the Shadow's heart, and it overwhelmed him. You already bear the mark of the Shadow, and I can't afford to let Toby's fate become yours."

"I'm with you there," I said.

She reached out, her hand hovering over my arm, not touching but close enough that I felt a chill, as if the mark recognized her.

"The Shadow doesn't trust you, Buck. It sees the mark as a chain, binding you to its will, but also a risk. If you falter, it will consume you."

I rubbed the mark on my arm, the wine amplifying its throb. "Is that what happens if I don't get to Avini in time?"

Nadie's words carried the weight of the night. "The Shadow will spread. It's not evil, but it's desperate. It'll shake the earth, poison the air, until its message is heard."

"I feel it," I said.

Nadie paused, her eyes searching mine, as if looking for the spark of resolve she needed.

"You're fighting for the hollow, for the spring, for the silver that must stay buried. Fail, and the miners will return, and this land will weep again."

"And Avini can quiet it?"

"Only if you reach her before David's zeal blinds her and turns her away from her own power," Nadie said. Her voice softened, almost tender, but laced with urgency. "Avini is young, untested, but her blood carries the old ways. You must help her see that, before David's visions twist her path."

The fire blazed, casting long shadows that danced across the camp. The breeze picked up again, and as the wind chimes began to sing, Ahanu lifted his head, a low howl escaping his throat. Pard pressed closer to me, his warmth grounding me against the wine's intoxicating pull. Tess checked her camera, her fingers steady despite the weight of Nadie's words. She glanced at me, her eyes reflecting the fire, and I saw a flicker of fear—not for herself, but for me, for what the mark might mean.

"The world needs to know about the poisoned earth, and I have the footage," she said.

Nadie held up a palm. "You captured something important: the mines, the glow, Toby's ravings. It's a start, but we need more."

"What if Jake's audience doesn't see the truth in the film?" Tess asked.

Nadie leaned forward, her voice a quiet command.

"Your images can speak, Tess. Jake's audience will understand the images through their hearts even if their eyes remain blind."

"If the Shadow's already this bold, we need to act," I said.

"Buck's right," Tess said. "When do we go to the commune?"

Nadie rose, her silhouette framed against the moonlit cottonwoods.

"Tomorrow, at dawn. The moon's power lingers, and the land will guide you. Rest here tonight—my blankets are yours. The wine will help you sleep, though keep your dreams clear. You'll need them."

She gestured to a stack of woven blankets near the fire, their patterns echoing the loom's design, each thread a silent prayer for the land's protection.

I nodded, the weight of the pouch from Nadie pressing against me. The mark on my arm pulsed, a reminder of the mines, of Toby's wild eyes, of the shadows that weren't just echoes but something alive, waiting.

Tess drained her cup, her face set with determination, and Pard curled up beside the fire, his breathing steady. I watched the flames, their dance mirroring the unease in my chest. The mark felt heavier now, not just a scar but a tether, pulling me toward a choice I wasn't sure I could make.

As Nadie stoked the flames, the encampment settled into a quiet rhythm, the spring's bubble and the cottonwoods' whisper blending with the frogs' distant chorus.

The air carried a faint hum, as if the earth itself were singing a lullaby laced with warning. I lay back on the blanket, the ground cool beneath me, and felt the hollow's pulse, steady but urgent, as if it knew time was running out.

# CHAPTER 18

The morning sun rose over Chat Creek, painting the sky in hues of gold and rose, a glorious dawn that belied the chaos of the previous night's earthquake. The air was crisp, carrying the scent of dew-soaked sage and the faint tang of disturbed earth.

Jake waited in the parking lot of the old high school, drinking coffee from a plastic cup. The world felt too quiet, as if the land were holding its breath after the tremor's upheaval. He'd given the crew the day off, a rare chance to shake off the dust and fear of Picher's restless ground, but his mind churned with unease.

His phone buzzed in his pocket, and he pulled it out to see a text from Tess. His brow furrowed as he read: 'Spent the night at Nadie's encampment. Buck and I are headed to the commune. Buck predicts trouble. Hope you and Colley can bail us out if things get too sticky.' She'd included the commune's coordinates, precise as always, a pin dropped in the unknown.

Jake's jaw tightened. He glanced toward Mama, who was leaning against a nearby tree, her silver braid catching the morning light as she sorted through a stack of texts on her phone. Colley was prepping the chopper, its blades gleaming under the sun's first rays.

"Tess just texted," Jake said. "She and Buck stayed at Nadie's last night. They're on their way to the commune."

Mama looked up, her eyes sharp despite the early hour. "Nadie's place, huh? That's no small thing. What'd they find out?"

Jake hesitated, rubbing the back of his neck. "She didn't say. Part of the text worries me."

"Like what?" Mama asked, folding her arms.

"She said, 'Buck predicts trouble. Hope you and Colley can bail us out if things get too sticky.' She sent the commune's coordinates."

Mama's lips pressed into a thin line, but her expression stayed steady.

"Trouble's Buck's shadow, always has been. What's your gut telling you?"

"I want to go there now," Jake said, his voice firm. "Get the chopper up, fly to those coordinates, and make sure they're not walking into a mess we can't pull them out of."

Mama shook her head, her braid swaying. "Nadie, Sage, Clara, and the Sheriff all want Buck and Tess to handle the commune. They're not kids, Jake. They've got the mark of the land on them, especially Buck. Let it play out."

Jake's grip tightened on his cup, the coffee's warmth doing little to ease the knot in his chest.

"And if it goes south? That earthquake last night wasn't just a tremor. Something's awake out there, Mama. You felt it."

She nodded, her gaze drifting to the horizon where the hills rose, their slopes dusted with the morning's glow.

"I felt it. But rushing in now might do more harm than good. Nadie's got her reasons, and Tess is sharp. Trust them."

Jake exhaled. "Fine. But I'm not sitting idle. Colley's got the chopper ready. Let's take a look at what that quake stirred up."

Mama raised an eyebrow but didn't argue. She grabbed her jacket, and they crossed the old football field to where Colley was finishing his checks, his lanky frame half-buried in the chopper's cockpit.

"Ready when you are, Bossman," he called.

The chopper lifted off with a roar, the blades slicing through the morning air as they climbed above the little town of Chat Creek. As they neared Picher, the landscape below unfolded like a scarred tapestry, the golden light unable to hide the wounds left by the quake.

As they flew closer, the ground revealed its secrets: rivers of black sludge oozed from cracked earth, remnants of the old mines' poison seeping through breaches in the makeshift dams.

Chat piles, once contained, had spilled into the waterways, their gray-green silt swirling like venom in the clear streams. The air carried a faint metallic tang, and patches of dead earth gaped like open sores, exposing rusted machinery and jagged rocks flecked with unnatural hues of green and yellow.

Fissures had opened, venting wisps of acrid vapor that shimmered in the sunlight, a toxic haze that seemed to pulse with an eerie glow. The land looked like it was bleeding, its scars raw and angry, a testament to decades of greed now torn open by the earth's own rebellion.

Jake's stomach churned as he leaned toward the window, his eyes tracing the devastation.

"This is worse than I thought," he said, his voice barely audible over the chopper's hum. "The quake didn't just shake things up—it tore the lid off hell."

Mama's face was grim, her hands gripping the edge of her seat. "The land's speaking, Jake. It's been poisoned too long, and now it's fighting back. If this is what's leaking already, imagine what's in store unless something is done."

"I know," Jake said. "And I feel so helpless."

"The whole world will see the devastation when your Tsisdetsi's Shadow episode airs," Mama said. "Maybe there's someone out there with the wherewithal to address the problem."

Jake smiled and shook his head. "Or scare the holy bejesus out of them."

Colley banked the chopper lower, skimming over a collapsed mine shaft where the ground had caved in, revealing a dark maw that seemed to swallow the light. The surrounding soil was slick with oily residue, and a flock of crows scattered, their caws sharp and accusing.

Jake's mind flashed to Tess's text, Buck's mark, and the shadows she'd caught on film. The commune felt like a potential powder keg, ready to blow, and he worried that he should have

Colley take them there, even if Mama was against it.

As the chopper climbed back toward the football field, Mama broke the silence, her voice steady but heavy.

"What now?"

Jake's jaw tightened, his mind racing. "Tess's interview with Lila Voss intrigued me. I think she knows more than she let on. I want to talk to her."

Mama frowned, shaking her head. "You gave everyone the day off. You have no cameraman."

"No, but you have a cell phone, my dear," Jake said, a faint smirk tugging at his lips despite the weight of the morning.

Mama rolled her eyes, her hand already reaching for her phone.

"Whatever."

The chopper's shadow swept over the scarred earth below, a fleeting silhouette against the rising sun, as Jake's thoughts turned to Lila Voss. Her words had carried a guarded edge in Tess's footage, a hint of knowledge she hadn't fully shared.

The chopper touched down back at the Chat Creek football field, its blades slowing to a low whine as Colley powered down. Jake and Mama climbed out, the morning sun now high, casting sharp shadows across the clearing. The air still carried the faint metallic sting from the flyover, a reminder of the land's wounds. Jake's mind was already racing, Tess's text and the ravaged landscape below fueling his urgency.

"Colley, stay with the chopper," Jake said, his voice clipped as he headed for the company Range Rover parked nearby. "Mama, we're going to Chat Creek. I want to talk to Lila Voss."

Mama slid into the passenger seat, her expression skeptical but resigned.

"You're like a dog digging for a bone, Jake. Based on Buck's interview, I can tell you Lila's a talker, not a sage. What do you expect to get out of her?"

"Answers," he said, starting the engine.

The Range Rover rumbled to life, its sleek black frame cutting through the dusty roads toward downtown Chat Creek.

"What answers?" Mama asked.

"She hinted at things in Buck's interview—stuff about Picher, the land. I think she's holding back."

"Whatever, Big Chief. I'm game," Mama said.

The drive was quick, the town unfolding in a patchwork of weathered storefronts and sun-bleached signs. The earthquake's touch was evident: cracks spiderwebbed across the brick facade of the bank, and a streetlight leaned precariously over the sidewalk. Lila's souvenir shop, a quaint corner store with "Voss's Trinkets" painted in faded blue, had taken a hit. The front window was shattered, glass glinting on the pavement, and a sign reading "Closed for Cleanup" hung crookedly on the door.

Inside, Lila was sweeping debris, her auburn hair tied back with a scarf, her denim skirt dusted with plaster. The shop was a chaos of toppled shelves, scattered mugs, and broken keychains shaped like Oklahoma's panhandle. She looked up as the bell jingled, her eyes widening when she saw Jake.

"Oh my stars," she gasped, dropping the broom with a clatter. "Jake Huntington! The Cryptid Hunter, in my shop!" Her hands fluttered to her chest, her voice pitching high with excitement. "I watched every episode of your show—Bigfoot in the Ozarks, the Chupacabra chase. I can't believe you're here!"

Jake flashed a practiced smile, used to the fanfare. "Good to meet you, Lila. Looks like the quake did a number on this place. Need a hand?"

He grabbed the fallen broom, but Lila waved him off, her cheeks flushing.

"No, no, I can't let the Cryptid Hunter push a broom! What would people say?"

Jake chuckled, leaning the broom against a shelf. "I'm not above pushing a broom, Lila. But if you're sure, how about we talk somewhere else? Somewhere with coffee."

Lila's eyes lit up. "The café down the street's open. It's past lunch, so it'll be quiet."

"Come on, I'm buying," Jake said.

The trio stepped out into the warm afternoon, the sun

glaring off the cracked pavement. The Chat Creek Café was a short walk, its neon sign flickering but intact. Inside, the air smelled of stale coffee and fried onions, the jukebox silent for once.

The place was nearly empty, save for two men at a corner table, their clean khakis and polished shoes standing out starkly against the worn linoleum. Jake's eyes narrowed as he took them in—too polished, too out of place.

Lila led them to a table by the window, still buzzing with excitement. A waitress poured coffee, black and steaming, and Lila launched into a stream of chatter about the quake, her shop, and Jake's show. Jake let her talk, his attention split between her words and the two men, who were speaking in low tones, their heads bent over a map.

"They don't look like locals," Jake said, nodding toward the corner table. "Khakis, clean shirts, shiny shoes. Not exactly farm attire."

Lila leaned in, cupping her hand as if sharing a secret. "The cute one's a geologist. The older guy's a landman. Been in town a few days, second visit this month. Nosing around, talking to farmers, poking around Picher."

Mama's brow furrowed. "What the hell is a landman?"

Jake kept his eyes on the men, his voice low. "Someone who works for an oil or mining company, taking mineral leases from locals. They're after something—either to drill a well or mine a lode of ore. Since there's no oil production in Ottawa County, I'd bet those two are with a mining company."

Lila nodded, her bangles clinking as she stirred her coffee. "They've been asking about old mine records, soil samples. Said it's for a 'survey,' but they're cagey. Won't say who they work for."

Jake's jaw tightened. "I'm going to talk to them."

He crossed the café, his boots thudding on the floor. The men looked up as he approached, their expressions guarded. The geologist, young and clean-shaven, adjusted his glasses, while the landman, graying and stern, folded the map with deliberate care.

"Afternoon," Jake said, keeping his tone friendly but firm. "Mind if I ask what brings you to Chat Creek?"

The landman's eyes narrowed. "Company business. Private."

Jake leaned on the table, his presence commanding. "I'm Jake Huntington. Working on a project in Picher. Just curious what kind of survey you're running."

The geologist shifted uncomfortably, but the landman's voice was cold. "Don't you understand what 'tight hole' means? We're not sharing details."

Jake pressed, undeterred. "Picher's a sensitive area. Folks here don't take kindly to outsiders digging up trouble."

The landman stood, tossing a wad of cash on the table. "We're done here." The geologist followed, and they strode out, the bell above the door jingling sharply.

Jake watched them climb into a nondescript sedan, memorizing the license plate as they peeled out. He pulled out his phone and dialed Angie, his assistant in Tulsa.

"Angie, run a plate for me. Oklahoma, XJ4-289. Find out who they're with, and fast."

Back at the table, Mama raised an eyebrow. "What was that all about?"

"Trouble," Jake said, his voice grim. He turned to Lila, who was watching with wide eyes. "What else do you know about those two? Anything specific?"

Lila launched into a ramble—names of farmers they'd visited, snippets of overheard conversations about "high-grade deposits," and a vague mention of a company jet at the regional airport. Most of it was chatter; her gossip-prone nature filled in the gaps with speculation. Jake listened patiently, sifting for nuggets of truth, but his patience wore thin.

"Thanks, Lila," he said, standing. "I'll be back to interview you properly once your shop's back in order. Appreciate your time."

Lila beamed, oblivious to his haste. "Anytime, Jake! You're welcome at my shop, quake or no quake!"

Outside, Mama fell into step beside him, her expression

disapproving. "You were bordering on rudeness back there, you know."

Jake shook his head, unlocking the Range Rover. "The Miami courthouse closes at five. We need to do some record checking before five."

Mama climbed in, skeptical. "So?"

Before he could answer, his phone rang. "Angie, what've you got?"

"The car's registered to Phoenix Minerals," Angie said, her voice crackling through the speaker. "Big mining company, publicly traded. I'm digging into their interest in Picher, but it'll take time."

"Do it," Jake said. "Find out everything you can." He hung up, his knuckles whitening on the steering wheel.

Mama glanced at him. "Phoenix Minerals. That's not small-time."

"Nope," Jake said, pulling onto the road toward Miami. "And they're sniffing around Picher. That's no coincidence."

The Ottawa County courthouse was a squat, red-brick building, its interior cool and musty, with a smell of old paper and dust. Jake led Mama to the basement, where land records were stored in towering metal cabinets. His fingers moved with practiced ease, pulling files and scanning titles, his experience as a landman—taught by his grandfather at Huntington Oil—coming back like muscle memory.

"Do you know what you're doing?" Mama asked, peering over his shoulder at the yellowed documents.

Jake snorted. "You forget my grandfather owned Huntington Oil. Taught me to check records when I was ten. I've spent more time in dusty courthouses than you can say grace over."

He flipped through deeds and mineral leases, his eyes narrowing as patterns emerged—recent inquiries, flagged parcels near Picher, and a handful of leases quietly acquired by Phoenix Minerals. A harried clerk appeared, tapping her watch.

"Closing time, folks. Five minutes."

Jake nodded, stacking the files. As they left the stuffy record room, he shook his head, his voice low and heavy.

"Holy Mother of God. This county is big-time screwed."

Mama's brow furrowed. "What'd you find?"

"Phoenix is moving fast," he said, stepping into the fading daylight. "They're leasing mineral rights around Picher, piece by piece. Don't know what they're looking for, but it's only a matter of time before they start digging holes in the ground."

The Range Rover's engine roared as they pulled away, the courthouse shrinking in the rearview. Jake's mind raced, the weight of Tess's text and the scarred earth from the flyover pressing against the new threat of Phoenix Minerals. Buck and Tess were walking into a storm, and the clock was ticking.

# CHAPTER 19

The Xpedition rumbled along a rutted dirt road, kicking up clouds of red dust that glowed in the late morning sun. Bone Hollow was behind us, its serene glow replaced by the rolling hills of Ottawa County, where the earth bore scars of old mines like battle wounds.

Tess sat in the passenger seat, her camera bag wedged between her feet, her fingers drumming on her knee. Pard lounged in the back, his ears twitching at every jolt, his nose pressed to the cracked window. The air was heavy with the scent of dry grass and a faint bite—Picher's legacy lingering in the breeze.

Tess glanced at me, her hazel eyes sharp despite the fatigue etching her face.

"You sure about this? Nadie's warning about David wasn't exactly comforting."

I gripped the wheel, the green tracery of the Shadow's mark pulsing faintly under my sleeve.

"Avini's the key to stopping the Shadow. We have no choice."

She nodded, but her gaze flicked to the road ahead, where a chain-link fence loomed, topped with barbed wire that glinted like teeth in the sunlight. The commune's entrance was a makeshift gate, flanked by two weathered watchtowers. A faded sign read "New Dawn Collective," but the armed men patrolling it screamed anything but welcome.

I slowed the Xpedition, my gut tightening. Four men in mismatched camo gear stepped forward, rifles slung across their chests, pistols holstered around their waists, their faces hard under sweat-stained caps. One, a broad-shouldered brute with a scar slicing his eyebrow, raised a hand to stop us. His partner, lean and twitchy, gripped a walkie-talkie, muttering something I couldn't catch.

"Stay calm," I whispered to Tess, cutting the engine. Pard growled low, his hackles rising.

The scarred man approached my window, his voice gravelly. "State your business."

"We're here to see David," I said, keeping my tone steady.

His eyes narrowed, flicking to Tess, then back to me. "Nobody sees David without a search. Out of the vehicle. Now."

Tess shot me a look, her jaw tight, but we complied. I opened the door, letting Pard stay inside, his eyes locked on the men. The lean guard gestured for us to step away from the Xpedition, while another began rifling through the back, tossing Tess's camera bag onto the dirt like it was trash.

"Hey, careful with that!" Tess said, stepping forward.

The scarred man blocked her, his rifle shifting slightly. "Hands where I can see them, lady."

The lean one, with a smirk that made my skin crawl, moved toward Tess.

"Got to check you for weapons," he said, his hands lingering too long as he patted her down, sliding over her hips with deliberate slowness.

"Get your hands off her," I said, my fists clenching.

Tess's eyes flashed with anger, but she held still, her voice low. "Buck, don't."

The guard's smirk widened, his fingers brushing her breast again. Something snapped inside me—the mark on my arm flared, hot and alive, and before I could think, I lunged. My fist connected, a satisfying crunch as he staggered back, blood spurting from his nose. He hit the ground hard, cursing.

"Big mistake," the scarred man snarled. The others moved fast, billy clubs swinging. I ducked the first blow, but a second caught my shoulder, pain exploding down my arm. Another club slammed into my ribs, and a final crack to the back of my head sent stars bursting across my vision. The world tilted, and I crumpled, the taste of dust and blood in my mouth as darkness swallowed me.

When I came to, my head throbbed like a drum, each pulse a reminder of the beating. I was slumped in a metal chair, my wrists bound behind me with cuffs that bit into my skin.

The room was bare, with concrete walls stained by dampness, lit by a single bulb swinging overhead, casting shadows that danced like specters. The air was stale, thick with the smell of mildew and something sharper—gun oil, maybe, or fear.

Four men stood around me, their faces a mix of anger and suspicion. The scarred guard from the gate was there, his pistol at the ready, his knuckles white around a billy club.

Another man, tall and imposing with a graying beard and eyes like cold slate, leaned against the wall, his presence commanding despite his silence. Like the others, he was dressed in camos, though his were starched, pressed, and bloused at the ankles, highlighting his highly polished military boots. His embroidered name tag identified him as David.

I knew him from Nadie's warnings—David, her son, the commune's leader, his zeal a spark that could ignite or destroy.

"Where's Tess?" I said, my throat dry, the mark on my arm pulsing in time with my headache.

David stepped forward, his voice low and deliberate, like a preacher sizing up a sinner. When my eyes began focusing better, I saw he was younger than expected, probably in his early fifties.

"She's safe for now," he said. "You, on the other hand, have a lot to explain, Buck McDivit."

He smiled and nodded when I asked, "I didn't need to see your nametag to know who you are. You have your mother's eyes."

"If you know my mother, then you know we haven't spoken in years," he said.

"She wants to change that. She sent something with me to

give to you," I said.

"Nadie's name doesn't give you a free pass to start fights."

I met his gaze, ignoring the pain radiating from my ribs. "Your man was out of line. And we're here to help, not cause trouble."

His eyes narrowed, a flicker of doubt crossing his face. "Help who? To what lies beneath this commune?"

"The only thing Tess and I are here to take from the commune is knowledge," I said.

David nodded to the man with the scar. "Release him," he said.

The pug-ugly bruiser wasn't happy to unlock the cuffs, and he used them to yank me to my feet. I didn't give him the pleasure of seeing me wince.

He was a good six inches taller and fifty pounds heavier than I was, and had to lower his big head to speak directly in my ear.

"Watch your ass, cowboy," he said. "I'm coming for you."

I ignored him, rubbing my wrists before handing Nadie's pouch to David.

David showed no emotion, although he continued to stare at the ceremonial pouch.

"How is Nadie?" he asked.

"Growing older and desperate to see her son and granddaughter," I said.

"Never going to happen," he said. "Bones, lock this man up."

David clicked his heels and left the room, leaving me with Scarface and the other three guards. When a wicked smile crept over his face, I knew I was in for another pounding. I beat him to the punch, kicking him in the nuts and then taking his feet out from under him with a kickboxing octagon maneuver. Scarface was on the floor, grimacing, but I had three handguns pointing at my head.

⸎⟡⸎

I came to from my second beating of the day in a jail cell. I wasn't alone. A big black man with an acne-covered complexion, dressed in an orange jumpsuit, sat beside me on the bottom bunk in a small cell.

"Boy," he said. "You got a death wish."

I rotated my jaw to see if it was broken. It wasn't. "What's your name?" I asked.

"Jonesy," he said.

"Buck," I said. "Glad to meet you, Jonesy." He laughed when I said, "You're only the second black person I've seen since arriving in Ottawa County. Sounds to me like you're the crazy one."

"Been telling myself the same thing for a week, now," he said. "Least I ain't been beat like you."

I smiled. "That big scar-faced mother fucker doesn't like me," I said.

"Hell, Buck, you're lucky you ain't dead. That guard whose nose you broke is Scarface's little brother."

"Just my luck," I said.

"I can tell you're a tough hombre," Jonesy said. "It'll get you killed in this place."

"I'm starving," I said. "When do they bring our food?"

Jonesy laughed and shook his head. "I been here three days and I've ate twice."

He laughed again when I said, "Yeah, well, I'm going to kill somebody."

"I seen men like you," he said. "You could and you would."

I didn't answer him, getting off the bunk and going to the bars to peer into the hallway. A janitor's mop bucket, a mop inside, lay near the cell. Jonesy saw me clutching for it.

"What are you doing?" he asked.

"Those pricks will be back. I need a weapon," I said.

"The mop?" he said.

"I can't quite reach it," I said.

"I can," Jonesy said. "I played basketball at Langston, and I have a standing reach of almost nine feet."

"Do it," I said.

"You going to kill somebody with it?" he asked.

I grinned and said, "If they don't kill me first."

"Buck, you're one crazy son-of-a-bitch," he said.

He grinned when I said, "What was your first clue?"

I crouched beneath the scratchy blanket in the cell, the mop handle's cool against my palms. My ribs ached from the earlier beating, but the pain only sharpened my focus. Jonesy, perched on the bunk above me, kept watch, his dark eyes flicking to the hallway.

The distant clatter of boots on concrete grew louder, and my grip tightened. Scarface—Bones—and two other guards were coming, their silhouettes looming in the dim light.

"Showtime," I said in a whisper.

The cell door rattled as Bones unlocked it, his scarred face twisted into a sneer. "Time for round three, cowboy."

The other two guards, one stocky with a buzz cut, the other wiry with a crooked nose, flanked him, cracking their knuckles like they were auditioning for a bad action flick.

I exploded from under the covers, the mop handle whipping through the air. I drove it into Bones' gut, doubling him over with a wheeze. Before the stocky guard could react, I spun, cracking the handle across his temple. The man crumpled like a sack of flour.

The wiry one lunged, but I sidestepped, slamming the handle into his knee with a sickening crunch. I followed with an elbow to the jaw, sending the guard sprawling, out cold. Bones, gasping, swung a wild fist, but I caught his arm, twisted it behind his back, and slammed him face-first into the bars. Blood sprayed, and Bones slumped, unconscious.

Jonesy stared, wide-eyed. "Damn, Buck. You don't mess around."

"Grab their keys and pistols," I said, tossing the mop handle aside. "We're leaving this hellhole."

Jonesy snatched the keyring from Bones' belt and locked the cell door behind him; the three guards sprawled in a heap.

"Where we going?" he asked, his voice steady despite the chaos.

"To find David, I said

"You going to kill him?"

Jonesy's question made me smile. "No, but I'll make him wish I had. Where'd you say you played basketball?"

"Langston," he said.

"Good school," I said.

We slipped out of the cellblock into the cool night air. The New Dawn Collective stretched before us, a patchwork of a hundred or so weathered structures—shacks and trailers mostly, their windows glowing with flickering light from candles or low-watt bulbs.

No telephone poles marred the skyline; No solar panels glinted faintly on rooftops, and no windmills creaked in the distance. The commune felt like a forgotten outpost, alive but untethered, its silence broken only by the hum of crickets and the occasional bark of a dog.

Jonesy led the way, his long strides eating up the dirt paths between the shacks.

"David's place is on the far side," he whispered. "Biggest house here, near the old barn."

We moved swiftly, shadows among shadows, avoiding the occasional patrol. My blood thrummed, the mark on my arm pulsing faintly, urging me forward. At the edge of the commune, a two-story cabin stood, its porch lit by a single lantern. Jonesy nodded at it.

I didn't hesitate, storming up the steps, boots pounding, and drove my heel into the door. It splintered inward with a crack that echoed like a gunshot, revealing the dark interior beyond.

# CHAPTER 20

The night air clung to my skin, sharp with the scent of pine and earth, as Jonesy and I stepped into the spacious interior of David's log cabin. Moonlight poured through expansive windows, illuminating the polished wood floors in silver and shadow.

The cabin was a fortress of rustic opulence, its walls adorned with elk antlers and woven tapestries, a stark contrast to the commune's ramshackle sprawl, reminding me of the Phillips family's lodge at Woolaroc, all grandeur and grit. This place carried a heavier weight, like a throne room built on secrets.

Jonesy's breath hitched, his lanky frame tense as we crept through the foyer. The air was thick with the faint musk of cedar and something sweeter, like incense burned too long. My grip tightened on the pistol, its weight a cold comfort as we walked past a broad staircase, each step creaking under our boots.

A hallway stretched into darkness, but a sliver of light glowed beneath a double door at the far end—David's bedroom. My pulse quickened, my arm tingling as I pushed the doors open, revealing a suite that could've belonged to royalty. A massive four-poster bed dominated the room, draped in velvet, flanked by carved oak nightstands. A crystal chandelier hung overhead, its prisms catching the moonlight and scattering it like stars.

David lay sprawled in the center of the bed, silk pajamas gleaming against the dark linens. I crossed the room in three strides, yanking him upright by the collar, the pistol's barrel pressed to his cheek. His eyes snapped open, shock giving way to fury as Jonesy flicked on a brass lamp by the bed, bathing the room in warm amber.

"You're going to pay for this," he said, his voice low and venomous, though his hands trembled slightly.

"Not me," I said. "I've been the victim for the last time in this zoo you call a commune. The next one of your men who lays a hand on me is going to die. Now, tell me where you're keeping Tess and my dog."

When a sharp bark cut through the tension, my head snapped toward the door. Pard stood there, tail wagging, beside Tess and a woman I didn't recognize. She was striking, with long dark hair cascading over a flowing nightgown, her eyes sharp and unyielding, like obsidian glinting in the lamplight. Tess, in a similar gown, looked more exasperated than afraid.

"Buck, what the hell are you doing?" Tess said, hands on her hips.

"Looking for you and Pard so we can get the hell out of here," I said.

"We aren't going anywhere," Tess said, her tone firm. "This is Avini. I've visited her lab, and we've been talking."

Avini crossed the room with a grace that seemed to defy the chaos, her gaze locking onto mine.

"If he moves, shoot him," she said.

"What are you going to do?" I asked.

"Put him back to sleep," she said, administering an injection into his arm with a needle.

We watched as David's eyes closed and he sank back onto the bed.

"Now what?" I asked.

"I don't like what's happening here at the commune," Avini said. "Things are getting worse. People are scared. Several of our citizens have left, and my father is a big reason for the decline. He's been coerced."

She nodded when I said, "Scarface?"

Avini shook her head. "I need you to go to Bone Hollow and return with my grandmother," she said. "She'll know what to do."

"Where will I find my vehicle?"

She pressed a set of keys into my hand, the metal cool against my palm. "Outside the main gate, where you left it."

"How will I get through the gate without the guards shooting me in the back?" I asked.

"There's an unguarded exit at the back of this cabin," Avini said. "I'll show you."

We followed her through the sprawling cabin, past walls lined with bookshelves and flickering oil lamps, to a narrow door hidden behind a tapestry. The night air rushed in as she opened it, revealing a path that snaked into the darkness. Tess stepped close, her hand brushing my arm.

"Are you coming with us?" I asked.

"Staying," she said.

"Too dangerous," I said. "You can't."

"Yes, I can. I'll be fine," she said, her eyes steady. "Go get Nadie. I'll be here when you return."

I nodded, though doubt gnawed at me. Jonesy, Pard, and I slipped into the night, the commune's eerie quiet swallowing our footsteps. The Xpedition waited beyond the gate, its classy frame a beacon under the moon's watchful gaze. We climbed in, Pard curling up in the back, as I gunned the engine, the roar shattering the stillness as we sped away toward Bone Hollow.

"Damn!" Jonesy said, holding on as I powered across a dry creek bed. "How much did you have to pay for this baby?"

"Not mine," I said. "My billionaire boss's vehicle."

"You work for a billionaire?" he asked.

"Right now, I do. Jake Huntington, the Cryptid Hunter."

"Get out of here," he said. "That's my favorite TV show. What's he doing in Ottawa County?"

"Filming an episode about Tsisdetsi's Shadow," I said.

"Any chance I might meet him?" he said.

"Damn good chance," I said.

The road unfurled like a ribbon under the stars, the hills of Ottawa County rolling past, their silhouettes jagged against the sky. Jonesy sat in the passenger seat, his long fingers tapping nervously on his knee, his gaze fixed on the horizon.

When we reached Bone Hollow, a campfire flickered in the clearing, its glow dancing across Nadie's weathered face. She sat on a log, her silver hair braided tightly, her eyes sharp as she watched us approach. The air was cool and heavy with the scent of wood smoke.

"What happened?" she asked.

"Trouble," I said. "This is Jonesy. David's men put me in a cell with him. We escaped."

"Where's Tess?" Nadie asked.

"She stayed. While I was fighting with David's goons, she was making friends with Avini. I think they're planning something, though I had no chance to speak to her about it."

"And David?"

"Acting more like a king than a preacher," I said, settling beside the fire. "The commune's a powder keg."

Nadie's lips tightened, her gaze distant. "I was afraid of that. I've spoken with some of those who fled—tales of chaos, violence. Tomorrow, you'll take me there. I'll see to it that the king is deposed."

Something hot and savory was cooking in Nadie's iron pot, the aroma wafting across the clearing. My mouth was watering, and I could tell that so was Jonesy's. Nadie smiled and motioned for us to sit on one of her colorful blankets near the fire. On the rise above us, Ahanu howled at the moon.

Kwanita came out of the shadows. Seeing Jonesy, she nuzzled up to him. With a grin, he put his rangy arms around her neck and hugged her.

"My grandparents have a donkey back home," he said. "Bet she's wondering where the hell I am."

"I'm starving," I said. "Let's eat, and then you can tell us how you landed in jail at the commune."

He smiled and said, "No need to ask me twice. Miss Nadie's food smells like heaven."

Jonesy was soon passing around plates of cornbread and venison stew Nadie had prepared, the warmth of the meal easing the night's chill. As we ate, Jonesy leaned back, his eyes tracing the constellations above.

"Want to tell us how you wound up in a commune jail cell?" I asked.

Jonesy drew a deep breath before beginning. "I wasn't supposed to end up in that place," he said, his words almost lost in the crackle of the fire. "I'm from Okmulgee, grew up on a little farm with my grandparents. My donkey's name is Esmerelda, a stubborn old girl, but she's family."

"A noble name," Nadie said.

Jonesy smiled and nodded. "I was studying ag science at Langston, dreaming of starting my own organic farm someday. I took a job delivering supplies to rural spots—thought it'd be a good way to see the state, save some money."

He paused, poking at the fire with a stick, sparks spiraling into the dark.

He nodded when I said, "The job brought you to Ottawa County?"

"Accidentally. Got off on the wrong road. Next thing I knew, I had no cell phone service and no GPS. It was dark when I reached this ghost town, with abandoned houses and stores, cracked asphalt, and huge piles of red dirt. Creepy as hell."

"Picher," I said. "What happened?"

"A couple of David's men found me, offered help. Said they had a mechanic at the commune. I didn't have much choice, so I went with them. Thought I'd be in and out."

Jonesy paused, glancing skyward as a shooting star flashed overhead. Kwanita brayed in the distance, Nadie's chickens roosting for the night.

"What happened?" I asked.

Nadie interrupted before Jonesy could answer.

"I sense the story is about to become more serious," she said. "Let's drink some herbal wine. It'll make us all feel better."

"No argument from me," I said.

Jonesy's smile had almost returned as he drank Nadie's magical wine. Almost.

His jaw tightened. "They fixed the truck, all right, but then they wouldn't let me leave. Said I was going to participate in a coon hunt and that I was the coon."

"What the hell does that mean?" I asked.

"They were going to give me a head start, then hunt me down like an animal, hinting at something horrible when they caught me."

My mouth opened, though nothing came out. Nadie refilled our mugs.

"The people who'd left the commune told me that a group of racists had infiltrated the 'People of the Earth.' I didn't believe them," she said.

"It's true," Jonesy said. "Scarface and his little brother are escapees from a prison in Tennessee notorious for its Aryan Nations population. They proceeded to indoctrinate many of the like-minded people at the commune, David being one of them."

"I heard as much," Nadie said. "I didn't want to believe it."

"That's not all," Jonesy said. "They began branching out, robbing farmers. I think they may have even knocked over a small town bank."

"A crime ring operating out of the commune?" I said.

"And David complicit as hell," Jonesy said.

I shook my head, the weight of Jonesy's words settling like dust. "You didn't deserve that."

"You saved my life, Buck. I'm grateful," Jonesy said.

Nadie's eyes softened. "You're free now. What will you do?"

Jonesy stared into the fire, his voice firm. "I'm not going back to that commune. That part's for sure. I'll leave tomorrow and walk to Okmulgee, back to my folks. Get the hell out of this God forsaken place."

"Don't do that," I said, clapping a hand on his shoulder. "I'll drive you when I return."

"Buck's right," Nadie said. "There's food and drink here, and you can watch my animals while we're gone."

"Don't go," Jonesy said. "You're just going to get yourselves killed."

"Pardon me a minute," I said. "I'm going to drive to the top of the hill and see if I can get cell phone service. Be right back."

Jonesy's smile was faint but grateful, the firelight catching the hope in his eyes. Above us, the moon hung heavy, its light weaving through the clouds, as Pard and I drove to the top of the hill. When I returned, Jonesy was asleep on the blanket.

"Who did you call?" Nadie asked.

"My boss," I said. "Reported to him what's happening at the commune. He's on it."

Nadie's expression was distraught. Ahanu noticed, nudging her with his big nose.

"I only hope Avini isn't part of the vile racist activity at the commune," she said.

"She isn't," I said. "She helped Jonesy and me escape, and she gave David a shot of something that knocked him out. She asked me to come get you because you would know what to do."

"That makes me feel better," she said. "Thank you."

"Maybe I should go alone," I said.

"We'll both go. You'll need my magic," she said. "And I'll need your muscle."

# CHAPTER 21

Mama and Colley sat at the bar of the company catering tent. After the chaos of the earthquake, Jake had given his people the day off to recuperate, and that included Norma, the bartender. He stood across the bar from them, mixing a martini for Mama.

"For you, my dear," he said.

Mama sipped the martini, a pleased look on her face.

"Very good," she said. "Who taught you to mix a martini?"

"One of my many talents," he said with a wink.

Jake's cell phone rang, interrupting their conversation. After excusing himself, he stepped away from the bar to answer it.

"Sounds like you two had one hell of a day," Colley said.

"We spent the afternoon in a dusty county courthouse. What we found has disturbed Jake."

"What did you find?" Colley asked.

"A public company is taking mining leases here in the county," Mama said. "They're even re-leasing the old mines."

"I thought the mines were condemned," Colley said.

"They are, most of the land now owned by the federal government," Mama said.

"There'd be a bunch of pissed off people here in Ottawa County if that little tidbit of information came to light," Colley said.

"Got that right," Mama said.

"What's the deal?" Colley asked. "I thought the mines were played out."

"That's the sixty-four-dollar question," Mama said, "and exactly what has Jake worried."

"Whatever the reason for the activity, it sounds to me like there's a rat in the woodpile," Colley said.

"Appears so," Mama said. "Angie's on it."

"She's good," Colley said. "She'll get to the bottom of it."

Colley's smile disappeared when Mama said, "What about the Thunder tickets?"

"Not my fault, Mama," he said. "Two was all I could get. You can take mine."

"Then how would Jake get to Oklahoma City?" Mama said.

"I'll wait in the chopper and listen to the game on the radio," Colley said.

"You're as big a Thunder fan as Jake is, and this is a once-in-a-lifetime event."

"I'm telling you, Mama," Colley said. "I've called in all my chits. I can't find another."

"I won't take your ticket," Mama said. "Jake's a billionaire. Surely someone will sell him an extra ticket, or two."

"This is the biggest game of the year, and Jake's not the only billionaire. Front row seats are nearing twenty-five grand each."

"Jake can afford it," Mama said.

"Heads up," Colley said. "He just got off the phone. We can talk about the tickets later."

Jake wasn't smiling when he returned to the bar. After pouring a double shot of scotch, he drained it in a single swallow.

"Uh-oh! Mama said. "Must have been a bad one."

Jake's smile was gone as he poured more scotch for himself and Colley and then mixed another martini for Mama.

"Why so glum?" she asked.

"That was Buck," Jake said. "He's at Bone Hollow with Nadie Red Eagle."

"And Tess?"

Jake shook his head, looking worried. "She's at the commune."

"Maybe you'd better explain," Mama said.

"Buck and Tess went to the commune this morning. Buck got into a fight and was put in a cell. He escaped with a man named

Jonesy, and now they are with Nadie, planning what to do next."

"Fight?" Mama said.

"Buck's a hot head," Colley said. "Doesn't surprise me."

"Sounds convoluted to me. He left Tess at the commune?" Mama said.

"She's with Avini," Jake said. "Two escapees from a Tennessee prison have settled in the commune. Avini asked Buck to go to Bone Hollow and return with Nadie to help solve an increasingly serious problem."

"Can you elaborate?" Mama said.

"The two men are violent racists who have recruited like-minded members of the commune. They've formed a theft ring and have already robbed a bank. David, Avini's father and head of the commune, is under their spell."

"Not good," Mama said. "What's your plan?"

"Angie's putting together a report on the two escapees and recent crimes in the area so that I'll be able to speak confidently with Sheriff Callahan."

"Does she have anything yet on Phoenix Minerals?" Mama asked.

Jake leaned against the bar, his expression darkening as he swirled the scotch in his glass.

"Oh, she has plenty," he said. "Phoenix Minerals isn't just sniffing around Ottawa County for lead and zinc out of some sudden geological epiphany. This stinks of a scheme so rotten it'd make a vulture gag."

Mama raised an eyebrow, setting her martini down. "Spill it, Jake. What's Angie dug up?"

He glanced around the tent, ensuring no one was within earshot, then leaned in closer.

"Phoenix's CEO, one Roland Carver, is cozy with Senator Hollis Grant—head of the Senate Committee on Environmental and Public Works, which, surprise, oversees federal land management in places like Picher."

"Oh, my!" Mama said.

"Carver and his top brass have funneled over two million

dollars into Grant's last campaign, with some donations so conveniently timed they might as well have 'bribe' stamped on them. Angie's got records of meetings between Carver and Grant's staff, off-the-books dinners, and a few 'consulting fees' that don't pass the smell test."

Colley whistled low. "That's bold, even for a mining outfit. But why Ottawa County? Those mines are dead, and the feds condemned the land for a reason."

Jake's lips curled into a sneer. "That's the diabolical part. Phoenix isn't after lead and zinc—at least, not primarily. Angie found internal memos buried in a leaked document cache. They're using the condemned federal land as a front."

When Jake paused to sip his scotch, Colley asked, "What's the real play?"

"Rare earth minerals," Jake said.

"No way! Here in Ottawa County?" Mama asked.

Jake nodded. "Deposits of neodymium and dysprosium, critical for tech manufacturing—batteries, magnets, you name it. That's not all."

"Hell, Jake," Colley said. "You have my attention. What else?"

"Stillwater is the home of the USA Rare Earth facility. They are establishing a domestic supply chain for rare earth elements and neodymium magnets."

"Sounds convenient," Mama said.

"Doesn't it, though?" Jake said. "They won't have far to go for their raw materials."

"About a hundred-fifty miles as the crow flies," Colley said.

"China has been choking the global supply, and prices are through the roof. Phoenix is quietly securing leases dirt-cheap, exploiting loopholes in the federal condemnation status, all while Grant's committee looks the other way."

Mama's eyes narrowed. "So they're planning to strip mine sacred land and make a fortune with a senator in their pocket?"

"Worse," Jake said, his voice dropping to a conspiratorial growl. "Angie's got evidence they're planning to 'rehabilitate' the Picher area as a cover, claiming they're cleaning up the environmental mess from the old mines."

"Damn, Jake," Colley said. "This story can't get much worse."

"Yes, it can," Jake said. "The mines Phoenix operates are case studies in cutting corners. Toxic runoff, dead rivers, and a couple of 'accidental' worker deaths swept under the rug."

"There's no good to what you just told us. What's the bottom line?" Mama asked.

"Phoenix will tear Ottawa County apart, pocket billions, and leave the locals with even more of a wasteland than what they already have."

Jake nodded when Mama said, "And if anyone asks questions, they've got Grant's influence to squash investigations."

Colley shook his head. "That's a hell of a racket. What's Angie doing next?"

"Cross-referencing Phoenix's lease agreements with federal records to see how deep the corruption goes," Jake said. "She's only just begun."

Jake winced when thunder shook the tent. Mama touched his hand,

"Nothing but a rainstorm, my dear, not another earthquake."

Colley poured himself more scotch and said, "This place has us all jumpy."

"Sounds like Angie's on to it. What else?" Mama said.

"My guess? They're planning to strong-arm any holdouts in Ottawa County, maybe even displace the Quapaw Nation's claims."

"Damn!" Colley said.

"It's not just white-collar crime—it's a land grab dressed up as progress," Jake said.

Mama's jaw tightened. "And the people here? The ones already hurting from the last mining disaster?"

Jake's eyes glinted with cold fury. "Collateral damage to Phoenix. They'll wave some jobs around, make big promises, then vanish when the rare earths are gone."

"We can't let this happen. There must be something we can do about it," Mama said.

"There is, and we are," Jake said. "Angie is building a case to take to the DOJ, but we need hard evidence to nail them before they start digging. If we don't move fast, Ottawa County's going to be a sacrifice zone for their greed."

Mama picked up her martini, her voice icy. "Then we'd better make sure Angie's got everything she needs. This smells like a fight."

Jake flashed a wicked grin, tipping his glass toward Mama.

"Partner, you ain't seen nothing yet. When the gloves come off, I play dirty enough to make the devil blush. Stick with me, and we'll burn Phoenix's house of cards to the ground."

"I believe you, baby," Mama said.

The glow of string lights bathed the catering tent in a warm haze. Outside, the Oklahoma darkness pressed close, the full moon casting long shadows through the canvas flaps, while frogs croaked in a steady rhythm.

Jake leaned against the bar, his scotch glass sweating in his hand, his TV-star charm fraying at the edges. Mama sat perched on her stool, her colorful shawl slipping slightly as she pointed a finger at him, her eyes flashing with New Orleans fire.

Colley cringed when Mama brought up the subject of Thunder tickets, her voice low, laced with mock betrayal, but her glare was real enough to make Jake shift uncomfortably.

"Hate to change the subject, but it's Thunder versus Pacers, and you're leaving me to watch it on TV?"

Mama sounded serious, though Jake spotted her smile, realizing she was only trying to lighten the moment.

"Take my ticket," he said. "You and Colley go."

Mama, not finished messing with him, pretended she didn't hear.

"You better hope I don't see you on TV sitting next to another woman," she said.

Colley raised his hands, his grin widening but cautious. "These tickets are gold dust—prime seats, courtside, Shai versus Halliburton. Everyone in the country wants a piece of the magic."

Jake grinned and took a sip of his scotch. "Mama would root for a tornado if it meant sticking it to my Thunder. But she's right, Colley. It's inhuman to dangle Game 7 finals tickets in front of a rabid fan."

Mama's lips twitched, a flicker of amusement softening her mock glare. "Don't sweet-talk me, Jake Huntington. You're a Thunder fanatic, and I know you'd sell your best camera to see OKC win."

Colley laughed, the sound casual but tinged with nerves as he tapped his glass of scotch with his finger.

"I'll call my guy tomorrow and see if he has one more seat. Problem is, anyone rich enough to pay twenty-five grand for a front row seat isn't going to sell it for any price."

Mama's smile disappeared. "You have two front row seats?" she said.

Colley nodded. "Best two seats in the arena; right on the center aisle."

Mama looked at Jake and said, "You didn't tell me that."

Jake set his glass down with a clink, his jaw tightening as he glanced toward the tent flap, where the moonlight spilled in.

"We've got enough going on with Buck and Tess chasing shadows. I need something normal, like screaming my lungs out at a game, to keep me sane. I'll think of something."

Mama leaned forward, her martini glass catching the light.

"Nothing's normal about this place, with quakes, cults, and that Shadow messing with us. I'm fine with you going to the game without me. I've only been joking. The Pelicans are my team, but this year, I'm rooting for my man and the Thunder, ticket or no ticket."

"We can worry about the Thunder game later," Jake said.

"What's on your mind, Bossman?" Colley asked.

"Fire up the chopper. Let's go to Tulsa and see what else Angie has dug up."

# CHAPTER 22

The chopper's blades sliced through the Oklahoma sky, the low hum vibrating in Jake's chest as Colley guided the sleek craft toward Tulsa. Below, the patchwork of fields and small towns gave way to the city's modest skyline, the Huntington Building's glass crown glinting in the late afternoon sun.

Mama sat beside Jake, her hands folded tightly in her lap, her eyes scanning the horizon like a hawk. She hadn't said much since they left Chat Creek, but Jake knew her silence meant she was thinking about something.

"Almost there," he said. "Angie has new information on Grant and Carver.

"What we need is two of her," Mama said. "Phoenix Minerals isn't playing checkers."

Jake nodded as Colley banked the chopper toward the Huntington's rooftop helipad.

"Good thing I brought my boots."

"I doubt anyone has ever caught you off guard," Mama said.

"Thanks for your confidence," he said. "I have a hunch I may need an extra pair before this problem is solved."

He smiled when she said, "Solve it, you will. Of that I have no doubt."

Colley handled the landing with his usual precision, setting the chopper down as if it were a feather on a pillow. The Huntington's roof was a stark contrast to Picher's scarred earth —a pristine slab of concrete with a view of Tulsa's sprawl, the Arkansas River snaking through it like a lazy python.

Jake and Mama stepped out, the wind whipping their clothes

as they made their way to the rooftop access door. The elevator whisked them to the top floor, where Angie's office waited.

Jake didn't skimp on his employee's offices, and Angie's was a study in understated power—mahogany paneling, a Persian rug that probably cost more than Jake's chopper, and a wall of windows framing the city below.

Angie stood behind a sleek desk cluttered with files, her tailored blazer and sharp gaze making her look every bit the Harvard MBA she was. At thirty-four, she had a presence that could silence a boardroom, and Jake trusted her instincts more than his own. At least sometimes.

"Jake, Mama," Angie said, her voice warm but all business. She gestured to a pair of leather chairs. "Sit. We have a lot to cover, and none of it's pretty."

Jake sank into a chair, his boots scuffing the rug. "Lay it on me, Angie. What's Grant and Carver cooking up?"

Angie slid a thick dossier across the desk, its edges bristling with sticky notes.

"Senator Hollis Grant and Roland Carver are tight. Phoenix Minerals has funneled over two million dollars into Grant's campaign through a web of PACs and shell companies. In return, Grant's been greasing the wheels for Phoenix to scoop up Picher's federal lands—condemned or not—for pennies on the dollar."

Mama leaned forward, her eyes narrowing. "Condemned land doesn't just get handed out like candy. What's the angle?"

Angie tapped a finger on the dossier. "Rare earth minerals. Neodymium, dysprosium—stuff that powers electric cars, wind turbines, you name it. Picher's old lead mines are sitting on a goldmine of this stuff, and Carver knows it."

"How did he know?" Jake asked.

"Hollis Grant somehow acquired a copy of an assay report concerning rare earth minerals at the New Dawn Collective," she said. "He shared it with Carver, who recognized the significance of the report."

"Who authored the report?" Jake asked.

"John Kane," she said.

"Wonder how the hell that got into Grant's hands?" When Angie paused, Jake said, "Tell me more."

"Grant's committee has been quietly reclassifying the land as 'rehabilitated' to bypass EPA restrictions. He has buddies in the Bureau of Land Management signing off on leases faster than you can say 'conflict of interest.'"

Jake whistled. "Two million's a lot of hush money. What's Grant getting out of this besides campaign cash?"

Angie's lips curled into a grim smile. "That's where it gets diabolical. I found a blind trust in Grant's name with ties to a Cayman Islands account. Guess who's a silent partner in one of Carver's corporate offshoots."

Mama's hand twitched. "Senator Grant is playing a dangerous game," she said. "What's Carver's end?"

"Carver's the brains behind the operation," Angie said, flipping open the dossier to a photo of Roland Carver—silver-haired and sharp-suited.

Jake shook his head and said, "Carver has the kind of smile that makes you check your wallet."

"He has Phoenix positioned to corner the U.S. rare earth market. Picher's just the start. If they pull this off, they'll have a monopoly on minerals China's been hoarding for years. Billions in profits, and Grant's cut could set him up for life."

"Movers and shakers are hard to control," Jake said. "Carver has the jump on us, and we're already behind the eight ball."

"And there's more," Angie said. "Phoenix is buying up properties around Picher, locking out locals and even strong-arming the Quapaw Nation with threats of federal audits."

"The Quapaws are involved?" Jake said.

Angie nodded. "I'm guessing the government is strong-arming them."

"The Fed's interests versus that of the Indian tribes," Mama said. "What else is new?"

Jake leaned back, his mind racing. "So Grant's selling out Ottawa County, and Carver's playing kingmaker. How do we stop them?"

Angie slid another sheet across the desk—a cryptic email from Grant to Carver, timestamped three days ago.

"The eagle flies at midnight—Picher's ours," it read. "That's code," Angie said. "Code for a final lease approval."

Angie shook her head when Jake asked, "When?"

"Don't know. Grant has a whistleblower scared silent, and he's leaning on local officials to keep quiet."

Mama's eyes glinted. "Hope you have a plan rattling around in that pretty little head of yours?"

Jake was worried, though Mama's comment made him smile. "Carver and Grant have a jump on us. Any chance of nailing Grant for political corruption?"

"Allegations of corruption and political malfeasance are everyday occurrences in Washington. Both parties protect themselves against such allegations," Angie said. "It has to stink pretty badly before anyone in Congress or the Senate reacts."

Mama looked at Angie and said, "There must be another way."

"I'm just the message bearer. Don't kill me," she said.

Mama reached across the desk and patted Angie's hand. "You gave Jake what he needed. Thank you."

"Bossman will figure it out," she said.

"Thanks, Ange," he said.

"I'll stay on it, Bossman," she said."

Jake grabbed the dossier, clutched Mama's hand, and pulled her to her feet. He stopped when they reached the door.

"One more thing," he said. "Get me a prospectus on Phoenix Minerals. Find out who's on the board and where their allegiances lie. Find out who the major stockholders are and how much they own."

"Yes, sir," she said. "I'm on it."

As they waited for the next elevator, Jake rubbed his jaw, staring out at Tulsa's skyline.

"You have an idea cooking in that little pea brain of yours, don't you, Sherlock?" she said.

Jake grinned. "When I was a senior at Duke, I was in the

NCAA finals in the 10K. The conference champ was a ringer from Ireland running for Arkansas. With one lap to go, O'Farrell and I had all but lapped the field. He had a kick, and I knew there was only one way to win that race."

"You tripped him?"

Jake shook his head as the elevator bell rang. "Nah, I finished second, but I thought about it."

"Good for you," Mama said.

"I would never trip a good person," he said. "On the other hand, Carver and Grant are anything but good guys."

Jake's office was a world apart from Angie's, a sprawling testament to his success that took up half the top floor of the Huntington Building. The walls were lined with polished oak, and a massive window framed Tulsa's skyline, now glowing under the amber hues of dusk.

His Duke MBA hung prominently beside a gleaming trophy case, its shelves packed with track and field awards—gold and silver medals glinting under recessed lighting, a reminder of the speed and grit that had carried him through life.

A sleek desk anchored the room, cluttered with maps of Ottawa County, mining reports, and a dog-eared copy of *The Art of War*.

Mama sank into a leather chair, her sharp eyes scanning the room as if it held the answers to their predicament.

"Fancy digs, Jake. You sure you're not overcompensating for something?"

Jake chuckled as he crossed to his desk. "Just making sure the world knows I'm not some small-town dreamer anymore."

"What now?" Mama asked.

Jake's office featured a fully stocked wet bar, complete with an ice maker.

"First things first," he said. "You need a martini, and I need scotch."

Jake presented Mama with her martini and then relaxed in the large chair beside her. Tulsa's neon was aglow, its nightlife beginning.

The neon lights of Tulsa flickered to life as Jake and Mama stepped out of the Huntington Building into the warm evening air. Downtown pulsed with energy—couples strolled along the sidewalks, music spilled from open bar doors, and the scent of grilled food wafted through the streets. The sky was a deep indigo, streaked with the last traces of a fiery sunset, and the city felt alive, vibrant, a stark contrast to the tangled web of corruption they'd just dissected with Angie.

"How about we grab some dinner?" Jake suggested, loosening his tie. "I know a place not far from here. Best fettuccine Alfredo in town."

Mama raised an eyebrow, her lips curling into a sly smile. "You buying, hotshot?"

"You know it," he said with a smile.

They walked a few blocks to a cozy Italian restaurant tucked between a boutique and a jazz club. The place was called Vito's, its exterior draped in ivy, with small round tables spilling onto the sidewalk under strings of Edison bulbs.

Inside, the air was thick with the aroma of garlic and fresh basil. A waiter in a crisp white shirt led them to a corner booth by a window, where candles flickered in amber holders, casting a warm glow across the checkered tablecloth.

Jake ordered a bottle of Chianti, and Mama, ever the skeptic, eyed the menu like it was a legal document.

"You sure this place isn't too fancy for a couple of country folks like us?"

"Speak for yourself," Jake teased, leaning back in his seat. "I'm a man of refined tastes now."

Mama snorted, but her eyes softened as she looked at him. "You've come a long way, Jake. This city suits you, even if you don't like to admit it."

The waiter poured the wine, and they ordered fettuccine Alfredo for Jake, chicken cacciatore for Mama. As they waited, Jake's gaze drifted out the window, where Tulsa's skyline shimmered against the night. His expression grew distant, and Mama, ever perceptive, tilted her head.

"What's on your mind, boy? You're looking like you're carrying the weight of the world."

Jake took a slow sip of wine, his fingers tracing the stem of the glass. "Just thinking about this place. Tulsa. Growing up here wasn't exactly a fairy tale."

Mama leaned forward, her elbows on the table. "Tell me about it. You don't talk much about your folks."

Jake hesitated, his jaw tightening. He rarely spoke about his parents, but something about the night—the warm glow of the restaurant, Mama's steady presence—loosened the knot in his chest.

"My parents were... well, let's just say they were more interested in their social calendar than their kid," he began, his voice low. "Dad was an oil man, always chasing the next big wildcat. Mom was a socialite, flitting from one charity gala to another. They had money and status, but no time for me. I was an accessory, something to trot out at parties when it suited them."

Mama's eyes narrowed, but she stayed quiet, letting him continue.

"I spent most of my childhood in an empty house. Marble floors, crystal chandeliers, but it felt like a museum. Cold. I'd wander the halls, wondering if they'd even notice if I disappeared." He gave a bitter chuckle. "Most of the time, they didn't."

The waiter arrived with their plates, the steam rising from creamy pasta and tomato-drenched chicken. Jake paused, twirling his fork absently as the memories flooded back.

"When I was about ten, I had... let's call it a bad day. I flunked a math test, got into a fight at school—nothing major, just kid stuff. But it felt like the end of the world. I came home, went to my room, and just... broke down. Sat there on the floor, crying my eyes out, thinking nobody cared."

Mama's hand reached across the table, resting lightly on his wrist. "Go on."

Jake's lips quirked into a faint smile. "That's when Grandpa

Hunt found me. He was living with us then, after Grandma passed. He'd been out back tinkering with his old Chevy, grease on his hands, smelling like motor oil and pipe tobacco. He didn't say anything at first—just sat down on the floor next to me, cross-legged, like he was a kid too."

Jake's voice softened, his eyes distant. "He let me cry it out, didn't try to fix it or tell me to toughen up. When I finally stopped, he looked at me and said, 'Jake, the world's a hard place, and it doesn't always notice you're hurting. But you gotta keep running your race, even when the crowd ain't cheering. You don't run for them. You run for you."

Mama smiled, her eyes crinkling. "Sounds like Hunt was a wise man."

"He was," Jake said, nodding. "He told me something else that stuck with me. He said, 'People will try to put you in a box— tell you who you are, what you can do. Don't let them. You decide your own shape.' That's when I started running track, you know. Not for medals or glory, but because it was mine. Something my parents couldn't touch."

Mama took a bite of her cacciatore, chewing thoughtfully. "Hunt sounds like he raised you more than your folks did."

"He did," Jake admitted. "He taught me how to change a tire, how to throw a punch, how to read people. Everything I know about grit, I got from him. My parents... they gave me a last name and a trust fund. Hunt gave me a spine."

The restaurant hummed around them, the clink of glasses and soft laughter filling the air. Jake took a bite of his Alfredo, the creamy sauce rich and comforting, but his mind was still in that room with Hunt, the old man's steady voice cutting through the chaos of his childhood.

Mama sipped her wine, studying him. "You're still running that race, aren't you? Carver, Grant, Phoenix Minerals—it's just another lap."

Jake met her gaze, a spark of determination flickering in his eyes. "Yeah. And I'm not letting those bastards put me in a box."

Mama raised her glass, a glint of mischief in her smile. "To Hunt, then. And to winning the race."

Jake clinked his glass against hers. "To Hunt."

As they ate, the weight of the day seemed to lift, if only for a moment. The city sparkled outside, and Jake felt the familiar fire in his chest—the same one Hunt had stoked all those years ago. Whatever Carver and Grant were planning, he'd run them down. For Picher, for the Quapaws, for himself.

"Ready to head back to the office?" Mama asked, wiping her mouth with a napkin. "Or you got more stories to tell?"

Jake grinned, tossing a few bills on the table. "Let's get back to work. I have a race to finish."

They stepped back into the Tulsa night, the city alive around them, and Jake felt the weight of Hunt's words settle over him like armor. The fight was far from over, but he knew one thing for sure: he wasn't running for anyone else.

# CHAPTER 23

The New Dawn Collective hummed with an undercurrent of unease, its patchwork of shacks and trailers bathed in the pale glow of moonlight filtering through a haze of dust.

The commune's silence was deceptive, broken only by the distant bark of a dog and the faint creak of a windmill that didn't exist. Instead, the air thrummed with an invisible energy, a pulse that seemed to rise from the earth itself, powering the flickering lights in the cabins without a single wire tethering them to the outside world.

Tess followed Avini through a maze of dirt paths, her camera bag slung over her shoulder, its weight a grounding reminder of her purpose. The commune's main gate loomed behind them, its barbed wire glinting like a warning. Avini led her toward a concrete building tucked behind a grove of twisted oaks.

Unlike the ramshackle structures around it, this one was solid, its walls smooth and unweathered, with a heavy steel door that looked out of place in the rustic sprawl. A faint hum emanated from within, like the drone of a distant hive.

Avini paused at the door, her fingers hovering over a keypad, her dark eyes shadowed with worry. A practical jumpsuit had replaced her flowing nightgown, its sleeves rolled up to reveal arms smudged with grease and chemicals. She glanced at Tess, her expression a mix of determination and doubt.

"This is my lab," she said, her voice low, as if the night itself might overhear. "Grandfather's legacy lives here. If we're going to save this place—or stop it from imploding—you need to see it."

Tess nodded, her journalist's instincts prickling. "Lead the way."

The door hissed open, revealing a cavernous space that felt like stepping into a different world. The laboratory was a marvel of modern science grafted onto the commune's earthy roots. Polished steel tables gleamed under LED lights, their glow steady and bright, powered by no visible source.

Banks of computers lined one wall, their screens displaying complex graphs and molecular models that danced in real-time. Centrifuges whirred softly, and glass vials filled with luminescent liquids cast eerie reflections across the room. The air smelled faintly of ozone, undercut by the earthy tang of the commune's soil, as if the lab were an extension of the land itself.

At the center of the room stood a cylindrical device, its surface etched with intricate copper coils that pulsed with a faint blue light. It was the size of a water heater but radiated a quiet power, its hum resonating in Tess's chest. Avini gestured toward it, her voice tinged with pride and reverence.

"That's the Kane Resonator," she said. "Grandfather—John Kane—built it based on Tesla's principles. It harnesses geothermal energy from the Earth's core, a clean and endless source, without disturbing the land. This commune runs on it —no grid, no pollution, just the earth's heartbeat."

Tess's eyes widened, her fingers itching to pull out her camera. "Tesla, as in Nikola Tesla? That's... incredible. How does it work?"

Avini's lips twitched into a half-smile, but her eyes remained distant.

"It's a harmonic oscillator, amplifying the Earth's natural electromagnetic fields. Grandfather was Tesla's apprentice in the 1940s, one of the few who understood his vision for free energy. He brought that knowledge here, built this place as a sanctuary for those who wanted to live in harmony with the land."

Tess approached the resonator with respect, reaching out to touch it but stopping just before her fingers made contact with the metal.

"Awesome!" she said.

"Touch it," Avini said with a smile. "It won't bite you."

When Tess touched the resonator, a tear appeared in the corner of her eye and dripped down her cheek.

"I felt this way once before when touring the Los Alamos National Laboratory. The bomb."

Avini touched her shoulder and said, "Are you crying?"

Tess turned and embraced Avini, tears pouring from her eyes, her body trembling.

"I'm sorry I'm so emotional," she said. "It's just that..."

Avini wiped away Tess's tears with her sleeve and said, "No need to explain. I feel the same every time I enter this building."

"It's like touching God," Tess said.

Avini paused, her fingers brushing the resonator's cool surface, as if drawing strength from it.

"It's not enough anymore. Not with what's happening out there."

She nodded toward the lab's small window, where the commune's shadowed outlines loomed.

Tess set her bag down, her voice steady but probing. "You're talking about David. And Scarface."

Avini's jaw tightened, and she turned away, busying herself with a tablet displaying a 3D model of a molecular structure.

"My father... he's not the man he was. He used to talk about Grandfather's dreams—living free, healing the earth. Now he's paranoid, obsessed with control. Scarface and his brother feed that darkness. They've got half the commune under their thumb, whispering about 'purity' and 'strength.' It's poison, Tess. And it's spreading."

Tess leaned against a lab table, her tears gone and her mind racing.

"You think David's lost it? Mentally, I mean."

Avini's hands stilled, her gaze fixed on the tablet, though her eyes were unfocused.

"He's not sleeping. He hears things—voices, maybe the Shadow itself. He talks about protecting the commune, but it's not protection. It's fear."

"How did Scarface gain so much control?" Tess asked.

"He and his goons make Father feel powerful, but they're the ones really running things, and it's tearing us apart."

"How?" Tess asked.

"People are leaving, scared of what this place is becoming." She looked up, her obsidian eyes meeting Tess's. "I barely remember Nadie, my grandmother. I was a baby when she and Father fell out. You say you've met her?"

Tess nodded. "Your grandmother is quite the person. I cut my leg to the bone. Nadie's herbal potions took away the pain. There's barely a scar."

"Grandfather revered her. Said she could harness the land's energy and perform miracles with her herbs and words. If anyone can pull Father back, or stop him, it's her."

Tess frowned, her journalist's skepticism warring with the memory of Nadie's wine and the pulsing mark on Buck's arm.

"You're banking a lot on Nadie. What's your plan when Buck brings her here?"

Avini's shoulders sagged, and for a moment, she looked younger, vulnerable.

"Don't know. I thought... maybe she could talk to him, remind him who he was. Or perhaps she knows how to quiet the Shadow, keep it from tearing this place apart."

"If anyone can, it's Nadie," Tess said.

"My experiments." Avini gestured to the vials and computers. "They're close to neutralizing the toxins in Picher's soil, using microbial enzymes to break down heavy metals. But the Shadow... It's not just science. It's bigger than that."

Tess's gaze flicked to the resonator, its blue glow casting shadows that seemed to writhe against the walls.

"This all leaves me speechless," she said.

"The Shadow—it's tied to something beneath the commune."

"You know about the vein?" Tess asked.

Avini nodded, her voice dropping to a whisper. "What lies below us is not a vein," she said.

"What, then?" Tess asked.

"Rare earth," Avini said. "Grandfather knew about it. Said it was sacred, the land's blood. It's why he put the resonator here."

"Rare earth?"

"Crucial in high-tech devices and applications," Avini said. "Electronics, clean energy, and military equipment. Grandfather had an assay report."

Avini nodded when Tess said, "And that's why he located the commune here?"

"Until recently, no one except Grandfather, Father, and I knew about the deposit."

"Scarface?" Tess said.

"Father bragged to him about it. Shared the report with him."

"Doesn't sound good," Tess said.

"Scarface knew someone who knew someone. A corrupt senator with lots of power, I heard. Now, men have visited the commune, wanting to lease the minerals beneath it."

"Your father wouldn't do that, would he?" Tess said.

"He's talking about it, saying it's a gift we should use. Scarface is pushing him."

Avini shook her head when Tess said, "Who's trying to take the lease?"

"Phoenix Minerals, a large public company. I have a sick feeling about it."

"Scarface didn't tell them about the resonator, did he?" Tess asked.

"He doesn't know about it. At least not yet."

Avini nodded again when Tess said, "Your father?"

"Grandfather guarded the 'knowledge' with his very life," she said. "Except for David, the rest of the commune has no clue what powers their lights."

"What will happen if Scarface learns about the resonator?" Tess asked.

"Probably kill me and David to possess it," Avini said.

"Oh, my God!" Tess said.

Avini's eyes darkened. "If the company takes the lease, they'll rip this land apart. I fear the Shadow will…"

"Will what?" Tess asked, her voice sharp.

Avini met her gaze, fear and resolve warring in her expression.

"It'll fight back. The tremors, the glow in the mines—it's just the beginning."

"Maybe a good thing," Tess said. "What else can stop the human monsters?"

"I've seen it in my dreams—rivers of poison, skies choking with dust. I can't let that happen."

The lab's hum seemed to deepen, the resonator's glow pulsing in time with Tess's heartbeat. She thought of the green shapes in Picher's mines, Toby Red Hawk's wild laughter, and Buck's mark, pulsing like a warning.

The air felt heavier now, as if the Shadow were listening, its presence seeping through the concrete walls. Tess pulled out her camera, her hands steady despite the chill creeping up her spine.

"I have footage from the mines—glowing shapes, shadows that moved like they were alive. If we can show people what's at stake, maybe we can stop the miners before they start digging."

Avini's eyes lit up, a flicker of hope cutting through her worry.

"You'd share that? With the world?"

"It's why I'm here," Tess said, her voice firm. "But we need to move fast. If Scarface and his crew are working with outsiders, they won't wait for us to get organized. And David

—"

Avini had left the lab door ajar, and she and Tess froze when it creaked open, revealing a wiry figure in camo, his crooked nose still swollen from Buck's earlier blow. His eyes glinted with malice as he stepped inside, a pistol dangling loosely in his hand.

"Father wants you at the meeting hall. You're coming too," he said, pointing the pistol at Tess.

Tess's heart pounded, but she kept her voice steady. "What does David want?"

His smirk widened. "He's got plans. Big ones. And you're either with us or against us."

Avini stepped forward, her posture rigid though her voice calm.

"Tell Father I'll be there. I need to shut down the lab first."

Scarface's little brother hesitated, his eyes narrowing, but he nodded.

"Five minutes. Don't make me come back for you."

He turned and slipped out, the door clanging shut behind him.

"Damn it!" Avini said. "Can't believe I forgot and left the lab door open. If those cretins only knew what was in here, they'd be all over it."

Tess exhaled, her grip tightening on her camera. "We're out of time, Avini. Whatever you're planning with Nadie, it needs to happen fast."

"Buck will bring her. But if Father's meeting with Scarface and his men, they're planning something."

"He'll bring her," Tess said.

"I hope so. We need her to deal with the Shadow... and Father."

Tess slung her camera bag over her shoulder, her mind racing. "I'm with you. But if David's gone as far as you think, we're walking into a lion's den."

Avini's eyes met hers, a spark of defiance igniting. "Then we'd better be ready to fight."

Tess clutched her arm, stopping her. "What about the resonator?" she asked.

"It'll never leave this building," she said. "Grandfather booby trapped it. If someone comes for it, it will destroy them, this building, and everything in it."

Avini's words burned in Tess's mind as they went outside, locking the door behind them. The commune's lights flickered, the resonator's hum faltering for a moment before steadying. The night seemed to press closer, the air thick with the scent of earth and something sharper, like the promise of a storm.

Tess felt the weight of her camera, the footage within it a weapon as potent as Nadie's vial. Somewhere out there, Buck and Nadie were coming, but the clock was ticking.

# CHAPTER 24

The steel door of Avini's lab clanged shut behind them, the sound swallowed by the commune's eerie stillness. The night air was cool, heavy with the scent of damp earth and pine, but it carried a sharper edge—a faint metallic tang that reminded Tess of Picher's poisoned streams.

The moon hung low, its silver light casting long shadows across the dirt paths, where the commune's shacks stood like silent sentinels. The Kane Resonator's hum pulsed faintly beneath their feet, a heartbeat that felt both alive and restless.

Avini led the way, her jumpsuit catching the moonlight as she moved with purpose. Tess clutched her camera bag, her heart thudding, the guard's warning echoing in her mind.

The path to the meeting house wound through a grove of gnarled oaks, their branches clawing at the sky like skeletal fingers. Tess's eyes darted to the shadows, every rustle amplifying her unease.

A figure emerged from the darkness ahead, his wiry frame unmistakable. Scarface's little brother, his crooked nose swollen and bruised from Buck's fist, stood blocking the path.

Dirt covered his camo fatigues, and his eyes shone with a combination of spite and anticipation. The pistol he held gleamed, its barrel reflecting the moonlight as he pointed toward a wooden building, its steeple forming a dark outline against the starry sky.

"Move," he growled, his voice thick with menace. "Father don't like to be kept waiting."

Tess exchanged a glance with Avini, whose jaw was tight, her obsidian eyes flickering with fear but also defiance.

"Stay close," Avini whispered, her voice barely audible. "The meeting house... it used to be our sanctuary. A place for prayer and reflection. Now it's something else."

"What kind of something else?" Tess asked, her voice low as they followed Scarface's brother, his boots crunching on the gravel path.

Avini's lips pressed into a thin line. "Scarface and his men... they've twisted it. It's not a church anymore."

The meeting house loomed closer, its weathered planks and sagging roof a stark contrast to the lab's modernity. The windows glowed with an unnatural orange light, flickering like a fire that couldn't decide whether to burn or die.

The air grew thicker, the metallic tang sharpening, mingling with a sickly sweet scent—like rotting fruit or incense gone wrong. Tess's stomach churned, her fingers tightening on her camera bag. She wanted to film, to capture whatever lay inside, but the pistol kept her hands still.

The door creaked open, revealing a cavernous interior that felt like stepping into a nightmare. The sanctuary's pews were pushed haphazardly against the walls, their wood scarred and splintered. The once-holy space was now a grotesque tableau of pagan and mystic symbols—spirals and jagged runes carved into the beams, smeared with what looked like ash or blood.

Tattered banners hung from the rafters, emblazoned with white supremacist emblems—crosses and lightning bolts that made Tess's skin crawl. At the far end, a limestone slab served as an unholy altar, its surface stained dark, surrounded by flickering candles that cast writhing shadows.

David stood at the altar, his silk pajamas replaced by a flowing robe of deep crimson, its hem embroidered with symbols that twisted like veins under the candlelight.

His graying beard framed a face that was both regal and unhinged, his slate-gray eyes wild, darting as if seeing things no one else could. He clutched a large knife, its blade etched with runes that seemed to pulse with a faint green glow—the same hue as the Shadow's mark on Buck's arm.

Scarface and a dozen of his minions flanked the altar, their camo traded for hooded robes that mimicked Klan regalia, their pointed headgear casting sharp shadows.

The commune's members—fifty or so—sat in the remaining pews, their faces pale and uneasy, some clutching each other, others staring at the floor. The air was thick with fear, the kind that clung to the skin like rotting flesh.

An organ groaned to life in the corner, its notes discordant and jarring, not a melody but a cacophony that grated against Tess's nerves. The player, hidden in shadow, hammered the keys with no rhythm, the sound twisting like a scream trapped in metal. Tess's heart pounded, her breath shallow as she and Avini were pushed toward the front, the pistol at their backs.

"Welcome," David said, his voice a disjointed rasp, as if pulled from a dream. "You're just in time... for the cleansing."

Avini's hand brushed Tess's, her fingers trembling, though her voice was steady.

"Father, what are you doing? This isn't you."

David's head tilted, his eyes unfocused, as if listening to a whisper only he could hear. "The Shadow speaks, Avini. It demands... blood. Sacrifice. To protect the rare earth... to keep the land pure."

Tess's blood ran cold. She glanced at the altar, its stains suddenly too vivid, too real. The organ's wail grew louder, a screeching dissonance that seemed to vibrate through the floor, syncing with the faint pulse of the Kane Resonator—and something darker.

Scarface stepped forward, his scarred face twisted into a grin beneath his hood. He raised his arms, his voice booming.

"The land cries for justice! The impure must be purged!"

His minions chanted in response, their voices low and guttural, words Tess couldn't understand, though she felt in her bones—ancient, wrong, that had warped into something vile.

Two of Scarface's men pushed through the crowd, dragging a young woman from the pews. She was barely twenty, her dark hair tangled, her eyes wide with terror as she struggled against their grip.

The commune members gasped, some crying out, but none moved to help, their fear trapping them in place. The men forced her onto the limestone slab, pinning her arms as she whimpered, her pleas drowned by the organ's relentless wail.

Tess's hand slipped into her bag, her fingers brushing the camera. Scarface's little brother had moved away from them. Tess pointed her camera and began filming the unfolding scene.

When Avini spoke, her voice was a desperate whisper. "Father, stop this! This isn't what Grandfather wanted!"

As if hearing her plea, David's eyes snapped to her, a flicker of recognition drowned by madness. The unholy congregation grew silent as he began to speak.

"John Kane... he was weak. He hid from the Shadow's truth. But I see it. I hear it. Blood will bind us to the power beneath us."

David raised the knife, its blade catching the candlelight, the green glow intensifying. The organ's notes reached a fever pitch, the air thickening with a pressure that made Tess's ears pop. The floor trembled faintly, a low rumble that wasn't just the resonator—it was the land, the Shadow, stirring.

Tess's mind raced. She thought of Buck, Nadie, and the footage on her camera that could reveal this chaos. She kept the camera aimed at the altar, filming, as she leaned toward Avini, her voice barely a whisper.

"We can't let this happen."

Avini's hand flexed, her eyes locked on the altar.

"I know."

David's voice rose, disjointed and fevered. "The Shadow demands... purity... sacrifice... the land will rise!"

He positioned the knife above the young woman's chest, his hands shaking but resolute. Before Tess could move, the earth roared. A deafening explosion shook the meeting house, the floor splitting with a jagged crack that snaked toward the altar. Dust and splinters rained down, the candles toppling, their flames licking at the banners.

Tess's camera kept recording as smoke billowed from the rift, thick and acrid, tinged with the same green glow Tess had seen in Picher's mines.

The organ came to a sudden stop, replaced by screams as the commune members scrambled—some fleeing, others frozen in terror. The young woman on the slab fell to the floor, then quickly got up and ran through the smoke to the door.

Avini grabbed Tess's hand, her voice urgent.

"Run for it!"

They bolted, weaving through the chaos as Scarface's men shouted, their robes tangling as they tried to regain control. Scarface's little brother saw Tess and Avini running into the smoke.

He started after them but stumbled, his pistol clattering to the floor as the ground bucked again; a second tremor sending pews toppling. Tess clutched her camera bag, her heart pounding as she and Avini sprinted for the door.

David's voice cut through the smoke, wild and unhinged. "The Shadow rises! You can't escape its will!"

The air was choked with dust and the stench of sulfur, the green glow pulsing from the rift like a heartbeat. Tess's lungs burned, but Avini's grip was iron, pulling her through the splintered doorway into the night.

The commune was in chaos, lights flickering as the resonator faltered, screams echoing from the meeting house. The moon hung above, its light now sickly, filtered through a haze of smoke and ash.

"Where to?" Tess gasped, her eyes scanning the shadows for Scarface or his brother.

Avini's face was set, her voice fierce despite the fear in her eyes.

"Into the woods. If the Shadow's this angry, we're running out of time."

They ran, the ground still trembling beneath them, the earth's pulse syncing with the green tracery Tess could almost feel, as if Buck's mark were calling to her across the miles.

The rain poured down in sheets, a relentless flood that

turned the commune's dirt paths into rivers of mud. Thunder rumbled in the distance, a deep growl echoing the earthquake's aftershocks, as if the land itself was still reeling from the rift in the meeting house. Avini stopped at the bottom of the stairs after entering David's regal log cabin.

She clutched Tess's arm and said, "Be right back. Wait here."

Tess thought the house was going to splinter and fall as she waited for Avini at the foot of the stairs. The steps and the banister began collapsing behind her as she hurried down the stairs.

"You have something," Tess said.

Avini nodded and showed her the jump drive in her hand.

"Grandfather's knowledge. Now, let's get out of here before this place comes down on our heads," Avini said.

Tess and Avini stumbled through the hidden door at the back of David's cabin, the tapestry flapping behind them like a wounded bird. The night swallowed them, the forest's dense canopy offering fleeting shelter as they ran, their breaths ragged, the glow of the commune's flickering lights fading into the dark.

Tess clutched her camera bag, its strap biting into her shoulder, the weight of her footage grounding her against the storm's chaos.

Avini's jumpsuit was soaked, her dark hair plastered to her face, but she moved with purpose, her hand still gripping the glowing vial in her pocket. The forest loomed around them, its pines and oaks swaying in the wind, their branches creaking like whispers of warning.

The air was thick with the scent of wet earth and ozone, undercut by that same metallic tang Tess couldn't shake—a reminder of Picher's poison, of the Shadow's pulse.

"We can't stop," Avini said, her voice nearly lost in the rain's roar. "Scarface's men will be after us."

Tess nodded, her lungs burning as she kept pace. "Where are we going?"

"Deeper into the forest," Avini said. "There's a place... I'm not sure if it's safe. It's a shot until Nadie gets here."

The hidden door had led them to a narrow path snaking through the underbrush, its stones slick with moss and rain. When Tess's boots slipped, Avini's hand steadied her, their eyes meeting in a shared resolve.

The commune's chaos—David's wild eyes, the knife's green glow, the rift's acrid smoke—felt like a nightmare they'd barely escaped. The storm seemed to chase them, lightning cracking the sky like a warning from the Shadow itself.

They pushed deeper into the forest, the trees closing in, their branches knitting together to form a tunnel. The rain softened to a steady drizzle, but the air grew heavier, as if the forest were holding its breath. Tess's skin prickled, a sensation beyond the cold, like the feeling she'd had in Picher's mines—something watching, waiting.

A soft glow flickered ahead, not the harsh orange of the commune's candles but a golden light that seemed to pulse with life. As they rounded a bend, a clearing opened before them, ringed by towering roses that swayed in the storm's breeze.

Their petals, crimson and velvet, gleamed with raindrops, and their thorns glinted like blades. At the center stood a figure, neither fully human nor plant, her form woven from vines and blossoms, her eyes glowing like amber embers. Sage, Clara's rose garden creature, radiated an otherworldly calm, its presence both comforting and unsettling.

"Welcome," Sage said, her voice a melodic hum, like wind through petals. "The storm drives you here. The land offers shelter."

Tess froze, her hand tightening on her camera bag. She'd heard Buck's stories about Sage, but seeing it—her?—was like stepping into a fairy tale laced with dread. Avini stepped forward, her fear giving way to awe.

"Sage," she said softly. "You... you know Clara?"

Sage's vine-like arms swayed, petals drifting to the ground.

"Clara's heart blooms in me. She tends the roses, and I tend the land's secrets. You carry its burden, Avini. And you—" Her amber eyes fixed on Tess. "You carry its truth."

Tess swallowed, her senses warring with the surreal moment.

"We need a place to hide. Scarface's men are coming, and David... he's lost it."

Sage's form shimmered, the roses around the clearing parting to reveal a hollow beneath their roots, a natural cave lined with moss and glowing faintly with bioluminescent fungi.

"Enter," Sage said. "The storm will mask your trail."

They ducked into the hollow, the air warm and earthy, the fungi's glow casting soft patterns on the walls. The rain's drumbeat faded to a muffled rhythm, and Tess sank to the ground, her back against the moss, her camera bag cradled in her lap. Avini sat beside her.

"We're safe for now," she said, her voice shaky but resolute. "We can't stay long. Father's... That ritual—" She shuddered, her eyes distant. "He thinks the Shadow wants blood, but it's Scarface twisting him, using his fear."

Tess nodded, her mind replaying the meeting house's horrors—the discordant organ, the limestone slab, the young woman's terrified eyes.

"Your father's hearing voices. The Shadow, maybe. But Scarface and his brother... they're turning the commune into something ugly. Racist. Violent."

"Grandfather built the commune to honor the land, not destroy it. His resonator, my research... It's all about healing. But Father's letting Scarface push him toward something else."

Tess's stomach lurched. "If outsiders get that lease, the Shadow won't just shake the ground—it'll bury us all. We need to get your research to someone who can use it. Jake, maybe. My footage could help, too."

Avini's eyes met hers, a spark of hope cutting through her exhaustion. "You'd share it? With the world?"

"Maybe the only way," Tess said. "But we need to get out of here first. Buck and Nadie are coming. We don't know when, and Scarface won't stop looking for us."

Sage's voice drifted from the cave's entrance, where her vine-like form stood silhouetted against the rain.

"The land stirs. The Shadow feels your intent. Though it does not trust, it listens. Stay until the storm passes, then choose your path."

Tess frowned, her hand brushing the camera. "What path? Back to the lab? The commune's crawling with Scarface's men."

Avini shook her head. "The lab is impenetrable. Grandfather saw to that. We need to find Nadie. Someone who can stop this before it's too late."

The fungi's glow pulsed, syncing with a distant rumble of thunder. Tess felt a chill, the same unease she'd felt in the mines, as if the Shadow's presence lingered even here.

"Sage, what does the Shadow want? Nadie said it's not evil, just desperate. But that ritual... it felt wrong."

Sage's amber eyes glowed brighter, her voice a whisper of petals.

"The Shadow is the land's pain, its guardian, and its rage. It seeks balance, but blood awakens its hunger. She nodded to Tess's camera. "Your truth."

Tess exchanged a glance with Avini, the weight of their task settling like the rain outside.

"So, we try to stop David's madness. No pressure."

Avini's lips twitched into a faint smile, her first since the meeting house.

"Grandfather believed in miracles. Maybe Nadie's our miracle."

The cave was quiet, save for the drip of water and the soft hum of Sage's presence. Tess pulled her camera from the bag, checking the battery, her fingers steady despite the ache in her chest.

"Mind if I film you and the cave?" she asked.

Sage nodded and said, "Do it."

Tess smiled, focused her camera, and began filming. The footage—glowing shapes, Toby's ravings, now the ritual's horror —was a weapon, but only if they could get it out. Avini's eyes traced the fungi's glow, as if searching for answers in its patterns.

"What now?" Tess asked, her voice low, the storm's rhythm a reminder of the world waiting beyond the roses.

Avini's gaze hardened, her voice firm. "We wait for Nadie. She'll know what to do. But if Scarface finds us first, we fight."

Sage's form swayed, petals drifting to the cave floor. "The land will guide you, though its patience wanes. Choose swiftly, or the Shadow will choose for you."

Outside, the rain fell harder, lightning illuminating the roses' thorns like a warning. Tess felt the weight of her camera, and the unseen mark that bound them to Buck, to Nadie, to the land itself. The forest was a refuge, but not for long. The Shadow was stirring, and time was running out.

# CHAPTER 25

The cave's bioluminescence pulsed, a heartbeat in the dark, as Tess stirred awake, her neck stiff from leaning against the mossy wall. The air was damp, heavy with the scent of earth and roses, but the storm's roar had softened to a distant murmur. The quiet was shattered by a sharp trill—Tess's cell phone, its screen lighting up with Buck's name.

She fumbled for it, her heart leaping. "Buck?"

"Tess, you okay?" I asked.

"Surviving," she said.

"I'm with Nadie at Bone Hollow, and have the Xpedition ready. Where are you?"

"Avini and I are with Sage," Tess said. "We fled the commune last night after... everything."

"What happened?" I asked.

"An earthquake hit. It's bad, Buck."

"Are you in Chat Creek?"

"No," Tess said. "Sage is some supernatural creature. Not human and has a cave near the commune."

I decided to worry about Sage later, and said, "Got your location pinged. Stay put. We're coming."

The call cut out, and Tess exhaled, her breath visible in the cool air of the cave. Avini's eyes were fixed on Sage and her amber eyes.

"If Buck and Nadie are close, we might have a chance. But the commune... Scarface won't let us walk away."

Tess nodded, her mind flashing to the meeting house—the bloodstained altar, David's wild eyes, the rift's green glow. Her camera bag lay beside her, the footage a ticking bomb.

"We have evidence. Your research, my film. We just need to get it out."

Sage's voice hummed from the cave's entrance, her vine-like form swaying.

"The land stirs. Its anger lingers, but allies approach. Choose your path with care."

The faint rumble of an engine cut through the forest's hush. Headlights flickered through the rose-thorn curtain, and Sage parted the vines, revealing the Xpedition pulling into the clearing.

Nadie stepped out first, her dark braid swinging, her medic bag slung over her shoulder. I followed, scanning the shadows.

"Tess! Avini!" Nadie called, her voice sharp with relief as she ducked into the cave. She hugged Tess tightly, then turned to Avini, her gaze softening. "You both okay?"

"Barely," Tess said, her voice hoarse. "The commune's a mess. Earthquake tore it up, and Scarface... he's running some blood ritual with David. We got out, thinking they were after us. They never came."

"Probably dealing with the damage," I said. Might be a perfect time to go there. What's the plan?" I said.

"Check the lab," Avini said. "The Kane Resonator in the wrong hands..." She trailed off, her eyes haunted. "It'd be catastrophic."

Nadie's face hardened. "Then we move fast. Survey the damage, secure the lab, and get out before Scarface's goons regroup."

We piled into the Xpedition, Sage's amber eyes watching as the roses closed behind us. The drive to the commune was tense, the forest's shadows deepening as dawn broke, gray and heavy with clouds.

The commune's gate came into view, its chain-link fence twisted and sagging from the quake, metal posts jutting like broken bones. Beyond it, the compound was a scene of devastation—shacks collapsed into piles of splintered wood, dirt paths cracked open, and a gaping chasm yawned near the meeting house, its edges glowing faintly green.

An unfamiliar ATV sat parked outside the gate, its mud-splattered frame gleaming under the weak sunlight. Avini's eyes narrowed.

"That's not ours."

I parked the Xpedition. "Stay sharp. Let's split up—Avini, Tess, check the lab. Nadie, you're with me. We'll see what's left of this place and help where we can."

Tess gripped her camera bag, her pulse racing as she and Avini headed toward the lab. The commune was eerily quiet, the air thick with dust and the metallic tang of the Shadow's vein. They passed commune members picking through rubble, their faces drawn with shock and fear. Some had fled in the night, their absence leaving the compound hollow.

The lab's steel door loomed ahead, but Tess's stomach dropped—it wasn't just ajar; it was wide open, swinging on its hinges. Avini sprinted inside, her breath catching as she scanned the room.

The lab was untouched, its equipment gleaming under the flickering fluorescent lights, the Kane Resonator humming steadily in the corner. The water heater-shaped oscillator pulsed faintly, its panels intact, but Avini's face was grim as she checked its controls.

"It's still running," she said, her voice tight. "Thank God. But this door... someone's been here."

Tess filmed the lab, her lens capturing the open door, the untouched equipment, the Resonator's faint glow.

"Scarface's men?"

Avini shook her head, her fingers hovering over the Resonator's dials. "Maybe. If they try to move it, it's rigged to blow. I wasn't bluffing about that."

Nadie and I moved through the commune, stepping over debris and splintered beams. Someone had erected a makeshift medical tent near the meeting house, its canvas flapping in the wind. Inside, cots were crowded with the injured—scrapes, bruises, broken bones. Nadie dropped to her knees beside a young boy, his foot swollen and bruised, his parents hovering anxiously.

"I'm Nadie," she said. "Let's get that foot fixed, okay?"

The boy's parents exchanged wary glances. "I'm Sam Little Horse, and this is my wife, Scarlet, and son Sammie."

"I'm Nadie. I'm a healer. I'll fix Sammie's foot."

Sam, a lean man with tired eyes, said, "We wanted to leave last night. Everyone was running after the quake, but Sammie couldn't walk. This place... It's not what it was. Scarface and his thugs, Father's rituals—Everything has become disjointed."

Scarlet nodded, her voice low. "Blood sacrifices. Pagan nonsense. John Kane would've never allowed this."

Nadie worked quickly, splinting Sammie's foot, her hands steady despite the weight of their words. As she wrapped the bandage, a voice called from across the tent.

"Nadie? Nadie Red Eagle?"

Nadie turned, her breath catching. An older man approached, his gray braids swinging, his traditional garb pristine despite the chaos around him. The man's face was weathered but handsome, his dark eyes warm with recognition.

"Bert Little Crow," Nadie said, a smile breaking through her focus. "You haven't changed a bit in the past forty years."

He chuckled, kneeling beside her to hand her a roll of gauze.

"Liar. I was a medic in the army, and I stayed to help here. Couldn't leave these folks to suffer."

Nadie and Bert fell into an easy rhythm, tending to the wounded, their hands brushing against each other as they worked.

"You weren't here at the commune when I left," Nadie said.

Bert's voice softened as he spoke. "I came here after John Kane died, thought it'd be a refuge. But Scarface and David... they're poisoning this place."

"Whose ATV is that parked in front?" I asked.

Two white men showed up this morning in it. Phoenix

Minerals, they said. I heard they're offering a million dollars to lease the minerals beneath the commune.

Nadie's hands froze, her eyes meeting mine across the tent. "A million dollars? For the minerals under the commune?"

I shook my head, wondering if they'd somehow learned of the silver vein. I could tell by Nadie's expression that she was thinking the same thing.

"A lot of money," I said. "They must believe there's something there."

"This is hallowed ground," Nadie said. "If they dig here, the Shadow will tear this place apart."

Footsteps echoed at the lab doorway. Tess spun around, her camera falling to her side as Scarface's younger brother, his nose still swollen, stepped inside with a pistol in his hand.

"There you are," he said. "We need you at the big house."

Avini's eyes flicked to the Resonator, then to Tess, a silent warning. They followed, the gun at their backs, through the commune's wreckage to David's log cabin, its polished logs untouched by the quake.

Inside, the air was thick with tension. David sat at a desk in his office, his crimson robe discarded for a rumpled suit, his eyes bloodshot and distant. Scarface stood beside him, his camo-clad thugs flanking two strangers—a young geologist with a nervous smile, and an older landman with glasses. The same two men Jake and Mama had seen at the café in Chat Creek.

Scarface's little brother pushed Tess and Avini into the room, his grip tight on his pistol. In the hallway, out of sight, Scarface leaned close to Avini, his breath hot against her ear.

"You're signing the lease, girl. Or I put a bullet in your friend's head." Tess's heart pounded. Before she could react, Scarface yanked her to the floor by her hair, his voice a low growl. "Don't test me."

Avini's face paled, her eyes burning with defiance. Scarface shoved her toward the desk, where the landman named Jenkins slid a contract across the polished wood.

"New Dawn Collective," he said, adjusting his glasses. "The million-dollar bonus is wired to your account upon signing. Phoenix Minerals gets the 160-acre mineral lease."

David signed, his hand trembling, his eyes unfocused. Avini hesitated, her gaze flicking to Tess, then signed, her jaw tight.

Jenkins nodded, his fingers racing over the keyboard of his laptop.

"Funds are transferred to your New Dawn account," the young geologist said. "Pleasure doing business."

As the Phoenix men left, Scarface pulled another document from his pocket, his grin predatory.

"One more thing, David. Avini. Sign this."

"What is it?" David asked.

"Doesn't matter what it is," Scarface said. "Sign it or I'll kill you; right here, right now."

Tess peered at the paper—a transfer of ownership for New Dawn Collective to one Marcus Donaldson, Scarface's legal name. David signed without hesitation, his face blank. Avini's hand shook as she added her signature, her eyes locked on Tess, still on the floor.

Marcus folded the document, tucking it into his camo jacket. Then, without warning, he wrapped a garrote around David's throat. David gasped, his eyes bulging, but Marcus's grip was relentless until David's body went limp, collapsing to the floor.

Avini screamed, her voice raw, tears streaming down her face.

"You monster!"

Marcus's eyes were cold, unyielding. "You're safe for now because we need you to help with the Kane Resonator. Father said you're the only one who knows how it works."

Through her tears, Avini said, "Father wouldn't have told you about the resonator."

Marcus smirked. "Father bragged, and now it's ours. Bring her," he said. "We're getting it now and then blowing this hellhole."

They dragged Avini toward the lab. Inside, the Kane

Resonator hummed, its panels gleaming. Marcus's men circled it, tools in hand.

"It's booby-trapped!" Avini said. "Tamper with it, and it'll blow!"

Marcus laughed, his brother's knife now at Avini's throat. "Nice try. Get to work."

Tess pulled herself off the hallway floor and sprinted through the commune, dodging rubble, her lungs burning until she reached the medical tent.

"Buck! They killed David. They're dismantling the Kane Resonator—it's rigged to explode! Avini is with them. She'll die if we don't do something."

My mind raced. "Nadie, get everyone out. Now. The resonator's going to blow and take the commune with it."

"Where are you going?" she asked.

"To save Avini."

Nadie nodded, her voice calm but urgent. "Bert, Tess, help me clear the tent. We don't have much time."

Nadie, Bert, and Tess began ushering the injured out, Sam and Scarlet carrying Sammie, their faces pale with fear. I sprinted to the lab. Through the open door, I saw Scarface's brother holding a knife to Avini's throat, Scarface and his men prying at the resonator's panels.

Snatching the billy club from the brother's belt, I cracked it against his skull. He crumpled, his knife clattering to the floor, as I grabbed Avini's arm, pulling her toward the door.

Scarface glanced up, his eyes narrowing.

"Let them go. We need this thing loose. We'll hunt them down later."

We bolted through the commune, the gate in sight. Behind us, a deafening roar erupted, the ground shaking as a fireball tore through the lab. We hit the dirt, shielding our heads as smoke and debris spiraled upward, the Kane Resonator's explosion painting the sky in ash and flame.

Avini coughed, her eyes wide with horror, and said, "Good

God Almighty!"

I pulled her to her feet and said, "That was too damn close! Let's get the hell out of Dodge before something else blows."

# CHAPTER 26

The morning sun climbed higher over Bone Hollow, its rays piercing the cottonwoods to paint the meadow in a mosaic of light and shadow. Nadie's sanctuary, a spring-fed oasis carved from the Oklahoma wilds, stood as a bulwark against the devastation left in the earthquake's wake.

The air carried the sharp tang of wild mint, laced with the acrid trace of smoke that clung to the survivors' clothes—a haunting echo of the lab's explosion and the Shadow's restless pulse. The spring at the hollow's heart gurgled softly, its crystal waters catching the light like a beacon of hope, while Nadie's free-range chickens strutted through the grass, their clucks a defiant note of normalcy amid the chaos.

A ragged convoy of vehicles crowded the dirt path: Buck's Xpedition, its frame caked with dust and ash, sat beside a commune pickup crammed with survivors, their faces etched with shock and exhaustion. The rhythmic thump of Colley's helicopter cut the air as it lifted off again, ferrying another load of the critically injured—those with shattered bones or burns too severe for field treatment—to the hospital in Miami. Jonesy, his flannel sleeves rolled to his elbows, his face streaked with sweat and grime, orchestrated the triage with a steady hand, his voice rising above the murmurs of pain and fear.

"Next group! Severe lacerations and head trauma to the chopper, now!"

I knelt beside a young man, no older than twenty, whose arm was mangled from falling debris. I worked a torn shirt into a tourniquet.

"Hang in there, kid," I said. "You're tougher than this."

Tess moved through the crowd, her camera bag a constant weight across her chest, its strap biting into her shoulder. She filmed with quiet intensity, her lens capturing the raw tapestry of survival: a mother soothing her crying child, an elder staring blankly at the horizon, the flicker of hope in weary eyes as Nadie's hollow offered refuge.

Her footage—the bloodletting ritual, David's descent, the Kane Resonator's fiery end—was a weapon, but its weight pressed on her, a truth that demanded sharing. She paused to adjust her focus, framing a young girl clutching a tattered doll, her face smudged with ash but alive with gratitude.

Avini handed out water from Nadie's canteen, her movements mechanical, though her eyes sharp with purpose. Her face, pale from exhaustion, held a quiet fire, the loss of the Kane Resonator and her father's death warring with her resolve.

She stopped beside Sam and Scarlet Little Horse, who sat on a blanket with their son, Sammie, his splinted foot propped on a crate.

"You holding up?" Avini asked, offering them a tin cup of spring water.

Scarlet took it, her hands trembling. "We're alive, thanks to you and Nadie. But that place..." Her voice broke, her eyes darting to Sammie, who stared at the chickens with a child's curiosity. "It wasn't home anymore. Not with Scarface and those... rituals."

Sam nodded, his lean frame tense. "John Kane's dream died with him. We should've left sooner, but Sammie's foot..."

He trailed off, his jaw tight with guilt.

Avini said, "We'll make it right. For John. For all of you."

At the medical station—a folding table strewn with bandages and antiseptic—Nadie and Bert worked in seamless tandem, their hands a blur as they stitched wounds and set bones. Nadie's medic bag lay open, its supplies nearly depleted.

Her focus was unbreakable, her dark braid swinging as she leaned over a woman with a fractured wrist. Bert, his gray braids catching the sunlight, passed her a splint, their fingers brushing in a fleeting moment of warmth. His clothing, beaded and worn, seemed untouched by the morning's grit, a testament to his quiet dignity.

Their eyes met, a spark of something more profound—memory, possibility—flickering in the shared glance.

"You always this calm under fire?" Nadie asked, her voice teasing as she tied off a bandage.

Bert's lips twitched into a smile, his hands steady as he cleaned a gash on a man's forehead.

"Army medic training. You don't forget how to keep your head when the world's falling apart. You're not so bad yourself, Red Eagle."

Nadie's laugh was soft, rare. "Took years to learn. John Kane taught me to listen to the land, to people. This hollow's my proof."

Kwanita, Nadie's donkey, nosed curiously at a stack of blankets nearby, her ears twitching as she nudged a corner, earning a chuckle from Sammie.

Ahanu, Nadie's wolf-dog, loped through the crowd, his amber eyes alert, his bushy tail wagging as he pressed his flank against Tess's leg, nearly toppling her. She laughed, scratching his ears, her camera momentarily forgotten.

"Easy, big guy."

Pard, my dog, bounded across the meadow, his joy a burst of light in the heavy morning. He barreled into me, his tongue lapping at my face with unrestrained glee.

I grinned and ruffled his ears. "Missed you, too, boy. Stay close, hear?"

Jake stood at the meadow's edge, his lanky frame silhouetted against the pines, his eyes scanning the horizon for any sign of pursuit—Phoenix Minerals' men, or worse, the Shadow's stirrings. Mama stood beside him, her sharp gaze sweeping the hollow.

"Nadie's built something sacred here," she said, her voice low, resonant with a wisdom that seemed to echo the spring's murmur. "This land holds its own against the dark."

Bert paused, wiping sweat from his brow with a bandana, his eyes tracing the hollow's beauty—the spring's shimmer, the chickens' carefree strut, the survivors finding solace in the grass.

"Love this place," he said, his voice warm with awe. "It's like an Eden here, Nadie. You've done right by it."

Nadie glanced up, a rare smile softening her weathered face.

"Took years to make it mine. John Kane taught me to listen to the land's heartbeat. This hollow's my answer to his lessons."

Tess lowered her camera, her lens lingering on Nadie and Bert, their quiet bond a counterpoint to the morning's urgency. She turned to Avini, her voice hushed but urgent.

"We've got the footage, but the prize is still out there. Phoenix Minerals has that lease. We can't stop them from digging."

Avini nodded. "The Kane Resonator's gone, but my research lives in here." She tapped the jump drive she'd retrieved from her bedroom. "We protect the land as best we can, or the Shadow wakes again. And next time, it won't just be an earthquake."

I overheard, standing to join them, Pard trotting at my heels.

"Jake's got contacts—EPA, tribal councils, maybe even feds. We get your evidence to the right people, we might shut Phoenix down before they break ground."

Tess nodded, her fingers tightening on her camera bag. "My footage shows the ritual, the explosion, Scarface's takeover. It's enough to raise hell. We need to move fast."

Avini's eyes widened, a flicker of realization cutting through her grief.

"Wait—the lease. Scarface forced David and me to sign over New Dawn Collective to him. Marcus Kane, his legal name. They wired a million dollars to the Collective's account at Chat Creek Bank."

"You don't know much about the law, do you, kid?" I said.

Avini frowned, her exhaustion making her patience thin. "What do you mean?"

"Title's no good until it's filed at the courthouse," I said. "If

Scarface had that deed on him when the lab blew, it's ash now. No record, no transfer. Legally, the land's still in your name and David's. After probate, it's all yours."

Avini's breath caught, her eyes glistening with a mix of shock and hope.

"Oh my God... a million dollars in the bank, and the land's still ours?"

"Good for you," I said, clapping her shoulder. "Problem is, Phoenix's lease still holds. We'll need lawyers to untangle that."

Avini nodded, her resolve hardening. "Then we fight in court. Whatever it takes to keep them from digging up the commune."

Jonesy's voice cut through, urgent and strained. "Buck! Need you over here—bad fracture!"

I gave Tess a nod, my hand grazing her shoulder. "Keep the faith, kid. A million bucks buys a lot of good lawyers."

Tess forced a smile, but the weight of her footage pressed heavier. As I jogged to help Jonesy, Colley's chopper swooped back into the hollow, its blades whipping the grass flat, sending Kwanita trotting away with an indignant bray.

The meadow pulsed with life—wounded healing, animals weaving through the crowd, survivors clinging to fragile hope. Nadie and Bert continued their work, their hands steady, their bond a quiet anchor. Sam and Scarlet whispered to Sammie, promising him a new start, while Ahanu curled up beside Tess, his warmth a comfort as she resumed filming.

The final flight from Bone Hollow carried me, Tess, Avini, and Jonesy, the chopper's hum a steady rhythm as the meadow fell away below. Nadie stayed behind, her silhouette framed by the spring, Ahanu and Kwanita at her side, Bert standing close, their hands brushing as they waved.

I leaned back, my eyes on the horizon, Pard's head resting on my lap.

"Those two," I said, nodding toward Nadie and Bert's fading figures. "Match made in heaven. Saw it in Nadie's eyes—both of them acting like teenagers in the back of an old Ford."

Avini managed a grin, though her face was shadowed by her father's death and the commune's ruin.

"They deserve it. After everything..."

Tess, her camera stowed, turned to Avini, her voice soft. "What'll you do with the money?"

Avini stared out the window, the rolling hills blurring below. "Don't know yet. Rebuild, maybe. Not the commune. Something better. Grandfather's dream, not Father's madness."

Jonesy, seated across from them, stared at the floor, his usual energy dimmed. Jake, noticing, leaned forward, his voice cutting through the chopper's drone.

"Why so glum, Jonesy?"

Jonesy sighed, rubbing his neck. "The company I was with fired me. They're suing me for the car I was driving, too. My grandparents... they're old, used to me helping out."

Jake's eyes narrowed, thoughtful. "I'll give you a job."

Jonesy blinked, wary. "I don't need charity, Jake. Just a gig."

"Charity's not my style," Jake said, his tone firm but warm. "Chase Johnson, my theatrical director, is retiring at the end of the year. I need someone to step up."

Jonesy shook his head, unconvinced. "I've got no experience directing films. I can't take your money for something I don't know."

Jake leaned back, a faint smile playing on his lips. "I watched you today, Jonesy. You ran that triage like a general—command voice, kept everyone moving, no hesitation. You're a natural, and Mama will tell you I'm good at recognizing talent."

"Like I said, I'm not into charity."

"You have a master's in management from Langston, right? Chase'll apprentice you until he retires. Teach you the ropes. I'm offering a hundred grand a year, full benefits, company vehicle."

Jonesy's jaw dropped, a grin breaking through his gloom. "Damn! Champagne's on me when we hit Chat Creek."

"First round, maybe," Jake said, chuckling.

Mama tapped Jake's shoulder. "If you're dragging me to that Thunder game tonight, you'd better drop me off first. I'll watch it in the catering tent."

Jake grinned, pulling a handful of tickets from his jacket. "Got five for the game, sixth row. Traded two for first-row seats. You're coming, Mama."

"No, I'm not," she said, her tone final but fond. "Jonesy, you're tall enough to play basketball. Want the extra ticket?"

Jonesy's grin widened, though he shook his head. "I'm taking the bus to Okmulgee to see my grandparents and my donkey, Esmerelda. They'll lose their minds when I tell them about the job."

"Bus, my hind foot," Jake said. "We'll drop you at your grandparents' farm on the way to OKC. Colley'll pick you up when you're ready."

As the chopper banked toward Chat Creek, the hollow's green heart faded from view, but its spirit lingered—a fragile Eden holding fast against the Shadow's threat. Tess clutched her camera bag, and me, my resolve.

# CHAPTER 27

T he Oklahoma sky burned orange as Colley's helicopter sliced through the dusk, its blades thrumming a steady rhythm over the rolling hills. The chopper's cabin was cramped, the air thick with the scent of engine oil and a hint of anticipation.

I sat up front beside Colley, his broad frame pressed against the co-pilot's seat, his eyes scanning the horizon. Tess, clutching her camera bag like a lifeline, stared out the window, her mind still tangled with the commune's ruins and the weight of her footage. Avini sat beside her, her face a mix of grief and resolve, the potential windfall and her father's death battling for space in her thoughts.

Jake sprawled in the back, his lanky frame relaxed but his eyes sharp, five sixth-row tickets to the NBA Finals—Game 7, OKC Thunder versus Indiana Pacers, winner takes all—tucked in his jacket.

We dropped Jonesy in Okmulgee, the chopper touching down on a dusty strip beside his grandparents' farm. Jonesy's grin was infectious as he hugged his grandparents, Esmerelda the donkey braying in the background, thrilled at his new job with Jake's production company.

"Champagne's on me when I'm back in Chat Creek!" he shouted as the chopper lifted off, his grandparents waving, their pride brighter than the setting sun.

Colley banked toward a private airstrip near the arena in Oklahoma City, the city's skyline glinting like a promise.

"Ten minutes out," he said, his voice crackling through the headsets. "Hope you're ready for madness."

Jake grinned. "Two courtside seats for five sixth-row babies. Still close enough to smell the sweat."

Tess managed a half-smile, her fingers brushing her camera bag. "I have so much work to do. I feel like I should be editing film instead of watching basketball."

"We've all been hard at it, and that's exactly why we need this break," Jake said, his tone firm. "One night to breathe. Tonight, we're Thunder fans. Tomorrow, we get back to work."

Avini nodded, her voice quiet but steady. "Grandfather loved basketball. Said it was like the land's heartbeat—wild, but in rhythm. Let's do this for him."

The chopper touched down on the airstrip, the arena's lights blazing in the distance, a beacon of chaos and glory. We piled out and boarded a waiting shuttle to the arena.

The streets buzzed with Thunder fans in navy and orange, their chants—"OKC! OKC!"—a pulsing wave that rolled through the night. Scalpers hawked last-minute tickets, vendors slung pop and hot dogs, and a street drummer pounded a frenetic beat, the air electric with playoff fever.

Inside the arena, the sixth-row seats put us just behind the Thunder bench, close enough to hear the squeak of sneakers and the coaches' shouted plays. The arena was a cauldron of noise—twenty thousand fans roaring, air horns blaring, the Jumbotron flashing highlights of OKC's playoff run.

The court gleamed under blinding lights, the Thunder's navy jerseys a stark contrast to the Pacers' gold. Tess's eyes widened, her love of sports kicking in as she pulled out her camera, filming the sea of waving Thunder towels and the players warming up, their shots arcing with precision.

"Hell of a sight," I said. "Reminds me of a stampede, only louder."

Colley, wearing a Thunder cap, grinned. "Moments like this are why I love flying."

Avini clutched her ticket stub, her eyes tracing the court where a player drained a silky three-pointer in warmups, the crowd erupting like a volcano.

"It's… alive," she said, her voice soft, almost reverent. "Like the Bone Hollow, only wilder."

Jake nudged her, pointing to the Jumbotron, where a fan cam caught a kid in a Thunder jersey dancing wildly.

"That's the spirit. Let's ride this wave."

The game tipped off, and the arena detonated. Thunder's point guard darted through the Pacers' defense, dishing for a thunderous dunk that shook the rafters. The crowd surged to its feet, Jake screaming, Tess filming, Avini clapping despite herself.

The pace was relentless—steals, fast breaks, alley-oops— each possession a battle in a war for the trophy.

By the second quarter, the score was knotted at 48, the tension palpable. Tess zoomed in, capturing the sweat flying off a player's brow, the crowd's roar a living thing.

Halftime brought a brief reprieve, the arena buzzing as a local band rocked the court and cheerleaders launched T-shirts into the stands. Jake passed around a tray of nachos, laughter cutting through our shared excitement.

The second half exploded with even more ferocity. OKC surged ahead in the third, a crossover leaving defenders sprawling. The Pacers clawed back in the fourth. The arena was a pressure cooker, with fans screaming and stomping, the air thick with sweat and desperation.

The final play was chaos as an extended arm swatted the final desperation shot into the stands as the buzzer screamed. The arena erupted, fans hugging strangers, confetti raining down, the Thunder victorious.

"We did it," I said. "Let's blow this joint before the crowd storms the arena."

As we filed out, the crowd still chanting, Jake draped an arm over Colley's shoulders and said, "A cold scotch and a dark Bricktown bar are calling my name."

"Yours, maybe," Colley said. "If we're flying tonight, I'm going to have to make do with soda pop."

Jake shook his head and said, "Bitch, bitch, bitch!"

The Oklahoma City arena pulsed with raw energy as we

spilled out into the chaotic night, swept along by a tide of euphoric Thunder fans. The air crackled with the aftershock of the victory—Game 7, a nail-biter that ended with the Thunder's last-second block, sealing their championship triumph over the Pacers.

Horns blared, strangers high-fived, and chants of "OKC! OKC!" rolled like thunderclaps through the streets. Confetti swirled in the breeze, catching the glow of streetlights, while vendors hawked commemorative shirts and kids darted through the crowd, waving Thunder flags.

The scene was a glorious mess—part carnival, part riot—fans drunk on victory, their voices hoarse but unrelenting.

We wove through the madness, shoulders brushing against strangers, the air thick with the scent of spilled beer, grilled hot dogs, and the faint tang of sweat.

Bricktown loomed ahead, its neon signs blazing like beacons, promising refuge and revelry. The district was alive, its cobblestone streets packed with fans streaming from the arena, their navy-and-orange jerseys a moving sea.

Live music spilled from open bar doors—a gritty blues riff here, a country twang there—mixing with the laughter and shouts of celebration. Street performers juggled glow sticks, and the canal's water shimmered under strings of fairy lights, reflecting the city's electric pulse.

Jake led the way, cutting through the crowd with purpose, his eyes scanning for the perfect spot.

"Something loud, something alive," he said, dodging a group of tipsy fans chanting the Thunder's fight song.

"Find us a bar with character, man," I said. "No corporate nonsense—a place that feels like Oklahoma."

We passed a rowdy sports bar, its TVs replaying game highlights. It was too packed, bodies spilling onto the sidewalk. A sleek cocktail lounge caught Tess's eye, though its sterile vibe didn't fit our group's raw energy.

Then Avini pointed to a tucked-away spot down a side street: The Rusty Anchor. Its weathered brick facade and flickering neon anchor sign promised grit and soul. A chalkboard out front read, "Victory Shots: $3!" and the muffled thump of a live band seeped through the walls.

"This is it," Avini said, her voice carrying a spark of excitement.

Inside, the Rusty Anchor was a haven of controlled chaos, the bar a polished slab of oak, scarred from years of spilled drinks and carved initials. Dim Edison bulbs cast a warm glow over mismatched tables, and the walls were plastered with Thunder memorabilia, vintage license plates, and faded photos of Oklahoma's oil boom days.

A three-piece band—guitar, bass, and a drummer with a handlebar mustache—belted out a raucous cover of "Sweet Home Alabama," the crowd singing along between swigs of beer. The air smelled of whiskey, fried pickles, and possibility.

We snagged a large table near the back, its surface sticky from spilled drinks but perfect for us. Jake slid into a chair, Avini claiming the spot beside him, her dark eyes glinting with purpose.

Tess plopped down across from them, her camera bag tucked safely under her chair, while Colley and I flanked the ends, already eyeing the drink menu scrawled on a chalkboard above the bar.

A server in a Thunder jersey swung by, dropping off a round of local IPAs and a basket of onion rings, her grin as infectious as the crowd's energy.

Colley sipped his soda with a frown. "This is the part of flying I hate: drinking soda pop while everyone else is having fun and getting shitfaced."

"Stop whining," Jake said. "You just watched the game of the century, and when we get back to Chat Creek, you can drink all the scotch you want."

Colley was smiling when he said, "Yes, sir, Bossman."

As the band transitioned to a soulful rendition of "Mustang Sally," Jake leaned back, his fingers drumming the table, his mind clearly still churning over Picher's toxic legacy.

"It's party time," I said. "Why the frown?"

"I can't stop thinking about Phoenix Minerals, Tsisdetsi's Shadow, and Picher. I want to fix things, but the numbers don't add up," he said.

"Then stop worrying about it," I said.

"I can't. Cleaning up Ottawa County is a money pit. Phoenix Minerals has the leases locked down, and I don't have the capital to fight them."

"Maybe you're coming at the problem from the wrong direction," I said.

"What do you mean?" he asked.

"There's always more than one way to skin a cat," I said.

"Like what?" he said.

"Hell, Jake," I said. "I don't know. A hostile takeover of Phoenix, maybe."

Avini turned to him, her gaze sharp, cutting through the bar's din.

"Besides, Jake, you're thinking too small. You don't just clean up Picher—you turn it into a win."

"Sounds great," he said. "How do I accomplish that particular feat?"

"Remediation technology has advanced," she said. "You could extract residual minerals while detoxifying the soil. Turn a profit, create jobs, and restore the land. Grandfather always said the earth gives back if you know how to ask."

"What about the waste?" he asked.

"There are fifteen miles of mineshafts beneath Picher," I said. "Refill the open shafts with the rock you mill from the reclaimation."

"Is that even possible?" he asked.

"Hell, Jake," I said. "That's why God invented engineers. There are hundreds of them out there itching to solve the riddle and provide you with answers."

Jake's eyes widened, a spark igniting behind them. He leaned forward, elbows on the table, the bar's noise fading as his mind raced.

"You're saying… mine the cleanup? Use the waste to fund the fix?" His voice carried a new edge, the gears turning. "That's… possible. But Phoenix still holds the leases. They're the gatekeepers."

I let out a bark of a laugh. "Hell, Jake, I thought you were a landman. If you conduct a hostile takeover of Phoenix, the leases are yours. The whole operation gets Congress's stamp of approval. It's like the Thunder's win tonight—a slam dunk."

The table erupted in laughter, the tension breaking like a wave. Tess raised her glass, her smile wide.

"To slam dunks and big ideas!"

Colley clinked his soda bottle against hers, and even Avini's reserved expression softened into a grin.

Jake's face, though, held something new—a quiet resolve, the blueprint of a plan taking shape. The bar's raucous energy swirled around us, but in that moment, the table was an island of possibility, the Thunder's victory echoing in Jake's newfound clarity.

# CHAPTER 28

The Briar Patch Inn sat at the edge of town, a cozy two-story house with ivy climbing its stone walls and a wraparound porch decorated with hanging ferns. Its windows glowed warmly, welcoming, like a beacon in the fading light.

Jake and Mama sat on a park bench in Clara's rose garden, holding hands and spending some quality time alone. A breeze shimmered through the old oaks surrounding the property.

"This place is perfect," Mama said. "How did you find it?"

"By accident," Jake said. "Someone posted a business card on the bulletin board at the café. Colley saw it, did a flyover, and told me about it. Sounded a lot better than staying at the Highway 69 Motel."

"It's so quiet and peaceful here," Mama said. "I almost hate to leave."

"Funny thing," Jake said. "Angie tried to check it out on the internet. That lone business card seems to be the only advertising out there."

"The place is so homey and the food so good, word of mouth is all the advertising it needs."

"I guess," Jake said. "It's so strange that there's no record of Clara anywhere, and none of the locals have any idea where she came from."

"Have you told her yet that we've wrapped the episode?"

"I told her. She probably already knew because most of the crew left town yesterday."

"Even with all the problems, the episode came together faster than I thought," Mama said.

"Tess saved our bacon with film of the earthquake and the Shadow."

"She's a keeper," Mama said. "Hope someone doesn't hire her away from you."

"I know it," Jake said. "There's a raise in her future."

"You haven't said how the Thunder game went," Mama said.

"Hell of a game. My ears are still ringing."

"So sorry you and Colley didn't get to sit in the front row."

"Traded two for five and only had to move back six rows," he said. "The game was awesome except for the fact you weren't there with me."

Mama put her free arm around him. "I'll go next year when the Pelicans win."

"Dream on," he said.

"What about Avini?" Mama said.

"A remarkable young woman. After the game, we all walked to Bricktown and had drinks," he said.

"Bricktown?" she said.

Jake smiled and said, "I keep forgetting you've never been to Oklahoma City."

Mama squeezed his shoulder and said, "A little detail we need to rectify."

"Bricktown is the former industrial part of downtown Oklahoma City. Converted to bars and restaurants, and has a canal snaking through it."

"My kind of place," Mama said.

"You'd love it," Jake said. "Upscale hotels catering to visitors, lots of dark bars, and a ballpark home to their minor league team. The Bricktown entertainment district is within walking distance from the arena where the Thunder play ball."

"Why do you think so highly of Avini?" Mama said.

"She made me realize why I'm an entrepreneur and why they are so important to the world."

"Tell me more about her," Mama said.

"You're soon going to meet her," he said. "You'll see for yourself."

Jake's fingers traced the edge of the bench, his eyes drifting over the garden's impossible lushness.

"Hard to believe this place is real," he said, his voice soft but thick with the ache of leaving. "Feels like we stepped into a dream and now we have to wake up."

Mama, her braided hair catching the moonlight, nodded slowly. Her hands rested in her lap, clutching a single rose she'd plucked earlier.

"This place... It's more than real. It's alive in a way most people never notice. Like it's holding its breath, waiting to tell you something."

A shooting star arced across the sky, for a moment outshining all the fireflies lighting the rose garden with a phosphorescent glow. The tree frogs and bullfrogs in the nearby pond suddenly quietened.

A ripple moved through the air, subtle as a sigh. The roses seemed to lean inward, their petals trembling, and there she was —Sage, stepping from the shadows as if woven from the garden itself.

Sage's dress, a patchwork of shifting colors, shimmered like the surface of a pond under moonlight, and her storm-cloud eyes held a quiet sorrow. Her bare feet made no sound on the gravel path, but the air around her seemed to hum, alive with the same strange energy that made the garden feel like a world apart.

"Sage," Jake said. He stood, brushing imaginary dirt from his jeans, suddenly aware of how ordinary he felt in her presence. "Didn't think we'd see you again."

Sage smiled, wistful and sharp, like a blade hidden in silk. "The garden always calls, Jake. Especially when it's time to say goodbye."

"You know we're leaving?" Mama asked.

Sage's gaze flicked to Mama. "I knew. You've felt it, haven't you? The pulse of this place. The way it remembers."

Mama's fingers tightened around the rose. "I've felt... something. All week, it's been like the air's talking, whispering things I can't quite hear."

Sage nodded, her hair streaked with blues and greens that flickered like fireflies, swaying as if caught in a breeze that wasn't there.

"Tsisdetsi's voice is loudest here, where the earth still sings. The pain in the soil, the cries in the water. It's all here, woven into every root and petal."

Jake shifted, his boots crunching on the gravel. "Now that we've seen Tsisdetsi, it feels... bigger. Now, it's not just Picher's story, it's ours, too."

Sage's eyes, deep and unyielding, met his. "It is yours, Jake. You and Mama, you've walked these paths, breathed this air. You've carried Tsisdetsi's weight. The Shadow doesn't just watch —it binds. It holds you to the truth of what's been done."

Mama's voice was barely a whisper. "And what is that truth?"

Sage knelt before the bench, her fingers brushing a rosebush, its petals glowing faintly under her touch.

"The mines, the poison, the children who suffered—it's not just history. It's alive, and it needs voices to speak it."

"Tsisdetsi's about to become a household name," Jake said. "You have my word on it."

Sage looked up, her gaze piercing. "You're leaving, but you're not done. Tsisdetsi will follow you, in your dreams, in the quiet moments. It always does."

The air grew heavier, the night lush with the fragrance of roses and poignant memories. From the path leading to the inn, a figure emerged—Clara Hensley, her gray braid swinging gently. She moved with grace, her dark eyes catching the moon's light.

"Clara," Mama said, standing, her voice warm but tinged with something unspoken. "We were just... saying our goodbyes to Sage and the garden."

Clara's smile was soft. "The garden doesn't like goodbyes. It holds onto folks."

She glanced at Sage, and for a moment, a flicker of understanding passed between them.

"This place... It's changed me," Jake said.

Clara's eyes softened, and she stepped closer. "The Briar Patch doesn't just give you rest—it takes something in return. A piece of your heart, maybe. Or a promise."

Sage tilted her head, her smile fading. "The garden keeps what it loves. And it loves you both."

Clara's fingers brushed Jake's hand, leaving a faint warmth that lingered.

"Don't forget what you've seen here. The fairy ring, the stars, the Shadow. They're all part of you now."

Mama clutched the rose tighter. "We'll see you both again."

Clara's laugh was soft, like wind through the roses. "Maybe you will. The Briar Patch is never far from the earth."

Sage stepped back, her form blending with the shadows of the rosebushes. "Go gently," she said, her voice fading. "And listen. Tsisdetsi's still speaking."

In a blink, she was gone, leaving only the faint glow of rose petals scattered on the path. Jake and Mama stood frozen, the garden suddenly quieter, the fireflies dimmer. Clara lingered a moment longer, her gaze distant, as if she, too, were part of the garden's magic, tethered to its secrets.

"Time for me to go," she said.

Jake nodded, his throat tight. He took Mama's hand, feeling the warmth of her skin. Together, they watched Clara return to the inn, the rose garden fading behind them, its colors burning into their memories like a dream they'd never quite wake from.

"Amazing," Mama said. "This place is so haunting. It could give the French Quarter a run for its money."

"That's a fact," Jake said.

"What about Buck?" Mama said. "Will you use him again?"

"You kidding? He's a natural. My audience will love him, especially my female audience."

"If Hollywood doesn't discover him first," Mama said.

She smiled when Jake said, "Don't get any ideas. I'm still the best man you've ever met."

"The very best, my dear," she said.

As if he'd forgotten something, Jake grabbed his cell phone, his fingers hovering over the keypad as a plan solidified in his mind.

"Who are you calling?"

"Ava," he said. "Our work here isn't quite done."

He dialed Ava Baltimore's number, the line ringing twice before her warm voice answered.

"Cryptid Hunter," she said. "Didn't expect to hear from you so soon. What's brewing?"

"Ava, I need a favor," Jake said, his tone steady but urgent. "You mentioned you're tight with the Quapaw chief."

A low chuckle came through the line. "Sure am. Tommy Red Eagle, my sister's boy. He has been the chief for nearly six years now.

"Any relation to Nadie Red Eagle?" he asked.

"His great aunt," Ava said. "The Quapaws are a small tribe. What do you want with Tommy?"

"I have a plan," he said.

"To do what?" she asked.

"I'll explain when I see you, but this has to stay quiet. Can you set up a meeting with Tommy? Somewhere discreet, maybe outside Ottawa County?"

Ava paused, the silence heavy with curiosity. "Kansas work for you? I have a cousin in Cherokee County, just across the border. Tommy and I visit her often—won't raise any eyebrows."

"Perfect," Jake said.

"She owns a diner called Ruby's Roadside in Galena. Nice little spot, off the main drag. Why the secrecy?"

"I don't trust anybody right now. Eyes are everywhere. We'll meet at Ruby's," Jake said, jotting down the name.

"How soon do you need us there?"

"How long will it take you to get to Galena?" Jake asked, glancing at his Rolex.

"Give us two hours," Ava said. "Tommy's in Miami, but he'll make the drive. Ruby's got a back room we can use—private, no questions asked."

"Two hours it is," Jake said. "And Ava? Tell Tommy I'll explain everything when we get there."

"You're stirring up a hornet's nest, Cryptid Hunter," Ava said, a hint of admiration in her voice. "I like it. See you at Ruby's."

Jake hung up, his pulse quickening as he turned to Mama.

"This is it for Chat Creek," he said. "I'm going to miss the place."

"Me too," she said. "Where to from here?"

"Kansas," he said.

"How far away is that?" she asked.

"Not far," he said. "We're meeting the Quapaw chief at Ruby's Roadside Diner in Galena, Kansas, in two hours."

"What's the deal, Bossman?" she asked.

Mama's response resulted in a grin dominating Jake's face.

"Stop it," he said.

"You like it, you know you do," she said.

"Part of my plan," he said. "If we can get the tribe on our side, we might have a shot at stopping Carver and Grant before that lease approval goes through."

Mama raised an eyebrow, her lips curling into a sly smile. "You're not just tripping the ringer from Arkansas this time, are you? You're aiming to blow up the whole track."

Jake grinned, grabbing his jacket. "Something like that. Let's move."

Their bags were already packed in the Range Rover. As they drove away from the inn, Jake glanced back one last time. The garden was still, but in the heart of the fairy ring, a single rose glowed under the moonlight, its petals curling inward.

Though Mama and Jake didn't see it happen, the inn and the rose garden flickered in the moonlight and then disappeared like Tess and Buck's mirage.

# CHAPTER 29

The drive to Galena was a quiet one, the Oklahoma plains giving way to the rolling hills of southeast Kansas. Jake's black SUV hummed along Route 66, the road's faded markers glowing faintly under the headlights. Mama sat in the passenger seat, her fingers drumming on the armrest.

"You think the Quapaws can help stop Phoenix?" she asked, breaking the silence as they crossed the state line.

Jake's hands tightened on the wheel. "They have leverage. The feds have been strong-arming them, but the Quapaws have treaty rights and a moral claim to that land. And, not to mention, I have a plan."

Mama nodded, her eyes glinting with approval. "I never had a doubt, my dear."

Ruby's Roadside Diner was a low-slung building with neon signs buzzing in the windows, its gravel lot sparsely filled with pickups and a lone motorcycle.

The air smelled of fried onions and diesel, and a faint hum of country music spilled out as Jake and Mama stepped inside. The diner was half-empty, a few locals nursing coffee at the counter, their eyes flicking curiously toward the newcomers.

Ava was already there, seated in a booth at the back with two men. One was probably in his forties, his dark hair closely cropped. The other man stood behind the booth, his arms folded across his chest. Ava waved them over, her expression calm but expectant.

"Jake, Mama, this is Tommy," Ava said, sliding over to make room. "Tommy, Jake Huntington, and Mama Mulate."

Tommy's handshake was firm, his gaze steady as he sized

Jake up. Ava didn't introduce the second man, and his unnerving stare bothered Jake.

"I'd hoped you would come alone," he said.

"Si Makes Rain," Tommy said. "Tribal police and my right-hand man. He goes where I go."

Si Makes Rain's braided hair reached the shoulders of his dark sports coat. He hadn't bothered removing his black Stetson.

Jake nodded and said, "Okay, let's talk."

"Ava says you've got a plan. I'm listening, but I'll warn you now—my people have been burned by promises before."

Jake slid into the booth, Mama beside him, and leaned forward.

"I'm not here to make promises, Tommy. I'm here to discuss a plan."

Tommy's expression remained unchanged. "Like I said, I'm listening."

"Phoenix Minerals has been nosing around, taking mineral leases. They're trying to steal Picher's land from under you, and they're using federal loopholes to do it."

"We're aware of what Phoenix offers," Tommy said.

"You have rights—treaty rights—and a story that can't be ignored," Jake said.

"We've been fighting the feds for decades," Tommy said. "Picher's poisoned, but it's still ours. What's your angle? You're not Quapaw. What's in this for you?"

Jake met his gaze without flinching. "I came here to film an episode of Cryptid Hunter. That project is complete, though I now have other interests."

"Such as?" Tommy said.

The neon glow of Ruby's Roadside Diner flickered across the table, casting long shadows. Jake leaned forward, his eyes locked on Chief Tommy Red Eagle, whose dark hair gleamed under the dim light.

Si Brings Rain stood behind him, his face unreadable, but his presence a quiet promise of protection. Ava's fingers traced the edge of a coffee mug, her gaze darting between Jake and her nephew. Mama watched the exchange with a glint of anticipation, sensing Jake was about to drop a bombshell.

Tommy leaned back, his white shirt creasing as he crossed his arms.

"The government's been sticking it to the Quapaws since before my grandfather's time. Treaties broken, land stolen, promises turned to ash—Picher's just the latest scar."

"All the reasons to remain proactive," Jake said.

"The feds strong-arm us with audits, threaten our funding to keep us quiet. That's how they play."

Si shifted, his dark eyes narrowing, but he said nothing, letting Tommy's words hang in the air like smoke.

Jake leaned closer, his voice dropping to a conspiratorial growl. "Let's get some payback."

Tommy raised an eyebrow, intrigued but wary. "Payback's a nice word, Cryptid Hunter. What's your play?"

Jake's grin was pure mischief, the kind he'd flashed before outrunning the best in the NCAA finals.

"We're going to do a hostile takeover of Phoenix Minerals. But I need your help."

Ava let out a low whistle, her henna-streaked hair catching the light as she leaned forward.

"You're talking about buying out a multi-billion-dollar company? Jake, you're a billionaire, sure, but Phoenix is a beast. You got that kind of cash lying around?"

Jake's grin didn't waver. "I don't need to outspend Carver—not yet. We start smart, quietly, buying as much Phoenix stock as possible without raising suspicions."

"Is that possible?" Tommy asked.

"We buy small blocks, through proxies, shell companies, whatever it takes to stay under the radar. My assistant is digging into their board and major stockholders."

"Still listening," Tommy said when Jake paused.

"We find the biggest noninvolved shareholder—someone who doesn't have Carver's or Grant's stink on them—and we make them an offer too good to refuse. A tender offer that'll tip the scales."

Tommy's expression remained guarded, but a flicker of interest crossed his face.

"The Quapaws are a small tribe. We can't offer much help," Tommy said.

Jake's answer carried the weight of a man who'd already run the numbers in his head.

"The feds have fucked over more than just your people. The Cherokees, the Chickasaws, the Choctaws—they've all been burned, same as you."

"And?"

"And they're sitting on casino money, millions in cash flow, political clout, and networks that stretch from Tahlequah to D.C. We get them all involved."

"What exactly are you suggesting?" Tommy asked.

"A coalition of tribes, a united front no one can ignore. We'll take control of Phoenix and use it as a vehicle to clean up Oklahoma—Picher first, then every poisoned creek and scarred hill the feds left behind. Are you with me?"

Tommy's eyes narrowed as he processed the audacity of Jake's plan. He glanced at Si, whose faint smirk suggested he was already imagining the chaos this could unleash.

Ava let out a soft chuckle, shaking her head.

"You don't think small, do you? You're talking about a tribal alliance—a war council with casino cash and a billionaire's playbook. That's a hell of a storm to stir up," she said.

"The Indians will be activist investors," Jake said. "Changing a company for the good of everyone. Independent investors will respond to our message and vote with us during the proxy and director's fight."

"But the storm it'll create," Ava said.

"A storm is what we need," Jake said. Carver and Senator Grant think they're untouchable. Perfect because we can poke a rod into their bike spokes before they realize they've reached the end of the road."

"The other tribes have no love for the feds," Tommy said.

"Picher's story could light a spark. If we frame this as a fight for all our lands, our rights..." He trailed off, a flicker of hope in his eyes. "It could work."

Si spoke up, his gravelly voice cutting through the room like a blade.

"You're talking big money, Cryptid Hunter. Casino tribes don't part with cash lightly. What's your pitch to get them on board?"

Jake's grin was pure Duke track star, the kind that said he'd already seen the finish line.

"They earn a stake in the game. The Quapaws lead—your story, your land, your Shadow—it's the heart of this fight. But we bring in the other tribes as investors in the takeover."

"Full partners?" Tommy said.

"Better than full partners," Jake said. "Once we have control of the vehicle, I cede all of my interest back to the coalition. The tribes will control their own destiny."

"How's it going to work?" Tommy asked.

"We buy into Phoenix stock through proxies to keep it quiet. We tender offers to the largest non-involved shareholder that are so sweet that they can't say no. Once we have a majority, we boot out Carver and his board of directors and install ours."

"And you'll be the CEO?" Tommy asked.

"Nope," Jake said. "Though I have someone in mind."

"A white man?" Si said.

Jake shook his head. "An Indian woman," he said.

"A woman?" Si said.

Si smiled slightly when Jake said, "Stow your sexism, Brings Rain."

"Sounds good, but..."

"No buts," Jake said. "We direct the vehicle's resources to clean up Picher, restore the land, and share the profits with the tribes. It's not just payback; it's justice, and it's good business."

Tommy nodded slowly. "I know folks in the Cherokee Nation, and I have cousins tied to the Chickasaws. I can make some calls, set up a meeting."

"Fantastic," Jake said.

"But Cryptid Hunter, you'll need to bring more than charm. They'll want numbers, timelines, guarantees."

"I have my assistant working on it," Jake said. "She's pulling every detail on Phoenix's board, their stock structure, and their vulnerabilities. By tomorrow, we'll know exactly how much stock we need and who we're targeting. My lawyers are already setting up shell companies to start buying—small, quiet, under the radar. We'll move fast."

Mama's voice cut in, sharp and commanding. "And don't forget Nadie Red Eagle. If she can tie the Shadow to this fight, it's not just about money or land—it's about the spirit of the tribes. That's what'll pull the Cherokees and Choctaws in. They'll see this as more than a business deal; it's a reckoning."

"You're offering Phoenix Minerals and a chance to stick it to the feds? That's a pitch even the Cherokee council might bite on. They've been itching to flex their muscle since their gaming compact got renegotiated."

"I'm nowhere near full blood, but I was born in Oklahoma and have Indian roots," Jake said.

Tommy grinned. "Everyone trusts the Cryptid Hunter," he said. "Even the Cherokees."

"Glad of that," Jake said.

Tommy exchanged a glance with Si, a silent conversation passing between them. Ava broke the tension, her infectious smile returning.

"You're crazy, Cryptid Hunter, but it's the good kind of crazy. Tommy, he's got the fire. We can work with this."

"You've mentioned cleaning up Picher and our land more than once," Tommy said. "If the feds can't afford the cleanup, how do we do it? Even all the casinos put together don't generate that kind of money."

"The chat piles," Jake said.

"What about them, Cryptid Hunter?" Tommy said.

"Mining techniques have progressed since the original companies abandoned Picher," Jake said. "They left millions of dollars behind in the chat piles. That's what's leaching into the groundwater and poisoning the earth."

"What are you getting at, Cryptid Hunter?" Tommy said.

Jake's hands and arms began waving like a wild man, his voice loud enough for everyone in the diner to hear.

"I'm talking about cutting-edge tech: bioreactors that leach minerals from the toxic piles, leaving clean soil behind; nanobots that filter groundwater until it sparkles clear. The collapsed mine shafts, once yawning traps, filled and stabilized with the processed remains of the chat; the land stitched back together, like a wound finally healing."

Everyone's mouth was open when Jake finished his impassioned speech. Si was the first to speak.

"God damn!" he said.

"Who knows enough about this technology you speak of to make it work?" Tommy said.

"One of your own," Jake said. "Avini Kane, granddaughter of Nadie Red Eagle. She has a double PhD from OU and is smarter than all of us put together."

Ava's eyes sparkled, her henna-streaked hair swaying as she leaned forward.

"Jake's words are true. Nadie has often spoken to me of Avini."

"She's not full-blood," Si said.

"You're right," Jake said. "She's half white and half Indian. Seems to me that's the perfect damn percentage you need to slay all your dragons."

"There's a problem," Ava said. "Avini lives in the commune with the 'People of the Earth.' She would never leave."

"She already has," Jake said.

The sound of a chopper landing nearby interrupted their conversation. As Ruby, Ava's cousin, appeared with menus, coffee, and iced tea, Avini and Colley joined them. After introductions, Jake spiked his coffee with scotch from his flask.

Tommy smiled and shoved his cup toward Jake. Jake topped it up with scotch and then passed the flask around the table.

# CHAPTER 30

Jake's idea progressed as planned and sometime later, the private dining room at Le Diplomate buzzed with the clink of crystal and the murmur of power. Tuxedoed waiters glided like shadows, delivering plates of seared foie gras and Château Margaux to Senator Hollis Grant and Roland Carver, CEO of Phoenix Minerals.

The air was thick with the scent of truffles and ambition. Grant, his silver hair swept back, his weathered face a bulldog scowl, leaned back in his chair, a smirk curling his lips. Carver, mid-fifties, his tailored Brioni suit gleaming under the chandelier, adjusted his Patek Philippe watch with manicured fingers, his face taut from subtle Botox and a narcissist's confidence.

"Roland, it's done," Grant said, swirling his wine. "Johnson's bill sailed through the House. My committee'll rubber-stamp it in the Senate. A few million for Picher's 'cleanup,' funneled straight to Phoenix after my friends get their cut. No one's looking too closely."

Carver's lips twitched, his Ivy League polish barely masking his unease.

"Cleanup, Hollis? We both know that money's for our pockets, not Picher's rivers. But I'm hearing whispers—stock purchases, small but coordinated. Someone's buying Phoenix shares, and I don't like it."

Grant scoffed, his jowls quivering. "You're paranoid. Who'd dare? The tribes? Those Indians don't have the cash or the brains to play at our level. We've got the Bureau of Land Management in our pocket, and the EPA's too spineless to sniff around. Picher's neodymium and dysprosium are ours—billions, Roland,

230

billions."

Carver's eyes narrowed, his fork pausing over a slice of Wagyu. "Don't underestimate them, Hollis. The Quapaws have been loud, and now I hear the Cherokees and Choctaws are sniffing around. If they're pooling casino money—"

"Casino money?" Grant laughed, loud enough to draw a glance from a nearby waiter. "They're too busy fighting each other to organize. We'll keep screwing them over, same as always. No one cares about a few poisoned creeks in Oklahoma."

Carver leaned forward, his voice low. "I'm telling you, something's off. My analysts say proxy votes are shifting. Activist investors—splinter groups—are backing a potential takeover. They want me and my board out."

Grant's face reddened, a vein pulsing in his temple. "Out? You? That's absurd. You're Phoenix Minerals. I've got your back in D.C.—nobody's touching us."

Before Carver could respond, a young aide in a crisp suit slipped into the room, his face pale. He whispered urgently into Carver's ear, his hands trembling as he handed over a tablet. Carver's Botox-smooth facade cracked as he scanned the screen. His fork clattered to the plate.

"What is it?" Grant said, his voice sharp.

Carver's jaw tightened, his eyes darting like a cornered animal.

"It's over, Hollis. The tribes—they've done it. They've got enough proxy votes. The Quapaws, Cherokees, Chickasaws, Choctaws—they've allied with some billionaire, bought up stock through shells, and rallied independents. They're ousting my board. I'm done."

Grant sputtered, wine sloshing onto the tablecloth. "That's impossible! Who the hell—"

"Jake Huntington," Carver spat, his voice venomous. "That damned Cryptid Hunter. He's behind this. He and that coalition of tribes. They've got Avini Kane lined up to take my place—some Indian scientist with a vendetta and a double PhD."

Grant's face went purple, his fists slamming the table.

"Huntington? That reality TV clown? I'll bury him! I'll stall the Senate, kill their funding, sic the IRS on—"

He froze as a shadow fell over the table. A man in a charcoal suit, DOJ badge gleaming, stood before them, flanked by two agents. His voice was calm, cold as steel.

"Senator Hollis Grant, Roland Carver, I'm Special Agent Torres, Department of Justice. You're hereby served." He slid two thick envelopes across the table. "You're to appear before the House and Senate Committees on Ethics and Oversight to answer charges of fraud, corruption, and conspiracy related to Phoenix Minerals' operations in Picher, Oklahoma. Evidence includes leaked memos, donation records, and offshore accounts tied to a shell company in your allies' names."

Grant's mouth opened, but no sound came out. Carver's hands shook as he tore open the envelope, his eyes scanning the summons. The room seemed to shrink, the opulence of Le Diplomate mocking their fall.

Torres leaned in, his voice barely above a whisper. "The tribes send their regards. And the Cryptid Hunter? He says to check the chat piles. You'll find more than neodymium there— your whole scheme's buried in them."

As Carver and Grant left the restaurant, the chatter faded to stunned silence. Outside, a crowd had gathered—TV reporters asking embarrassing questions as cameras rolled, Jake Huntington leaning against his black SUV, a grin splitting his face. Beside him, Mama Mulate and Nadie Red Eagle watched Carver and Grant, frowning as they shoved microphones out of their faces.

Nadie glanced skyward, whispering to the wind, and the Shadow of Picher stirred, its presence a silent vow that the land would heal, and the tribes would rise.

# EPILOGUE

**W**eeks later, the Oklahoma air carried a crisp edge, the late summer haze giving way to the first whispers of fall. The world had shifted in the wake of Tsisdetsi's Shadow, the Cryptid Hunter episode that had gripped the nation.

Tess's camera work—raw, haunting, and unflinching—had woven a tapestry of Picher's scars and Bone Hollow's resilience, earning her accolades from critics and viewers alike.

The public devoured the footage: the commune's descent into madness, the Shadow's eerie pulse, and the survivors' fragile hope. Social media buzzed with #TsisdetsiLives and #PicherReborn while Tess, ever the perfectionist, was unbelieving, though reveling in her unexpected success.

In Tulsa, Jake Huntington's audacious gamble had paid off. The hostile takeover of Phoenix Minerals was a masterstroke, executed with surgical precision. With the Quapaw Nation and a coalition of tribes—Cherokee, Chickasaw, Choctaw—backing him, Jake's proxies had quietly amassed enough stock to oust Roland Carver and his board.

Senator Hollis Grant, blindsided by the maneuver, could only watch as Congress, swayed by the tribes' unified voice and the public outcry from Tsisdetsi's Shadow, rubber-stamped the deal.

Carver and Grant were left reeling, with significant jail time in their futures because the stink of corruption was too putrid to ignore from either side of the aisle. Their empire was crumbling, unable to counter the tidal wave of tribal clout and Jake's relentless strategy.

Jake, true to his word, sold his stake in Phoenix to the Indian Compact for a tidy profit, stepping back with a grin that said he'd outrun the ringer from Arkansas after all.

Avini Kane, now CEO of Phoenix Minerals, stood at the helm of a company transformed. From her office in Miami, Oklahoma, she oversaw the cleanup of Picher and Ottawa County with a fierce determination.

Bioreactors hummed across the chat piles, leaching rare earth minerals while detoxifying the soil, just as she'd envisioned that night in Bricktown. Nanobots scrubbed the groundwater, and the collapsed mine shafts were filled with processed waste, stabilizing the land.

Jobs poured into the region, many of which were filled by Quapaw and other tribal members, breathing life into a community that had long been left for dead. Avini's grandfather's dream—a land healed, a people empowered—was taking root, and she carried it forward with a quiet pride.

Jake and Mama, their work in Oklahoma done, boarded a private jet bound for New Orleans. The Crescent City's sultry embrace awaited—a much-needed respite of jazz, gumbo, and long nights on Bourbon Street. Over beignets at Café du Monde, Jake sketched ideas for their next project.

"Haiti," he said, his eyes glinting with mischief. "Vodou, zombies, maybe a chupacabra or two."

Mama laughed, her sharp wit undimmed. "You'll chase anything with claws and a story. Just don't expect me to wrestle it."

"Or we could take a trip to Las Vegas and catch Ava and her newly-formed Pegs. She finally got her one-hit wonder," Jake said.

"*Time* won't be her last hit, just her first," Mama said.

At Bone Hollow, Nadie and Bert were inseparable, their bond forged in the crucible of survival. They'd begun plans to restore the commune, not as it was, but as a haven for healing, rooted in John Kane's original vision.

With Kwanita the donkey grazing nearby, Ahanu the wolf-dog patrolling the meadow, and the chickens clucking contentedly, the couple lived a quiet, joyful life. Their love, like the spring at the hollow's heart, was a steady current, grounding the community they were rebuilding.

Sage and Clara had vanished, slipping into the shadows as mysteriously as they'd appeared. So too had sightings of the Shadow, its restless energy quieted, at least for now. Some whispered it had retreated to the earth's depths, others that it had never existed at all. But the land around Picher felt lighter, as if a weight had lifted.

Sheriff Callahan and his deputy had closed the book on Scarface's crime ring, dismantling the last of its tendrils in Ottawa County. The meth labs were gone, the dealers rounded up, and the commune's dark chapter sealed. Callahan, ever the performer, had tipped his Stetson to Jake before he left.

"You stirred up hell, Cryptid Hunter, but you cleaned it up, too."

Tess and I were back on the open road, the highway unspooling like a ribbon under a sky wide enough to swallow your troubles. My old pickup rumbled along, hauling a trailer where Lady, my chestnut mare, bobbed her head contentedly.

We were bound for Texas, heading to Tess's family ranch, where her spirited palomino, Rio, awaited. The plan was simple: pick up Rio, then tear off to Las Vegas for a week of rodeo thrills —barrel racing, bronc busting, and neon-soaked nights. We'd even catch Ava's latest performance, her voice sure to light up the Strip.

Tess, her camera bag tucked at her feet, flashed a grin as I butchered a Willie Nelson tune, my off-key warbling filling the cab.

"You're going to love the rodeo, Buck," she said, her eyes dancing with mischief.

I shot her a wink. "Long as I'm with you, darling, I'd cheer for a tractor pull."

She laughed, then her tone softened. "You kept your promise to Nadie."

I raised an eyebrow, hands steady on the wheel. "What promise?"

"The silver vein. You, me, and Nadie swore never to tell a soul. She said you'd break that vow. You didn't."

I chuckled, glancing at her. "Nadie was right. I broke it."

Tess's jaw dropped, her arms crossing tight over her chest. "You didn't. Who'd you tell?"

"Avini," I said. "She had to know."

"Why didn't you tell me?" she asked, her voice sharp but curious.

"'Cause then you'd be in on it too," I said. "Avini needed the truth to finish what we started in Picher. Forgive me?"

Her arms unfolded, and a slow smile spread across her face. She leaned over the console, her lips brushing mine in a kiss that tasted of dust and promise. Pard, never one to miss a moment, joined in, his wet tongue slobbering across our faces. We laughed, the cab alive with warmth.

As the sun sank below the horizon, painting the sky in fiery gold and molten crimson, hope pulsed through the plains, strong and unbroken, ready for whatever the road brought next.

End

# BOOK NOTES

The story of Picher, Oklahoma, reads like a fevered tale spun by a writer drunk on imagination—but it's no fiction. Picher's tragedy is all too real, a scarred landscape of broken promises and poisoned earth.

As a young geologist at the University of Arkansas, I chased the dream of mineral wealth; my thesis focused on the Copper, Lead, Zinc, and Antimony Deposits of Sevier County, Arkansas. (Go ahead, chuckle at the title—I did.)

Back then, I never set foot in Picher, but I was captivated by tales of mineralogists unearthing stunning crystals in its condemned crawlspaces. Youthful ignorance was indeed bliss.

This year brought a personal storm that reshaped this story. My beloved wife, Marilyn, battled a relentless, undiagnosed illness that worsened over months, culminating in her tragic death from sepsis in the hospital.

Her loss seeped into every page of *Tsisdetsi's Shadow*, infusing it with a depth of heart I hadn't anticipated. Writing this book became a refuge, a way to navigate grief while telling a story of resilience and redemption.

The reclamation of Picher depicted in the novel isn't just wishful thinking—it's grounded in reality. Cutting-edge technologies, such as AI-driven bioreactors and nanobots, could transform Picher's toxic waste piles into clean soil and clear water, generating a profit in the process. If only I'd had this vision in my younger, bolder days as a geologist—I could've been somebody.

*Tsisdetsi's Shadow* is the fourth installment in my *Paranormal Cowboy Series*, starring the rugged soldier-of-fortune

Buck McDivit. Crafting this tale was a joy, a way to escape my sorrow and immerse myself in a world of mystery, justice, and the supernatural. I hope you find as much thrill in reading it as I did in writing it.

Fans of my *French Quarter Mystery Series* will recognize familiar faces in *Tsisdetsi's Shadow*. Mama Mulate and Jake Huntington, the charismatic Cryptid Hunter, are spinoffs from the moody, haunted streets of New Orleans, where my primary character, Wyatt Thomas, reigns as a private investigator.

Speaking of Wyatt, he makes his debut on Oyster Island in *Oyster Bay Mambo*, a standalone mystery that bridges two series with recurring characters. Oyster Bay Mambo is Book 5 of my Oyster Bay Mystery Series set on a barrier island in the Gulf of Mexico about fifty miles from New Orleans. And for those who love the French Quarter's blend of mystery and hauntings, mark your calendars: *Blood and Ashes, Book 15* of the *French Quarter Mystery Series*, arrives in February 2026.

To my readers, thank you. Your support breathes life into my stories, keeping them from fading like morning fog over a forgotten lawn. Without you, my words would vanish into the Great Unknown. Here's to shared adventures and the stories yet to come.

# ABOUT THE AUTHOR

Eric Wilder is an American author known for his gripping mystery novels set in New Orleans. He was born and raised in Louisiana, where he discovered his love for storytelling at a young age. After completing his education, Wilder spent several years in the oil and gas industry before pursuing a career as a writer.

Wilder's breakthrough came with the publication of Big Easy, which introduced readers to his signature blend of suspense, action, and local color. The book instantly succeeded, drawing critical acclaim and a devoted following. Wilder followed up with a collection of thrillers set in the heart of New Orleans.

Wilder's writing is characterized by his deep knowledge of the city and its unique culture and his skillful use of suspense and plot twists to keep readers on the edge of their seats. His books have been praised for their authenticity, vivid descriptions, and compelling characters.

Today, Eric Wilder is a respected author with a loyal fan base and a reputation for delivering top-notch thrillers that transport readers to the heart of New Orleans.

Wilder is the author of twenty-four novels, several cookbooks, many short stories, and Murder Etouffee, a book that defies classification. His series features characters who often find themselves involved in the paranormal.

Eric Wilder lives in Oklahoma near historic Route 66 with his two dogs, Moe and Buddy.

# OTHER BOOKS BY ERIC WILDER

**French Quarter Mystery Series**

Big Easy, Book 1

City of Spirits, Book 2

Primal Creatures, Book 3

Black Magic Woman, Book 4

River Road, Book 5

Sisters of the Mist, Book 6

Garden of Forbidden Secrets, Book 7

New Orleans Dangerous, Book 8

Cycles of the Moon, Book 9

Half Past Midnight, Book 10

Thief of Souls, Book 11

Krewe of Illusion, Book 12

Wild Magnolias, Book 13

Night People, Book 14

Blood and Ashes, Book 15

**Paranormal Cowboy Series**

Ghost of a Chance, Book 1

Bones of Skeleton Creek, Book 2

Blink of an Eye, Book 3

Tsisdetsi's Shadow, Book 4

Adobe Moon, Book 5

**Oyster Bay Mystery Series**

Oyster Bay Boogie, Book 1

Oyster Bay Tango, Book 2

Oyster Bay Two Step, Book 3

Oyster Bay Limbo, Book 4

Oyster Bay Mambo, Book 5

**Standalone Novels**

Of Love and Magic

Diamonds in the Rough

Ben's Magical Midnight Garden

**Anthologies and Cookbooks**

Murder Etouffee
Over the Rainbow
Lily's Little Cajun Cookbook

www.ingramcontent.com/pod-product-compliance
Lightning Source LLC
Chambersburg PA
CBHW011434240626
47153CB00011B/2989